O9-AHW-985

VAMPIRES NOT INVITED

C HEYENNE M C C RAY

Batavia Public Library
Batavia, Illinois

St. Martin's Paperbacks

NOTE: If you purchased this book without a cover you should be aware that this book is stolen property. It was reported as "unsold and destroyed" to the publisher, and neither the author nor the publisher has received any payment for this "stripped book."

This is a work of fiction. All of the characters, organizations, and events portrayed in this novel are either products of the author's imagination or are used fictitiously.

VAMPIRES NOT INVITED

Copyright © 2010 by Cheyenne McCray.
Excerpt from *Zombies Sold Separately* copyright © 2010 by Cheyenne McCray.

All rights reserved.

For information address St. Martin's Press, 175 Fifth Avenue, New York, NY 10010.

EAN: 978-0-312-53268-0

Printed in the United States of America

St. Martin's Paperbacks edition / December 2010

St. Martin's Paperbacks are published by St. Martin's Press, 175 Fifth Avenue, New York, NY 10010.

10 9 8 7 6 5 4 3 2 1

Praise for these other novels from *New York Times*
bestselling author
CHEYENNE MCCRAY

NO WEREWOLVES ALLOWED

"The suspense is well written, the villains are chilling,
and Nyx is a kick-ass heroine to admire. A captivating book in a fascinating series, *No Werewolves Allowed* is a tale I highly recommend."
—*Romance Reviews Today*

"Interesting characters, fast-paced plot and fascinating
world-building make this a must-read."
—*Fresh Fiction*

DEMONS NOT INCLUDED

"The hot new Night Tracker series promises plenty of
thrills and chills. McCray does an excellent job estab-
lishing this world and its host of intriguing characters.
The action is fast and furious, and the danger escalat-
ing. Add in some sexy sizzle and you have another pat-
ented McCray gem."
—*Romantic Times BOOKreviews* (Top Pick, 4 ½ stars)

"McCray weaves a supernatural tale of mystery, murder, and blossoming romance. *Demons Not Included*
has a well-rounded cast, a captivating storyline, and
plenty of suspense to keep readers guessing."
—*Darque Reviews*

DARK MAGIC
Winner, *Romantic Times* Reviewer's Choice Award for Best Paranormal Action Adventure of the Year

"McCray does a stellar job layering the danger, passion and betrayal. Awesome!"

—*Romantic Times BOOKreviews* (Top Pick, 4 ½ stars)

"Action, romance, suspense, love, betrayal, sacrifice, magic, and sex appeal to the nth degree! [McCray's] heroines kick butt and run the gamut from feminine to tomboy, and her heroes...well, they're all 200% grade-A male. YUM! Her love scenes left me breathless . . . and I'm surprised I have any nails left after the suspense in this last book."

—*Queue My Review*

"Vivid battles, deceit that digs deep into the coven, and a love that can't be denied."

—*Night Owl Romance*

"Besides a fabulous finish to a great urban fantasy that sub-genre fans will relish as one of the best series over the past few years, the romance is the one readers have been waiting [for] to see how it plays out since almost the beginning. Master magician Cheyenne McCray brings it all together in a superb ending to her stupendous saga."

—Harriet Klausner

SHADOW MAGIC
"Erotic paranormal romance liberally laced with adventure and thrills."

—*Romantic Times BOOKreviews*
(Top Pick, 4 ½ stars)

"A sensual tale full of danger and magic, *Shadow Magic* should not be missed."   —*Romance Reviews Today*

"Cheyenne McCray has created a fabulous new world. You won't be able to get enough!"

        —Lori Handeland, *USA Today* bestselling author

WICKED MAGIC
"Blistering sex and riveting battles are plentiful as this series continues building toward its climax."

        —*Romantic Times BOOKreviews* (4 stars)

"Has an even blend of action and romance. . . . An exciting paranormal tale, don't miss it!"

        —*Romance Reviews Today*

"Cheyenne McCray shows the best work between good and evil in *Wicked Magic*. The characters are molded perfectly…sure to delight and captivate with each turn of the page."   —*Night Owl Romance*

SEDUCED BY MAGIC
"Blistering passion and erotic sensuality are major McCray hallmarks, in addition to a deft and exciting storyline. This magical series continues to develop its increasing cast of characters and complex plotline; the result is erotic paranormal romance liberally laced with adventure and thrills."

        —*Romantic Times BOOKreviews* (Top Pick, 4 ½ stars)

"The slices of humor, the glimpses of the characters' world through fantastic descriptions, not to mention fascinating characters, landed this book on...[the] keeper shelf."

—*Romance Divas*

"Witches, drool-worthy warriors, and hot passion that will have readers reaching for a cool drink. Cheyenne McCray has created a fantastic and magical world where both the hero and heroine are strong and are willing to fight the darkness that threatens their worlds."

—*A Romance Review*

FORBIDDEN MAGIC

"Wildly erotic and dangerously sensual, this explosive paranormal thriller sizzles. McCray erupts on the scene with one of the sexiest stories of the year. Her darkly dramatic world is one readers won't mind visiting again... McCray knows how to make a reader sweat—either from spine-tingling suspense or soul-singeing sex... McCray cleverly combines present-day reality with mythological fantasy to create a world where beings of lore exist—and visit the earthly realm."

— *Romantic Times BOOKreviews* (Top Pick, 4 1/2 stars)

"McCray will thrill and entrance you!"

—Sabrina Jeffries, *New York Times* bestselling author

"A yummy hot fudge sundae of a book!"

—MaryJanice Davidson, *New York Times* bestselling author

"*Charmed* meets Kim Harrison's witch series, but with a heavy dose of erotica on top!"

—Lynsay Sands, *New York Times* bestselling author

"McCray's paranormal masterpiece is not for the faint-hearted. The battle between good and evil is brought to the reader in vivid and riveting detail to the point where the reader is drawn into the pages of this be-witching and seductive fantasy that delivers plenty of action-packed sequences and arousing love scenes."

—*Rendezvous*

"*Forbidden Magic* is a spellbinding, sexy, superbly written dark fantasy. I couldn't put it down, and you won't want to either...[a] fabulous plot... [Cheyenne McCray has an] incredible skill at keeping readers engaged in every moment of the action. Longtime fans and newbies alike will be enchanted and swept away by this enduring tale of courage, love, passion, and magic."

—*A Romance Review*

"If one were going to make a comparison to Cheyenne McCray with another writer of the supernatural/sen-suality genre, it would have to be Laurell K. Hamil-ton...*Forbidden Magic* definitely puts McCray in the same league as Hamilton. The book is a very sexy work... *Forbidden Magic* is dark and filled with dan-ger at almost every turn. Magic and mystery abound in San Francisco, with a major battle between the forces of good and evil, and the outcome is always in doubt when it comes to demons."

—*Shelf Life*

"Cheyenne McCray has written a sexy adventure spiced with adventurous sex."

—Charlaine Harris,
New York Times bestselling author

St. Martin's Paperbacks Titles By
CHEYENNE McCRAY

NIGHT TRACKER NOVELS
Demons Not Included
No Werewolves Allowed
Vampires Not Invited

LEXI STEELE NOVELS
The First Sin
The Second Betrayal

THE MAGIC NOVELS
Dark Magic
Shadow Magic
Wicked Magic
Seduced by Magic
Forbidden Magic

ROMANTIC SUSPENSE
Moving Target
Chosen Prey

ANTHOLOGIES
No Rest for the Witches

To Daniel James with love

ACKNOWLEDGMENTS

Thank you to my three sons for putting up with Mom on an intense deadline—and in the midst of moving, too!

Thank you to Chuck Andruis for your support of Brenda Novak's 6th annual online Auction for Diabetes Research. Congratulations, Brenda, and all of the auction's many supporters, for hitting the one million mark!

He who does not punish evil,
commands it to be done.
—Leonardo da Vinci (1452–1519)

WELCOME TO NEW YORK CITY'S UNDERWORLD

Dark Elves/Drow: we rock.

Demons: I am *so* through with Demons.

Doppler: a paranorm who can shift into one specific animal as well as their human form.

Dragons: you just never know if one might be living next door to you. Really.

Fae: shee-ya, right. Should have paid attention during our last case if you really want to know all of the different races.

Gargoyles: freaking ugly. And dangerous.

Incubus: no Adonis could begin to compare to these paranorms. Stay. Away.

Light Elves: mirror, mirror how art we better than all?

Metamorph: slimy paranorms who can take over the image of any human. And not in a good way.

Necromancer: exactly what you think. They talk to and raise the dead. Creeeeepy.

Shadow Shifter: a paranorm with the ability to shift from human form into shadows.

Shifter: can transform into any animal of their choosing as well as take their human form.

Sorcerer: scary. Seriously scary.

Specter: boo.

Sprites: belong in the Fae category, believe it or not. Ugly, disgusting, malicious beings.

Succubus: promises sex good enough to sell your soul for. One word: don't.

Werewolves: can take wolf form almost anytime, but at the full moon they go nuclear.

Witches: in a class all their own.

Zombies: I do not want to talk about Zombies. You can't make me.

Vampires: not invited.

ONE

Dealing with Sprites is like stapling raw eggs to a wall.

Slippery, nasty things that go bad when not cleaned up. And I don't mean giving them a bath.

This one was picking his hairy nose.

As he stood by the big toe of the Statue of Liberty, the Sprite flicked a booger off his finger. Gross. The breeze carried the sickly-sweet odor of burnt sugar to me. All Sprites smell like burnt sugar. At least all the ones I'd ever met.

The Sprite wiped the back of his hand across his brown, mottled face, streaking bright paint over his lumpy cheek. His worn clothing was drenched in the same color and he slid a paintbrush into the bucket he carried.

In the moonlight, paint gleamed on the statue's enormous toenails and I sighed.

Lovely. The Sprite had given Liberty a pedicure.

That reminded me that I needed to get together with the girls for a spa day.

Protuberant glassy blue eyes shifted in my direction but I was certain the Sprite couldn't make me out in the darkness. Most Dark Elves—Drow—can easily blend with the shadows and night and it's a talent I inherited despite my human half.

Don't get me wrong, I love my human side. Sometimes it's a disadvantage and sometimes it's an advantage. Just depends on who I am at the time.

After sunrise, I'm a normal-looking human paranorm PI with a penchant for designer clothing.

As a PI I get tough and usually dangerous cases that involve strategizing, investigating, and using my paranorm powers. Sometimes I bring in other paranorms to help shut down evil, like Demons and sick scientists bent on paranorm genocide. Cases that most don't even know exist—especially humans.

I have all of the typical human skills I bring to the job. But I'm also a trained fighter and I have powers—paranormal powers vital to defeat the kinds of enemies humans would never be able to deal with.

When the sun goes down I become Drow, my body changing, my skin and hair turning shades usually found only in the realm of the Dark Elves. My hair is cobalt blue and my skin like pale amethyst marble. I also have very small fangs that I'm not crazy about, and like all Elves, my ears become pointed. I'm fine with the pointed-ears thing.

By night I was a Night Tracker.

Trackers had the power and resources to do what humans could not. With our physical strength and powers, including magic, we could take down threats that no one else had a chance of doing. We were equivalent to a combination of covert ops in the human CIA and a military special forces like the Navy SEALS or the Rangers.

Tonight I'd just tracked down this booger-flicking mischievous, malevolent being.

When the Sprite looked away, I kept close to the instep of the statue and eased through the shadows while gripping one of my dragon-clawed daggers. The seventeen-inch-long, two-inch-wide Drow-made daggers had been designed just for me.

I gathered my elemental strength, my primary strength. The element I used most often was air, but there was plenty of water around if I needed it right now.

My leather fighting suit hugged my body as I moved. Most Trackers preferred leather because it was comfortable and helped protect against nasty scrapes. Black so we could blend in with the night.

I withdrew a step back into the darkness. I didn't want to give the Sprite a chance to escape.

I glanced at the moon, then at the Statue of Liberty's torch, and almost groaned out loud. How was *that* going to be explained? In the morning New York City's residents and tourists would get their first view of the statue and see that the formerly oxidized copper-green torch was now pink.

Neon pink.

The toenails would be easily taken care of . . . but the torch? Then I saw the Lady's lips and her glossy new pink lipstick. Sheesh.

This mess was probably too big for the Paranorm Council to cover up. There was only so much Soothsayers could do even as talented as most of them were.

As I looked up into the near darkness, I made out three Sprites swinging from the torch and then up and over the railing.

Muffled cries echoed from the base of the flame where other Night Trackers waited. Ice and Angel were taking care of their prey, no doubt with perfect efficiency.

Ice could be a jerk, but after working with him on

the Werewolf case I'd come to appreciate him, even if I could still do without his jerk side. We all could, as a matter of fact.

Angel was like an avenging angel. Truly an amazing Tracker.

At the same time I heard the sounds, my ugly target jerked his head up and dropped his paint can with a hard *clunk*. Neon paint splattered the side of the statue's foot. The Sprite started to shimmer and fade, but I was already moving.

"No way," I shouted as I used my air elemental magic to push me faster. I forward-flipped through the air and landed on the Sprite, slamming him face-first in a puddle of paint. "You are so not going anywhere," I said as I drove him down.

He was completely solid again. My teeth clacked as my knees hit the brutal surface and I winced as I landed and straddled his back. If another being is touching them, Sprites can't use glamours—become invisible—at all. Unfortunately, since he wasn't in glamour, I could smell him. Ugh.

Sprites are some of the only beings who can use glamours to mask themselves and their strong smell from other paranorms. Most paranorms can see through glamours—with some exceptions, like Vampires. Vampires can't see through paranorm glamours because they were born human.

Before his first scream could escape, I grabbed one of the Sprite's tufts of matted blond hair, jerked his huge head up, and put my dagger at his neck. The blade bit into the paranorm's throat and a trickle of blood rolled down the Drow-mined and -forged metal.

My cobalt blue hair fell over my shoulders as I leaned

close to the Sprite. I felt the dangerous white flash in my sapphire eyes. As a Tracker I was all business.

"Cooperate or I'll let you have a taste of Lightning, this pretty little dagger, later where the mess won't foul this place more than you already have." My voice was tight and low.

"Stupid purple bitch." The Sprite laughed, the sound like a scratchy cough. "You and the other idiot Trackers know nothing. We will tell you nothing."

Amethyst, came the instant but ridiculous thought.

Do not call me purple. Please. I'd hate to have to rough you up.

"I'm not worried." I moved my blade away a flash before I pushed his face against the copper-covered iron beneath us. "We'll encourage you plenty."

"Bitch," he shouted again before tacking on a few more foul words, these spoken in an ancient Fae language. Words that were *really* not nice. I brought his face down again.

The snap of his bulbous nose was loud to my pointed ears. Oops. I grimaced. Sometimes I forget my Drow strength can be a bit much.

Blood from his broken nose joined the neon pink paint coating his face. The Sprite howled a cry of pain. His words bubbled through blood as he spoke in a harsh breath. "There is nothing to tell you. We are just having fun, purple whore."

"Go ahead." I drew my 9mm Kahr and raised it. "Call me purple again." The whore part I let pass.

He glared at me with one eye as he twisted his head just enough that I could see him. "Purple—"

Okay, that was enough. "Nighty night." I swung my arm down and knocked him upside his temple with the handgun's grip. He slumped without making another sound. "We'll have our conversation later." I tucked my new luxury compact Kahr PM9 away and patted the leather holster. "It's nice to have more than one use for a weapon."

I used the 9mm mostly during my day job as a paranorm PI, but in this case maybe I'd been a little overzealous. I tended to be a lot tougher and rougher as a Tracker. Being a law enforcer brought out the hard side of me.

From my weapons belt I snagged a pair of elemental-magically-treated handcuffs and jerked the Sprite's arms so that I could cuff his wrists. He groaned a little but he didn't wake up.

Once Sprites started ganging up and creating chaos in New York City, all Night Trackers began carrying extra cuffs. The cuffs were the only thing that could keep Sprites from using their glamour skills before the Paranormal Task Force—PTF—put them behind elemental-magically treated cells.

Trackers enforce paranorm laws, and there were currently twenty-two of us in New York City including rovers. Twenty-three counting my human partner, Olivia.

Normally my territory was the Upper West Side of Manhattan. Thanks to all the crazy things that had been going on with Sprites, some of us had been assigned to be on special teams and had to go where the trouble was. Unfortunately we hadn't made it before the statue had gotten a makeover.

Pink lipstick and toenail polish. Crazy.

Lights winked and stared from the city's skyline in a colorful sparkle that I enjoyed, partly because of the contrast from the world I grew up in. Near the Ellis Island Ferry, the PTF agents waited on shore. When we got the

Sprites across the water, the PTF would haul the beings to the elemental-magic-treated cells in the Paranorm Center.

I sensed Joshua's presence around a drape of the statue's robe. He strode into sight, dragging an unconscious and cuffed Sprite by the scruff of his neck. With a disgusted look on his harsh features, the Shadow Shifter dropped the Sprite beside me and my prisoner.

As a Shadow Shifter, Joshua could become a shadow, virtually invisible when he drifted from one shadow to the next, whether on the ground or in and around buildings. When he was in his male form, he was so sexy, with a build and accent that any female couldn't help appreciating.

Joshua glanced at the Sprite I was still straddling. The being's face was covered in blood from his broken nose and scrapes. "Looks like you've had a bit of fun with that one." Joshua's Australian accent was thick as he spoke.

"A little more 'fun' than I'd intended." I looked at the glittering Manhattan skyline again, picturing some of the Sprites' latest "pranks."

Joshua kicked the unconscious Sprite at his feet. The Shadow Shifter's flail hung from his belt, the iron so black that I could barely make it out in the near darkness. I wondered if he'd used the spiked ball to handle his Sprite.

Ouch.

My senses told me that now one of my closest friends was near. In moments Nadia shoved a cuffed and gagged Sprite around the statue's massive foot. The being cried out behind his gag as he fell next to the other Sprites and banged his head on the hard surface beneath our feet.

"Oh, shut up," she said with obvious impatience. "Sprites are so aggravating. We're low on gags after all of this."

Joshua watched with amusement as Nadia made a point of ignoring him. She hated alpha males, especially those who made it clear they thought of her as a sex object. Joshua probably didn't know how lucky he was that she hadn't sung him to his death already.

"What in the name of the Underworld is going on, Nyx?" A gorgeous Siren from the Bermuda Triangle, Nadia shoved a thick length of her red hair over her shoulder. "Sprites never work in teams. They all have a mind of their own."

"Almost as bad as they hate leadership and authority." I pushed myself to my feet and stepped away from the Sprite I'd taken down. "But something's behind all of this chaos."

"No lie," Joshua said.

I twisted my lips as I thought of yesterday's events. "You have to admit that they were pretty creative at the mayor's office."

Joshua laughed, a deep, sexy laugh, while Nadia shook her head. If I wasn't in love with Adam, Joshua was the kind of male a girl could have a crush on.

With a grin I pictured what had become a hothouse of flowers. "Every electronic device in the mayor's office suddenly blossoming into bouquets the moment they were turned on—that was worth the price of admission."

It was hard not to laugh as I thought about the Soothsayers having to freeze the scene so that the PTF could clean up the mess while Olivia, my partner, and I searched for clues.

Olivia worked with me during the day as a paranorm

PI even though she was human. At night she was an honorary Tracker when we needed her. There wasn't another soul on this earth Otherworld that I would rather have worked with.

Joshua smirked as I added, "The Paranorm Council had to pay to have their flunkies rush out and buy all new office equipment for the mayor and his staff."

Nadia gave an exasperated huff. She was taking things a little more seriously than me. "How about the Museum of Natural History's dinosaur skeletons suddenly becoming animated, tearing out the doors of the museum, and chasing down taxis."

To be honest, that had been kind of amusing, too, although it had been a real pain to get under control. It had taken every Tracker we had and all of our individual magical abilities to take care of the dinosaur skeletons and get them back where they belonged. Not to mention six Soothsayers to freeze all of the norms—and erase their memories—so that the whole mess didn't end up on the evening news.

"My favorite by far was the Empire State Building's lobby entirely stuffed with hot dogs when the monument opened Wednesday morning." I got a grin out of Nadia when I continued in a mock-serious voice, "At least they had the decency to get Nathan's hot dogs. When Olivia and I got there we were pretty hungry. A couple of Nathan's with the works hit the spot."

Nadia shook her head. "This is all so absurd."

Joshua folded his arms across his muscular chest and shook his head. "How can you work with a human for a partner?"

I ignored him. What did I care what any of the Trackers thought about Olivia? She was the most kickass human female I knew.

"Chaos." Nadia put her hands on her hips. "The Sprites have caused nothing but chaos."

I tilted my head and saw Liberty's pink lips, then studied the illuminated neon pink torch.

"Yes." I sobered. Lady Liberty was a symbol of freedom, including my own freedom from the Drow realm. "Now they've gone too far."

I looked at Nadia. "What's really frustrating is that we're out chasing these guys while Vampire attacks are on the rise."

She frowned. "Not by much, but enough to be concerned."

Joshua nodded. "You're right on that one."

Vampires were far worse than Sprites. Even though they had been forced into passivity for over a century, since the Paranorm Rebellion, they always seem to have an undercurrent of evil to them. Sprites on the other hand thrive on creating mischief and chaos.

When Lulu, a Soothsayer, had the Statue of Liberty scene frozen, and the Paranorm Task Force had taken the Sprites to the detention center, Nadia and I started to head toward the Pit.

"How's your Detective?" Nadia asked me with a grin.

I smiled in return, a feeling of happiness warming my body as I thought of Adam. "As sexy as ever," I said, and Nadia laughed—probably at the goofy girlie look that was undoubtedly on my face.

"So what makes you so hot for this human, anyway?" Nadia asked.

I sighed, a happy sigh. "Adam is genuine, caring, and he understands me, accepts me." I looked at Nadia. "He *gets* me."

Nadia gave me a teasing look. "I'll bet he 'gets' you."

My cheeks felt pleasantly warm. "Well, he's also sensitive, while at the same time a tough man. I love that combination."

Something shadowy caught my eye near one of the darkened tourist charter boats and my smile faded. As soon as I saw it, the shadow disappeared.

I have fantastic night vision and the fact that I hadn't been able to make out what the shadow was made me frown. It wasn't a Shadow Shifter because it stood upright. Yet I sensed it had to have been some kind of being.

"Nadia." I lowered my voice and my friend looked at me. "Let's go that way." I indicated the place where I'd seen the shadowy figure. "I don't know what, but I saw something over there."

She rested her hand on the hilt of one of her serpent swords. "Any idea?" she whispered as we slipped out of the lighted area and into the darkness.

"No." I frowned again as we eased toward the location. "But I've sensed some kind of being nearby every time we've gathered up troublemaking Sprites." We moved closer and I kept my voice so low that I couldn't be heard by anyone but Nadia. "This is the first time I've actually seen something. I just don't know what it is."

I kept my own hand close to one of my daggers as we crept forward.

We reached the area where I'd seen the shadow. Like I had expected, nothing was there.

But the slightest hint of a familiar smell was. "Old dirt and musty leaves." I straightened and searched the darkness with my gaze. "A Vampire, and recently."

The fact I hadn't been able to tell that from where I'd been standing set me on edge.

"No sign of blood, not even the scent of it," Nadia said.

I ran my finger along my collar. "But why would a Vampire watch us round up Sprites?"

Nadia studied the area around us. "Probably in the neighborhood looking for a bite."

"Yes. Maybe," I said.

Something didn't feel right. Didn't feel right at all.

TWO

The night had a sharp snap to it and I smelled wood burning in fireplaces and the scent I associated with Otherworld holidays. It was a change in the air, the days having a different feel and scent to them than any other time of the year.

I wondered what it might be like to lie back on a beach in some tropical location, something I had never done before. Maybe even wear a bikini when I was under the sun and get a tan. The thought of walking on the beach at night as Drow made me smile to myself.

The Pit was the hottest paranorm nightclub in New York and probably the entire East Coast. The nightclub was hidden from human eyes, magically tucked away next to the supposedly haunted Dakota building at Seventy-second Street and Central Park West.

I say supposedly because I know for a fact the Dakota building wasn't haunted, not a single Specter in residence. All of the happenings over the years were thanks to Brownies who *love* to scare humans.

The Pit, owned by Rodán, was a "safe place" for paranorms. Rodán was of the Light Elves and served as Proctor over all of New York City's Peacekeepers. He was so magically dominant that it took incredible power to cross the threshold into the Pit.

Not that long ago, two Demons had managed to fool Rodán's magic, something that was unbelievable. But that's another story I don't have time to get into.

After almost catastrophic happenings with Demons, Rodán had strengthened his wards tenfold in and around and even above and below the nightclub. He had the place covered with magic and muscle, too. No one was ever in danger in the Pit.

Fred wasn't at the door tonight, but Matthew was. Like most bouncers and law enforcement, he was a Doppler. He was a black Labrador when he wasn't in his human form. Fred was a golden retriever in his animal form and often he and Matthew would go for runs in Central Park. It was always a competition between the two of them. Sometimes I brought them Milk-Bone treats.

Dopplers make great PTF agents, bouncers, and anything else to do with security and law enforcement. In most cases, Dopplers are tough, dependable, intelligent, and have a strong sense of right versus wrong.

Unlike the cool weather outside, inside the nightclub was excessively warm from all of the paranorms packed into the place. It smelled of pipe weed, bar food, and beer, along with the combination of all of the different paranorm scents.

Pixies smell like milk chocolate, Doppler females like tiger flowers, and Shifter males of warmed amber. So many types of paranorms, so many scents to sift through.

"Sweet Cat is playing tonight." I heard the band's signature sound as it pulsed through the nightclub and saw the group onstage. I glanced at Nadia. "Adele is on lead vocals, so it's good Olivia isn't here tonight. At least I don't think so. What time is it?"

"Around midnight." Nadia looked at one big-screen TV in a corner of the room. "Hey, the Paranorm Winter Olympics are on." She turned back to me. "Unless the rovers assigned to our territories can't handle the areas for the night, I'm ready for a drink and watching a little of the Olympics."

"With Mandisa covering yours and Nakano tracking my territory I think they're in great hands." I stopped and watched the screen for a moment. "I haven't had much time to watch the PWO. Not even the parts I recorded on my DVR."

Nadia brought her gaze to me. "They're better than the human Olympics."

Some of the world's best athletes are paranorms. Especially Shifters, who tend to be flashier than most paranorm races. Personally I had a thing for human quarterbacks.

"I think it's fun." I laughed. "Humans would never guess that the male who won five gold medals in skating and the seven-time gold medalist in swimming are actually Shifters. They supposedly don't use their abilities to help them win, so I don't see a problem with it."

Nadia stared at the screen, looking almost entranced at the hockey game on the screen, Shifters versus Dopplers.

Which reminded me of one of the greatest games in human Olympic history. "The USA hockey team in the 1980 Olympics, a bunch of college kids who beat the Russians. Shifters. All of them."

Nadia and I watched a Doppler shoot a puck past a Shifter goalie.

"I have to admit that I always loved watching Michael before he retired." I smiled. "Not only is the great number twenty-three a sexy Shifter, but his forty-eight-inch vertical leap was incredible."

Nadia sniffed. "You can jump higher than that."

"That's different, what I do is more acrobatics." I shook my head. "Michael has talent that most paranorms just dream of. And style. For a Shifter he's a really nice guy."

Yeah, Shifters are great at most athletics including anything that has to do with speed and agility, but Weres always give them a run for their money in the Paranorm Olympics.

Doppler athletes are at their best in events that involve strength. The Fae tend to be awesome in a variety of areas—Nymphs and Pixies are great at ice dancing, Abatwa and Elves excel at archery, and Tuatha are generally the best at sword-fighting.

"I still think the Paranorm Olympics are so much better than the norm Olympics. Both summer and winter." As she walked, Nadia's hip brushed one of the low round tables where a couple of Shadow Shifter males lounged.

One of the males, a blond who must have had more muscle than brains, said to Nadia, "Hey, redhead. Babe. Join us for a stiff one." He and the other male laughed in the way males laugh when they sound like they're in on some kind of sexual joke that they think is funny.

I winced.

Nadia went totally still. Her back was rigid as she slowly turned and faced the males. Oh, crap. Her skin had already started to turn sea green and gills were growing behind her ears. It had been a busy night and no doubt that wasn't helping her self-control.

Her sensual voice slipped into her Siren's song.

The males stopped laughing and stared at her with wonder and lust.

I tugged on Nadia's arm but she went up an octave and her song filled the nightclub.

All males paused whatever they were doing and stared at Nadia.

Sirens hate almost all males. Especially those who make sexual innuendoes or advances.

These males were doomed. Unless I did something and soon.

Nadia was entering a dangerous trance that would be harder and harder to control if I didn't stop it.

Her song was sensual and lovely, enticing and inviting. Only the females in the nightclub were immune, and I heard everything from anger to confusion and even amusement from some of them.

Nadia's hands were going for her serpent swords as she moved closer to the two Shadow Shifters' table.

I grabbed her arm. Shook her. Tried to get her to stop. She easily pulled away from my strong grasp. A Siren about to burst into full song is a Siren it's best not to get too close to.

Her voice rose higher and higher. Her mouth opened wider and she sang like an opera singer.

Bless it.

I looked around me and spotted a plate of whole lemons and limes on the bar. I released Nadia's arm long enough to grab a lemon.

Just as she started to draw her swords I stuffed the lemon in her mouth, cutting off her song.

The whole place went silent. Even the DJ wasn't playing music anymore.

The Shadow Shifter males blinked, looking drowsy and confused.

Nadia spit out the lemon and I caught it. "Ewww," she said as she made a face.

"Wha—" the blond Shadow Shifter male started. I stuffed the lemon into *his* mouth. He made a gurgling sound and he tried to spit out the lemon that I'd jammed in pretty tight. Well, it would help keep him from making an ass of himself again—in front of Nadia at least.

Nadia's skin began to lighten as I jerked her away from the table. "I almost killed them, didn't I?" she muttered.

"Uh-huh," I said.

Nadia looked over her shoulder. "Too bad you stopped me."

Heh.

Gotta love her.

The nightclub came to life as music started pounding and males and females began chatting again. Almost every male in the place was shaking his head as if trying to get a roomful of moths out.

We headed to the bar that Hector ran. He was a Shifter who preferred a lion form. Rowwwr.

"Extra dry martini with three olives for Ms. Nyx," Hector said as I approached and he began fixing my favorite drink.

"Thank you," I said as he handed me my drink. "You're the best, Hector."

"Of course." He grabbed grapefruit and cranberry juice and combined them with a shot of vodka before handing Nadia the drink. "And a Sea Breeze for the beautiful Ms. Nadia." Hector was one of the only males who could get away with referring to Nadia as beautiful.

Nadia smiled. "On our tabs, please."

Hector leaned forward, both forearms on the bar. "The drinks for both of you are on the house as a thank you for not killing the patrons."

Nadia's cheeks turned pink.

Hector started rubbing the bar down with a cloth. "All

that blood. Would have been such a mess." He winked at Nadia.

"Um, thanks, Hector," she said and I echoed her thank you.

Nadia's cheeks were still pink as we turned away from the bar.

"It's so crowded tonight." I looked for a place to sit and frowned.

The only spots open were two chairs in the Trackers' corner with its large black overstuffed leather couches and chairs. Three seats were available at a big round table.

But that table had two Vamps lounging on one end. I've never been crazy about Vampires. I didn't have to worry about Nadia getting friendly with one, but I'd always had to work to keep my partner Olivia away from them.

"Kelly and Fere are in the Tracker corner." Nadia looked from that part of the nightclub to me. "Don't you think it's better if we just sit here?" She pointed to the round table with the Vampires.

Hmmm. The two Trackers I disliked the most versus sitting close to a couple of Vamps. Well, I probably should avoid the chance that there might be a double paranormicide if Kelly and Fere made me mad enough.

I glanced back at the Vampires, weighing my options.

A brown-eyed Vampire wore a blue T-shirt and had short dark hair that curled just above his collar. Considering the fact that he was dead, he looked like he was in remarkably good shape, almost like a norm. His skin wasn't waxy-pale like every other Vampire I'd seen.

I sniffed. He smelled young, like freshly tilled soil and cool air. I frowned to myself. He couldn't have been a Vampire more than a couple of years. However, since the Rebellion it had been illegal to turn norms into Vampires. Apparently not everyone was following the ban.

The other Vamp had long dark hair and green eyes. His features were strong, angular. He was paler than the other Vamp and his scent told me he was old, very old. It was in the set of his lips, the age in his eyes, his scent of must and graveyard dirt.

"Okay." I let out a resigned sigh as I looked away from the two Vampires. "Just don't talk with the Vamps."

Nadia grinned. "Who, me?"

When we each settled ourselves in a seat, I met the gaze of the older Vampire. His green eyes were clear, focused, with a dangerous edge to them. A weird sensation crept down my spine and I suppressed a shudder.

I kept my gaze cool and casually looked away.

Vampires should really stay in their coffins and not come out.

THREE

Nadia and I turned our chairs so that our backs were to the table and we could see the dance floor and everything else that was going on.

My spine prickled and I frowned to myself again. I'd never seen a Vampire with anything but bloodshot eyes from too many fake blood cocktails.

"I didn't know there was a Faerie dart tournament tonight." Nadia caught my attention and gestured to the far side of the nightclub and a large elevated floor. Pinball machines, dartboards, and pool tables were on that level.

I cleaned up at pool—no one could beat me. I'd never gotten into Faerie darts.

Purple Faerie dust burst in a puff of glitter as one of the tiny Faeries hit the bull's-eye feetfirst, the point at the end of her leg sleeve burying itself into the board.

"Remember when the competitors used to throw the Faeries headfirst at the dartboard?" Nadia said.

I shook my head. "That was while I was still a youngling in Otherworld."

Nadia laughed, a beautiful laugh that was almost a song. "They strapped helmets with points onto their heads and hit headfirst. The new feet-first technique eliminated a lot of headaches."

"Ow." I grinned. "Well, Faeries *are* hard-headed Fae."

"It's better now." Nadia folded her arms across her chest. "At least for them."

We watched another contestant pick up his Faerie teammate and aim her at the dartboard.

"They sail with wings tight to their sides and their legs encased in a specially designed dart sleeve," Nadia said. "The guidance is a combination of the skill of the thrower, and the Faerie remaining as tight and straight a package as possible. It makes for an aerodynamic, accurate dart."

The long-haired Were holding the tiny Faerie dart took aim, then threw her. I couldn't help a giggle when the Faerie spun, with her little wings tight to her side and the sharp end of the sleeve burying itself into the bull's-eye in a cloud of sparkling blue dust.

"Nothing like paranorm watching," I said to Nadia as I watched a Doppler and a Tuatha arm wrestle. They were a pretty even match, but I would have put my money on the Doppler.

"Eh." Nadia made a dismissive gesture. "Boring. Same old, same old."

I didn't think so. The human half of me enjoyed norm-watching and paranorm-watching. It helped my PI and even my Tracker skills to really get an idea on what makes a norm or paranorm tick.

Compared to paranorm races, norms are pretty . . . normal.

Paranorms tend to stick within their own races. It's always been that way and no one seems inclined or cares to change it. I wondered what it would be like if the New York City paranorms were one big melting pot like norms were in that city. But I had a hard time seeing it.

Some beings from different paranorm races intermingled with everyone, like me. But most . . .

Fae with Elves? Dopplers with Shifters? Shadow Shifters with Metamorphs? Witches with Werewolves? Vampires with anyone?

Nope. Couldn't see it happening.

Even amongst Trackers, there were some personality or race conflicts. For the most part I got along with all races. Maybe it was because I was the only one of my kind around and I didn't have a choice. But I didn't think so. It was just my nature.

"Got him." I gestured to the Doppler who downed the Tuatha in the arm-wrestling match. "Could have made some money on that."

Nadia pointed to a group of pretty young females lounging on couches in a grouping on one side of the nightclub. Witches.

Witches have a mystical air about them, a sense of mystery and unpredictability. As was common with their kind, they wore flowing gowns of different colors and all wore loads of jewelry.

Most paranorms wear little adornments if any. My collar is one exception and that's only because Father insisted a Drow princess was required to wear one from birth. Keeping it on after I reached adulthood at twenty-five had been a battle I'd let him win.

To be honest, though, the collar had been a part of my life since I was a youngling and it kept me grounded in a way I can't really explain. I let my father think that his determination that I wear it caused me to relent.

Sometimes it was worth it to let the King of the Drow think he had "won."

"Witches don't come into the Pit often." Nadia looked thoughtful.

I nodded. "Guess they needed a girls' night out."

Nadia looked at me. "Spa day," we said at the same time and we both laughed.

"We need to get with Lawan and Olivia and pick a day," Nadia said.

I rolled my shoulders. "I could so use a deep-tissue massage."

"You and me both." Nadia nodded her agreement. "And a facial. I would loooove a facial."

An angry voice from behind me caught my attention.

"Look at them," one of the two Vampire males said. "Content to do nothing but go along with their pathetic little lives."

"I'm sick of this shit." The other Vampire kept his tone low. "We put up with the way these idiotic paranorms treat our kind. No respect."

It took some effort to not turn around and say, "Want respect? Why don't you start with doing something with your lives other than sucking blood?"

Then I remembered Vampires have no lives.

Heh.

Instead of making any kind of remark, I tried to watch a Shifter and a Doppler arm wrestle. They were at the same table, cattycorner to Nadia and me, where the first opponents had been competing.

Tried and failed to focus on the competition. I couldn't concentrate because of the Vampires who were talking on the other side of our table. I wanted to tell them to shut their traps.

But their traps were saying such strange and peculiar

things, like "It won't be long," "Things will change," and "He'll let us know when the time is right."

When one of them said "Volod," my pointed ears perked up. They were talking about the city's Master Vampire. I'd never met Volod—Vampires aren't exactly my favorite paranorms—but everyone knew about him in the paranorm world.

"Volod will see to everything, Charles," one of the Vampires said.

I turned just enough to set my empty martini glass on the table and see the two Vamps from the corner of my eye.

"Yeah, we won't have to worry about putting up with paranorm shit much longer," the Vampire called Charles replied. He was the young Vampire. "I've told you before to call me Chuck."

I wanted to laugh when he told the other Vampire to call him Chuck. Who ever heard of a Vampire named Chuck? He added, "Not Charles, just Chuck, okay, Dracula?"

Dracula?

The other Vampire stared at Chuck with his cold green eyes. "Drago," the Vampire said in a voice impossibly colder than his eyes. "Don't fuck with me, Charles Michael Andrulis."

"Yeah. Drago." Chuck shrugged but the act wasn't as nonchalant as the young Vamp tried to make it. "Whatever you want."

I took another sip of my martini, doing my best to act like I wasn't eavesdropping. Considering the pounding music and all of the voices in the crowded nightclub, I shouldn't have been able to hear them at all. A gift or a curse, sometimes I'm not sure, but my hearing is exceptional.

Trying to go unnoticed when you have blue hair and amethyst skin becomes more of a challenge. Fortunately the two Vampires weren't paying attention to me.

"So what's the plan?" Chuck said in a hurry, like he was trying to change the subject.

"Volod will make his plan known to all Vampire kind soon." Drago started to take a drink of his fake blood cocktail and made a disgusted face before he put the glass down again. "For now all you need to do is be prepared." His eyes locked with Chuck's again. "And keep your mouth shut."

"Like who am I gonna tell?" Chuck muttered, then looked away from Drago. "I don't even know enough to tell anyone what's gonna go down."

"Exactly." Drago's fangs glinted in the strobe lighting. "And that's the way we'll keep it. For now."

"Vampires don't belong in a paranorm nightclub," came a very hard, very drunk voice. I did turn then, just enough to see a Shifter named Jack who I didn't know very well, but had always avoided. He was well known as a real jerk.

Jack held a bottle of Bud and wore a more belligerent expression than usual. "Your kind shouldn't be allowed through those doors."

Drago raised his head and hissed, his fangs looked sharper, longer than before. The green-eyed Vampire slowly got to his feet. "Leave, Shifter. Or I will make you."

With a harsh laugh, the Shifter threw the contents of his beer bottle into Drago's eyes.

The Vampire moved so fast I barely saw it. He grabbed the Shifter by his neck and lifted the male so that his feet were dangling.

A gurgling sound came from the Shifter's throat a second before he shifted into a snake.

Drago looked disgusted and flung the snake to the floor. The snake immediately rose up back into his human form.

Chuck shot to his feet and slammed his fist into the Shifter's face.

The Shifter stumbled backward, then morphed into a cougar.

It pounced on Chuck, driving the Vampire to the floor.

The next thing I knew, the cougar was flying across the room.

The cougar landed on a table. It collapsed in a crash, drinks and broken wood flying, and knocking five screaming Pixies and Nymphs off their chairs.

Drago's green eyes burned with hate as he started to stalk the cougar. Before he'd taken a step, two of Rodán's Doppler bouncers, Tony and Kyle, grabbed the Vampire by his arms.

"You're out of the club." Tony dug his fingers into Drago's biceps as he began to drag the Vampire toward the door.

Kyle had the Vampire's other side. "Don't even think about coming back."

Drago hissed but didn't struggle. When they reached the door, the Vampire said loud enough for me to hear over the music. "You have failed to respect our kind, but you will."

"Whatever." Kyle shoved the Vampire out the door, and out of sight.

I looked at the other Vampire who was already following Drago. The cougar was licking his paw, never taking his tawny eyes from Chuck.

The second Vamp strode to the doorway where Kyle and Tony had just thrown Drago out.

Chuck paused a second as he looked at the bouncers. "You'll regret this."

Tony made a snorting sound. "Don't bother coming back. It's a wonder any of your kind are allowed in the Pit."

The Vampire snarled before brushing by Tony and Kyle, then past Matthew who still manned the front door in Fred's place.

I wondered why Jack hadn't been kicked out, as well. He'd started the whole thing.

Nadia and I looked at each other and she tossed her long red hair over her shoulder. "They should have thrown out those Shadow Shifters, too."

"Maybe almost dying at your hand was lesson enough." I watched as perhaps seven other Vampires in the room converged and started talking to each other in voices so low I couldn't hear them. "What's up with the Vamps? Why aren't they skulking over their synthetic blood cocktails and chewing on the celery sticks?"

"Maybe they're tired of celery." She looked in the direction the Vampires had left. "I've always wondered why Vampires sleep in coffins. At least I've heard they do."

I shrugged. "From what I learned since coming here is that they sleep in coffins because they appear dead to their families and friends when they are 'turned.' So they're buried in coffins."

Natalie looked thoughtful. "Still doesn't make sense why they sleep in them."

"Rodán told me it takes nine nights for a turned Vampire to wake." I looked across the room at a group of Vampires who had gathered together. I lowered my voice. "Once they're turned, new Vampires have a lot of strength and they dig their way out of their graves."

"What a way to become a paranorm." Nadia wrinkled her nose. "Get bitten, contract the vampire infection, buried, then claw your way out of a grave."

"It's weird that just because they're undead they can only come out at night," I said. "I still don't understand that."

Nadia was starting to look bored but then she asked, "How do they know what to do? Regular paranorms grow up in families and we're taught from the time we're younglings how to be part of our race."

"According to Rodán, a full-fledged Vampire is always waiting on the ninth night, when the new Vamp climbs out of his grave," I said. "Then the experienced Vamp takes the newly turned Vamp—along with his or her coffin—to a Vampire lair where they learn what's involved in being a Vampire."

Nadia laughed. "Vampire 101."

I grinned. "I guess that's about it."

"So Vampires sleeping in coffins came about because of being buried in them as turned humans," she said when she finished laughing.

I had a hard time stopping laughing too before I said, "The coffins are their last possession before they wake as Vampires. So I guess they get a little attached to them."

Nadia yawned, a pretty little yawn that she covered with her hand. "I think it's time to go home. I want to watch the rest of *The Little Mermaid* before I go to bed." She looked at me. "Last night's Sprite ordeal cut into my regular programming."

"What a strange night." I pushed my chair away from the table and stood. "If it wasn't for all the Weres in the bar, I would have thought it was a full moon."

We had to walk past the seven Vamps. One of them raised her head and her blue eyes flashed hatred strong enough to make me almost pause.

Almost. Vampires weren't worth pausing for. As far as I was concerned, Vampires should never have been invited.

FOUR

"How many?" Olivia made a hex sign with her fingers as I held up a report the moment she walked through the front door. Bells jangled as the door to our PI office slammed shut behind my partner. "Let me guess. Six."

"Make that seven." I leaned back in my chair and dropped the report on a teetering pile of other folders on my desk.

Olivia and I had been partners for going on two years now. I brought her into our PI firm about six months after Rodán had set me up in business and I had learned a lot of the tricks of the trade.

Our door sign was Pixie-made, sparkly purple and sapphire, which Olivia hated. She thought that it made us look too girly. I rather like girly.

NYX CIAR
Olivia DeSantos
PARANORMAL CRIMES
PRIVATE INVESTIGATORS
By appointment only

Nice. I thought so, anyway.

"Ready to get in on the fun we had last night?" I asked her.

A long strand of her hair hung loose from where she had pulled her hair back in a clip. The dark hair fell across her cheek. Half Kenyan and half Puerto Rican, Olivia's skin was like beautiful brown silk. "Bet your purple ass I want in on 'the fun.'"

"Amethyst ass." The response was automatic when she called me purple.

She tugged off her New York Mets sweat jacket and tossed it on a pile of folders on the credenza by her desk. Her desk was as bad as mine, only she preferred neon orange and green sticky notes and I liked hot pink.

When Olivia took off the sweat jacket, it revealed her side-holstered Sig Sauer. "You know how I feel about Sprites. I think they all need to be penned up and the locks soldered shut."

If I wasn't so tired from tracking Sprites all night, staying at the Pit for a few hours, and then another extracurricular activity, I would have grinned when I saw her T-shirt.

ONE BY ONE THE PENGUINS ARE STEALING MY SANITY

I pointed to the bright red T-shirt, obviously a new addition to Olivia's extensive collection. "You should X out penguins and change it to Sprites."

She leaned over her desk and grabbed a black permanent marker from the cup beside her computer monitor. She popped the cap of the marker. "Good idea."

Then I did laugh.

My cat jumped onto my desk, startling me. The blue Persian gave a loud yowl and I winced. "Okay, okay, Kali. I'll be up to give you your Fancy Feast."

Kali's tail twitched and I knew my underwear drawer

was in trouble. And I'd just bought new panties at Victoria's Secret yesterday.

I'd gotten a little bit smarter, though. I'd started buying as many as a dozen panties at a time. Took Kali longer to work her way through shredding my new ones.

Kali jumped off my desk and started toward a set of file cabinets. Tail still twitching, the cat looked over her shoulder at me in a way that said, "You. Will. Pay."

I groaned. Maybe I'd get lucky and a couple of pairs of panties and bras would survive.

As if I'd be so fortunate.

"Statue of Liberty," Olivia said and I turned to look at her. She grinned as she held the uncapped marker in her hand and shook her head with amusement on her face. "Saw it on CNN. I swear I thought the mayor was going to trip over his tongue and fall into the crowd of reporters when he tried to talk his way through this one."

I gestured in the direction of my weapons wall. "I think all of those press conferences might be harder to deal with than grabbing a sword or a bow and taking care of the Sprites."

Fine diamond-headed arrows were in quivers on one wall of our office. Light Elves fashioned the bows from precious Dryad wood and Dark Elves made the diamond arrowheads. Longswords and other Otherworld weapons were braced on my walls, mostly reminders of home. I preferred my dragon-clawed daggers, which were better for close combat.

Olivia patted her handgun. "I'll take a Sig or a Glock any day over one of those things."

I nodded. It depends on what form I'm in as to what my weapon of choice is.

As a human I usually have a much softer side than when I'm Drow. I can be tough then, too, but as a human I love being feminine. I enjoy wearing silks and satin, eating at nice restaurants, taking in a play, spending a day out with "the girls," and cuddling with Adam. But as a human I still have the same need for justice that probably makes me a little tougher than I might otherwise be.

At night, my heritage takes control when I track the bad guys—paranorms—down. Dark Elves are warriors, fighters, and most run the line of gray magic, some even dark magic.

My magic doesn't run dark or even gray, but on this level I'm more primal, the hunt for the wrongdoers almost a pleasure. It's a side of me that is sometimes hard to deal with when I face the aftermath in the morning. I never kill for the sake of the kill. I never harm any being for the sake of harming them. Never. I do my job as a Night Tracker and I'm good at what I do.

It's my strong sense of justice that determines how I act and react by day and by night. It's my soul that determines who I am.

The bells jangled again as the door swung open and heat flushed through me. *Adam.* My belly tingled as I met his warm brown eyes and he gave me his cute, almost shy smile.

There was nothing shy about Detective Adam Boyd.

He loved to watch me when I shifted, watching the change in my body, my skin tone, my hair. It still amazed me that once he learned about my other half, he had so easily accepted who and what I am. Not many humans can handle what I become at sunset.

After their initial surprise—and some serious convincing when it came to Olivia—she and Adam each took my differences in stride. More or less.

Now if I could just get Olivia to stop calling me purple and keep her from eating Lay's barbecue chips around me, our relationship would be nearly perfect. The crunch queen. Drove me nuts.

Adam gave Olivia a nod and a smile before reaching me. At five-two, Olivia was a full foot shorter than Adam, but in a wrestling match it was possible she could take the tall detective down. Never doubt Olivia. She was an explosive package.

She capped the marker and tossed it on her desk without desecrating her T-shirt. "Don't pretend you're here to see me too." Olivia's expression was sarcastic but amusement was in her tone. Her red Keds squeaked on the floor as she rounded her desk, then plopped in her leather chair.

He grinned and shoved his hands in his worn brown leather bomber jacket and eased into one of the client chairs in front of my desk. Even though it wasn't windy, his brown hair was tousled as if I'd just had my hands clenched in the thick, soft strands. Heat made its way through me, warmth that only filled me when I was around Adam.

"How was last night?" As a NYPD detective he had a hard edge to his voice when on the job. But not with me. His tone was low, caring, with a sensuality that was so natural it sent excited shivers through me.

At first I thought Adam was talking about being in my bed after I got home from the Pit in the wee hours of the morning. My cheeks burned as I did my best to keep from looking at Olivia.

Oh. He meant tracking.

Olivia snickered. I ignored her.

I cleared my throat. "It was busy last night."

"Nice touch to the Statue of Liberty." He dragged his

hand down his stubbled face. "Talk about a mess for the mayor to try to explain in a press conference how the statue ended up with pink toenails and lipstick."

With an exasperated sigh I added, "Not to mention the torch."

"Some idiot's going to start a rumor that the whole thing was done by space aliens." Olivia put her feet up on her desk. "Trust me."

"This can't be just Sprite mischief." I repeated the thought yet again as I had been doing for days now. I ran my fingers along my collar. "There are way too many Sprites around and they're wreaking havoc everywhere."

"It's getting harder to keep the knowledge of what's causing all of this from going public." Adam's brown eyes became intense like they always did when he was focusing on his job. "At least in the norm world it is."

"I think everyone is tired of cleaning up Sprite messes." Olivia pushed the loose strand of hair away from her cheek. "Need to round up every one of the little bastards and then we won't have to worry about it at all."

"We've got to figure this out." I jerked my thumb at Olivia. "Before she gets any bitchier than she already is."

Adam laughed and I tried to hide a grin.

Olivia grabbed a rubber band from her desk, loaded a good-sized eraser in it, and aimed it at me, her eyes narrowed. "Excuse me?"

"Kidding." I held my hands up and caught the eraser that Olivia let fly. Her first experience with the paranorm world had been with a nasty Sprite. She'd had no use for them after that and more than disliked the slimy beings.

Almost as bad as I hate Zombies.

No, not even close. Nobody can hate anything worse than I hate Zombies.

Olivia considered the black permanent marker again as I focused on Adam. I picked up the growing file folder from the last week of Sprite-related "mischief." I groaned. "They're practically tearing up the city. Manhattan will never be the same if we don't get them under control."

"Still can't believe what they did to Yankee Stadium." Adam frowned and shook his head as he mentioned the disaster at the baseball park. "Sacrilege."

"Send them all to Otherworld." Olivia pulled her slim XPhone out of the holster at her waist. Using a stylus, she started to jot down notes on the phone regarding the Sprite case. "Let the Great Guardian take care of them."

"Good idea." I rolled my eyes at her. "Why didn't I think of that?"

Adam shoved his hands deeper into his jacket pockets. "Without starting an extraterrestrial alien panic, how are they going to explain last night?"

Olivia snorted. "That's nothing compared to what they did to the Met."

I felt like banging my head against my desk and Adam clenched his jaw. "What's the point to all this sh—crap that these things are doing?"

Adam always did his best not to use "colorful language" in front of me. If he only knew—when I let loose with Drow curses, they made human expletives sound like making sweet cooing sounds to a baby.

"What we do know is that Sprites despise leadership." I frowned and concentrated on the problem instead of the crazy things that the Sprites had been up to. "Everything they've been doing has to have been organized, though. There must be a reason for all of this." I picked up a pencil and tapped it on a sticky note on my desk. "Now to figure out what that is."

"What's our next step?" Adam got to his feet. "I'm ready to bust these little SOBs."

"*My* next step is what happens." I stood and grabbed my Dolce & Gabbana handbag from a cubbyhole in my desk. "It's time for me to visit the Sprites in lockup again."

"Why the hell can't we go to the paranorm lockup with you?" Olivia asked with a scowl. "Who made up that lame-ass rule?"

The Great Guardian, of course. Every paranorm who knew about the Paranorm Center was sworn to secrecy about its existence or whereabouts. The only thing Olivia and Adam knew was that there was a paranorm lockup somewhere in the city.

"Can't help it." I held up my hands in a pleading gesture. "Just one of those things."

Olivia toyed with a rubber band. "We know everything else."

With a shake of his head, Adam said, "I doubt that."

"It's just not like Nyx to keep secrets from us." Olivia flipped another eraser at me.

Adam looked at me, understanding in his warm brown eyes. "Everyone has to keep one secret or another. Just the way things work."

Sunshine warmed my fair skin as Joshua and I walked from the Upper East Side and entered Central Park. We headed toward the Alice in Wonderland unbirthday party sculpture, at the northern end of Conservatory Water.

When I was a youngling in the Drow Realm, my mother would read human fairy tales and fantasy stories to me, and Alice in Wonderland had been one of my favorites.

We were on our way to interrogate the Sprites in lockup. The numerous miscreants were being held in detention within the confines of the PC, which was deep below Central Park.

As a Shadow Shifter, Joshua didn't make a sound when he moved or walked. That was quieter than I was used to in another paranorm being. Elves and some Fae are completely silent when they want to be. Shadow Shifters can be just as quiet.

The PC housed our version of a legal system, which included the Paranorm Council. I never considered it much of a legal system. It was more like a medieval version of New York City bureaucrats.

Peacekeepers across the earth Otherworld held the paranorm world together, not the Paranorm Council. The Pit headquartered New York City Peacekeepers. Rodán, of course, served as Proctor over all New York City Peacekeepers. That included Night Trackers, Soothsayers, Healers, and Gatekeepers. Multiple races served as Peacekeepers including Dopplers, Werewolves, Shifters, and Fae.

Night Trackers were some of the few beings allowed in the Paranorm Center since we were the elite of paranorm law enforcement. This was Joshua's first visit to the NYC Paranorm Center since his arrival from Australia.

When we reached the Alice in Wonderland unbirthday party sculpture, Joshua looked on in amusement as I walked counterclockwise the circumference the characters inhabited. As I did, I recited the engraved nonsensical poem to open the door. " ' 'Twas brillig, and the slithy toves did gyre and gimble in the wabe.' "

Joshua grinned, the first sign of humanity from him that morning. "And what might that mean?"

"No idea." I walked to the glamour-hidden entrance beneath the toadstool. "Comes from Lewis Carroll's poem called 'The Jabberwocky.' It's not in any paranorm language I'm familiar with."

But then I wasn't exactly familiar with the intricacies of more languages than those of Light and Dark Elves. Olivia was the linguistics expert and spoke several earthbound languages proficiently. She'd been learning Drow from me over the almost two years that we'd been partners. I wasn't sure if her learning Drow was a good idea or not, considering she'd picked up several Drow curse words too.

When we started down the steps beneath the sculpture, torches flared to life along the walls. The cold of the underground took away the warmth of the sun and cooled my skin.

My long black hair fell over my shoulders as I looked downward at the spiraling stone steps and held my handbag close to my side. Because we were headed to the detention center, I had chosen to wear black jeans and a cashmere sweater, forgoing my usual designer clothing.

We jogged down the steps, which led us almost as deep as the belowground realm of the Dark Elves in Otherworld. When we reached the enormous circular main foyer, we went through one of five archways, then passed the huge chamber used by the Paranorm Council. The Paranorm Center was out of a medieval picture book of a dungeon, only about twenty times larger. Some things never change.

"Security is tight." Joshua nodded in approval, no doubt recognizing that some of the shadows were not shadows at all. They were Shadow Shifters, Joshua's race.

I looked at the Dryads who pressed their faces out from their wooden columns. "After the Metamorph incident, they had to come up with something."

During the Metamorph op, the Dryads, who had previously been the only security, had blown it big-time. Metamorphs were worse than Sprites, and that was definitely saying something. Metamorphs could mirror any human and use it to their advantage. The beings had no redeeming qualities. None.

Well, at least none that any of us knew of. All of the Metamorphs in New York City that we'd ever come across had been seriously bad news.

"There's another good reason for the higher level of security, too." I paused as a Dryad in one of the columns partially came out. Like all Dryads her smile was wicked.

I cleared my throat and looked away from her to Joshua. "Archives are kept in another part of the Paranorm Center. Important information that needs to be well-guarded."

"Such as?" Joshua's expression and his voice remained even but there was curiosity in his intense eyes.

"Along with 'top secret' events, information is kept on every paranorm species," I said. "Knowledge that is kept from all paranorms for a reason."

Joshua looked away from me and stared down the hall. "Our operation in the Catskills would be considered 'Top Secret.'"

My hands suddenly felt dirty, just thinking about the whole case. I wiped my palms on my jeans. "Everything about that op should never come to light."

Joshua made a grumbling sound of agreement.

I pointed to the council chamber's closed heavy wooden doors as we passed. "Where the council meets." It must be in session because of the pair of black-robed Shifter guards standing to either side of the door.

Joshua focused on the door with an intense expression. "How many serve on the Paranorm Council in New York City?"

"Five." I counted them off on my fingers. "One female represents Dopplers, a Werewolf male represents all Weres, and another female council member, a Siren, serves for every race of Fae." I wasn't about to get into all of the Fae races. "Then there's a male Shifter who—"

Joshua scowled as he interrupted me. "I have heard of this. It is unacceptable for a Shifter to represent Shadow Shifters as well."

"Don't get me started," I grumbled. "A male of the Light Elves serves for the Dark Elves as well. The Drow aren't too happy about it.

"Vampires and Witches have been trying to get on the council, but they have been voted out every time." I glanced at the doors as I spoke. "Unfortunately the council still needs to work on things like 'cooperation,' and 'working together for the good of the many.'"

Yeah, right.

Joshua kept his normally long strides just a little shorter for me. I'm tall at five-eight, but he had me beat by quite a few inches in height. Only the guards were in the great hall as Joshua and I walked through it. The guards and whatever else that might be watching us.

As we were passing the heavy wooden doors of the council chamber, both doors flung open. They slammed against the walls, barely missing the guards who stood on either side of the door.

Instinctively I reached into my handbag for my Kahr as the pounding noise reverberated through the giant hall. My hand closed around the weapon's grip but I didn't take the Kahr out of my handbag.

My heart took another leap as a Vampire strode through the archway, fury on his pale but strong, aristocratic features. Behind him, through the great doorway,

I caught a glimpse of unrest among the five council members and heard their angry chatter.

The Vamp faced the five paranorm representatives. "You will regret your decision to not allow Vampires on the council." His words rang throughout the great hall as he repeated, "You *will* regret it."

"Volod—" one of the council members started to say.

But the Vampire had already raised one hand. The doors slammed shut so loudly it felt as though the thick stone beneath our feet vibrated and my teeth chattered.

So this was Volod. As far as I knew, he was the last remaining Master Vampire in New York State and he was lord over all of New York City's Vampires. When every one of the other Masters had been destroyed in the Paranorm Rebellion sometime in the nineteenth century, Volod had taken absolute control.

It had been too late for the Vampires, though. He was practically a king with no people to reign over. His kind had almost been wiped out completely. I wondered how many Vampires had been "made" since the Rebellion, like Chuck.

Volod's long hair streamed over his shoulders. His black Dockers and black polo shirt stretched snugly across his swimmer's build as his long strides took him toward Joshua and me.

I almost stepped back but forced myself to hold my ground. Volod's cold black eyes met mine. For the first time when facing a Vampire I felt a chill roll through me and I barely kept from shuddering.

As a Tracker I was used to dealing with his kind. Not one Vamp had ever made me feel the way I did right then . . . like he would easily have torn my head off, ripped my heart from my chest, and eaten it while my vision faded in my last moments on this earth Other-world.

Maybe I felt that way because it was daytime and I was in my human form, without my complete strength and abilities as Drow. My insides quivered as he walked past us. Threads of unease twined in my belly.

Volod left behind the bitter smell of anger and a Vampire's strong odor of graveyard dirt.

As a Vampire, for him to be up during the day was strange. No doubt he'd ventured out because the council meeting was during the daylight hours—probably to keep Vampires from attending. I didn't believe any Vampire but a Master Vampire could safely see at least some light of day without damage to them.

Guess that little ruse, to hold a meeting during daylight hours so that Vampires couldn't attend, hadn't worked. Likely Volod had taken one of the dank underground passageways that stretched out beneath the city like a spiderweb.

Joshua and I looked at each other after Volod passed. Joshua jerked his thumb in the direction Volod had just vanished. "Who is that?" Joshua sounded more bored than agitated unlike me.

"His name is Volod and he's the New York Master Vampire." I started walking and Joshua fell into place beside me. "The way he just stalked out of the council meeting can't be a good thing."

FIVE

Definitely not a good thing. The Master Vampire had stalked out of the council meeting in a way that left no doubt in my mind that he was serious about the Council regretting their decision.

My skin crawled, like grubs wiggling on my body.

I looked up at Joshua, mentally shook off the creepy feeling, and shrugged. "I should take into account that the Council fights regularly and pretty much accomplishes nothing. Rodán and the Night Trackers are the ones who take care of business." And we did.

As Proctor, Rodán took direction from the Great Guardian herself. From the first time she interfered—*helped*—I called her the GG. She ticks me off and has since I lived belowground in Otherworld. I'm probably going to end up in Underworld for my lack of reverence for her.

Joshua said, "Your Council. What does it do?"

"Very little," I said under my breath. "They don't accomplish much of anything. Peacekeepers do all of the work."

"It's the same where I come from," Joshua said with a smirk. "Hours behind doors but little results."

I gave a nod in the direction we were heading. "The Paranorm Task Force is great, though."

Primarily Dopplers ran the PTF. Somehow the fact that Dopplers changed into one animal form made them less flighty, more responsible than Shifters who tended to shift with whatever mood they were in.

Dopplers had a knack for cleaning up "messes" that we Trackers left behind, as well as hauling paranorms who broke our laws off to elemental-magic-treated jails. Where we were headed now.

We had to walk down a long, expansive hallway to the very end where it was dark with flickering shadows cast by two torches. I wondered if Joshua felt at home around plain old shadows.

Stairs wound deeper belowground. I scrunched my nose at the stench that grew worse the closer we got to the detention center.

"Too bad Dopplers don't clean the place as well as they handle roping up the bad guys we neutralize." I glanced at Joshua. He appeared deep in thought, so I didn't bother to say anything else to him.

Dopplers were also excellent in assisting in making sure magical disasters were erased as best as possible. They sure did a bad job of keeping the place clean, though.

That thought was reaffirmed as we entered what might be considered the administrative office of the PTF.

Crumpled papers surrounded a wastebasket like snowballs on the dirt floor. The basket itself was over-loaded with paper plates, plastic utensils, and unfinished meals—and more paper snowballs.

Three scratched and marred wood desks were crowded into the place. One of the desks was occupied by a male Doppler. GREG was embroidered on his blue jumpsuit. Greg had a big belly, buggy blue eyes, and skin so pale that it matched the paper snowballs on the floor.

"Could really use some Shifter cleaners in here," I muttered under my breath. It was a useless thought because there's too much animosity between the races. I would have been laughed at if I even suggested it.

The place smelled of rat poison and stale food along with the stench of way too many paranorms crammed in one location. In a place like this, all the scents of different paranorms meshed together can be knock-you-on-your-butt overwhelming.

I ran my fingers along my collar as I looked down the passageway leading to the cells. I dropped my hand away as I focused my attention on the buggy-eyed Doppler who was sitting behind the smallest desk in the cramped room. I had a feeling his animal form would be something with eyes as buggy as his human ones.

"Nyx Ciar. I'm a paranormal private investigator." I held out my hand to the Doppler, but he didn't take it. What a jerk. I gestured with the same hand to my partner for the day. "This is Joshua, a Night Tracker. We're here to interview the Sprites."

The Doppler chuckled, his belly jiggling like Olivia's huge boobs did when she ran. "All of them?" he asked with clear amusement. "Let's see your creds."

I kept my expression polite as I showed him my paranorm PI credentials.

Greg grabbed a set of keys and sort of hop-jumped down the hallway. Maybe he was a gray tree frog in animal form. Dopplers could be just about any type of creature, including amphibians.

Species from Otherworld never bothered to keep up with the times. Things stayed as medieval as they could be. Just a few examples were the decrepit stone walls and floor, and the hissing and spitting torches that were interspersed along the passageway Greg led us down.

As we passed cells, I recognized a lot of paranorms that I had taken down as a Tracker, but they didn't recognize me in my human form. Saved me from hearing what would have been plenty of curses as I walked through.

Instead I was on the receiving end of multiple propositions and comments about my attributes. It took a lot of willpower not to respond to each creep with a good kick or punch.

The Doppler led us down two levels. The stench was overpowering as we went down another level and I coughed. Being around that many Sprites at one time was not going to be easy.

Cells containing Sprites took up the entire bottom level, which was bizarre. Normally five Sprites at most were housed at one time in the detention center. The thirty or so Sprites that were there now were loud and obnoxious, shouting obscenities as we passed.

"Sprites in New York City have always been scum." While I spoke, I glanced at Joshua as we walked past several of the cells. "They're almost as bad as Metamorphs. Almost." I shook my head as I remembered the whole Metamorph incident that was the reason security was so much higher at the Paranorm Center.

Joshua nodded as he studied the closest cells with his intense gaze.

"Even though they tend to get in trouble," I said, "we've never had this many Sprites locked up at one time before."

The first cell the PTF agent, Greg, took us to was the one that contained the extra-ugly Sprite that I'd taken down last night. The Sprite hissed as he glared at me with his huge protruding eyes that made Greg's buggy eyes seem tiny in comparison.

I walked up to the cell and handed Joshua my purse containing my weapons.

His eyes narrowed. "I'm going in with you."

I ignored him as the PTF agent unlocked the cell and opened it just long enough for me to slip in and keep the Sprite from slipping out. Joshua looked at me with narrowed eyes.

As I stared at the Sprite, I said to Joshua, "You can have your fun next. My turn first."

"This one's name is Ordox, according to the register," Greg said.

My focus shifted entirely to the Sprite whose nose I had broken, his ugly face scraped from meeting a minuscule portion of the copper-plated statue. His ragged, dirty clothing hung on him like sails that had lost their wind.

Ordox had a wicked expression now, an evil smile, as if he'd just been handed a birthday present as I walked about ten feet from him.

Likely he was so delighted because he thought I was a mere human. That was no doubt what he sensed—my human side. He probably figured he could overpower me and make me his hostage.

He rushed me.

Enough room was between us that I was able to take one step, then forward-flip, using my air element to propel me faster.

I landed behind him on my running shoes, then I grasped his neck in one hand and slammed him up against the wall.

His head made a hard *thunk* and he howled in pain. It was a muffled sound considering how tight a grip I had

on his throat. My Drow strength made it impossible for
him to move.

He tried clawing at my hand but I raised my other
and aimed two fingers at his eyes. I felt the dangerous
white flash in my own eyes as I moved my fingers closer
to his face.

"You are going to give me the information I want,
Ordox." My fingers were almost to his eyes and he went
limp in my grasp. "I'm going to let go. You won't try
anything." I couldn't let him know that I was one and
the same Tracker who'd taken him down at the statue.
So I gestured toward Joshua who folded his arms across
his chest. "You know better than to mess with a Tracker,
don't you?"

At the word "Tracker," the Sprite's face went red
and he started cursing in a seldom-used Fae language
that is guttural and almost as ugly as he was. I didn't
understand but I had a pretty good idea what he was
saying.

"You're also going to learn to not mess with me," I
said in English before following that with a few Drow
curse words. Drow is similar to but not pretty like the
language of the Light Elves. It's harsh and was clearly
not complimentary to him in return. He looked surprised
as I spoke in my native language before his expression
went arrogant and evil again.

One more time I squeezed his neck, letting him know
that I was no idle threat. When I released him he dropped
to the hard stone floor of his cell in a ragged heap.

"Bitch," Ordox growled but didn't bother to stand.

"You are going to tell me," I said, "what is behind all
of this chaos you and the other Sprites have been causing in the city."

The Sprite grinned, which surprised me. I'd never even

seen a Sprite smile, much less grin. He laughed, which was even more startling and the sound grated down my spine.

I had Ordox's dirty collar clenched in my fists before he finished laughing. The Sprite glared at me and pressed his thick lips tightly together. I used everything I could to get Ordox to talk short of any kind of violence. To get a name, anything. Unfortunately this Sprite wouldn't give an inch. I couldn't get a word out of him, except his comments that the Sprites just enjoy mischief and like to cause chaos. All of this was true, but I sensed there was more to it this time. This was different.

Ordox actually laughed as I walked out of the cell. I glanced over my shoulder.

"No one knows anything," he said. "And no Sprite is stupid enough to tell you even if he does know."

"I doubt that." I turned back away from him and closed the cell door behind me with a hard *clang*. "Sprites aren't known for their intelligence. Someone will talk."

He laughed again, a sound that grated up and down my spine. "Go home, bitch."

I almost went back in that cell. Instead I turned away with Joshua and the Doppler and we walked to the next jailed Sprite.

This time Joshua dissolved into shadow and moved under the elemental-magic-treated bars. Trackers could pass through because we had each been given the power that made elemental-magic-treated confinements useless against us.

Although I had learned the hard way that when I'm human they do work on me. When I'm Drow it's not a problem.

The Sprite shrank back when Joshua rose to his imposing height and towered over the creature.

During the time Joshua interrogated the Sprite, the creature wouldn't say a word that would help us at all.

Twelve more rounds of interviewing Sprites, and what little patience I'd had was shot.

Lucky number thirteen, I thought as I entered Sprite's cell.

He was small for a Sprite. Looked younger than the rest and he sat in the corner with his arms wrapped around his knees. He wouldn't make eye contact with me. All of the other Sprites had been so defiant, most with an in-your-face attitude.

Hmmm. This Sprite might have possibilities.

I walked up to him. "What's your name?" I hadn't asked any of the other Sprites for their names but this one seemed different.

"Negel," he said quietly.

I crouched down so that we were nearly eye level. "Negel, we have some important questions to ask."

The Sprites were hiding something big and we had to find out. Somehow. Someway.

"What?" the Sprite asked.

"All I want is to know why Sprites are creating all of this chaos in the city," I said. "A reason and some names."

Negel looked past my shoulder and I followed his gaze to see the Sprite in the adjacent cell glaring at Negel.

"Do not say *anything*!" the Sprite shouted. "Or you will die, you stupid *hundoff*."

"See what you can get out of that slimy creep," I said to Joshua. "I'll take care of this one."

After Joshua dissolved into shadow and reappeared in the other Sprite's cell, I gave my full attention to Negel.

"Start talking." I made my voice sound deadly soft.

"They'll kill me." The Sprite's thick lips trembled. "I

have a wife and children to take care of. And a brother, too."

For a moment I just stared at him. I'd never thought of Sprites having families and siblings.

"We won't let them know you talked." I glanced at the Sprite screaming from the other cage for Negel to shut up. "I have an idea that will keep them from knowing you said anything."

His voice dropped so low I could barely hear him. "The—the one responsible can't know I told you. He'll kill me."

I shifted from my crouch onto one knee on the filthy floor. "You have my word that no one will find out you said anything."

Negel looked both scared and skeptical.

I called to my air elemental powers, and almost instantly all noise was cut off from around us. All that could be heard was the sound of Negel's quick breaths.

"I've just put an invisible shield around us." I focused on the Sprite and didn't look around at the others in lock-up. "No one can hear a word you say. I'll also make sure we let nothing slip that could endanger you."

Negel's huge eyes were wide as he stared at me. His throat worked as he swallowed. His lips barely moved as he said, "If this you promise, then I will tell you what I know."

"Why are the Sprites wreaking havoc in the city?" I asked.

His huge Adam's apple bobbed. "A distraction, a diversion."

I frowned and my mind raced. "From what?"

He shook his head. His dirty blond tuft of hair flopped as he moved and his ears wiggled. "That's all I know."

"Give me more," I said.

For a moment, Negel didn't say anything. "I will tell you this because I think it is wrong what is being done." Negel gave another nervous look over my shoulder. "We are not that kind of being."

Yeah, right.

The Sprite ran his tongue over his thick lips. "I did overhear a little. Just a little."

"What?" I said.

He grunted, then pushed a sentence out in a rush. "The night before I was captured, I was walking by our leader, Tobath—"

"Sprites don't have leadership." My gaze narrowed and I felt the ache in my eyes signifying the white flash that he would see, a flash that would tell him my patience with him wasn't as good as I had thought. "Sprites despise leadership and organization."

"It is true," Negel said. "Tobath gathered us together and has others who enforce his commands." The Sprite ran his tongue over his lips again. "My brother, Penrod, has been trying to find a way to stop Tobath, who is nothing but a dictator."

Negel's chest expanded beneath his rags as he took a deep breath. "Penrod said the only way we can do this is to join with Tobath and pretend to go along with him, and wait to find an opportunity to take him down." Negel looked down on his long, nubbly fingers. "After what I have seen, I am not sure it is possible."

"You know more than what you led me to believe at the start," I said.

Negel scooted up higher against the wall. I was too afraid. I fear that something might happen to my family."

That I could believe, that he was too scared. This Sprite was not bad guy material. I had a hard time imagining him doing much of anything when he was supposed to be creating chaos in the city.

"What did you overhear?" I said. "I want to know *everything*."

"I didn't see who Tobath was talking to." Negel wiped his hand across his forehead. "But he said the master is pleased with what my people had done so far and he said that the plan is proceeding nicely. That is all I heard. I swear, that is all I heard or know."

My skin started to chill and goose bumps prickled my skin. *Master.* There was only one being I had ever heard referred to as Master. "Who?" I asked.

The name tore from Negel like a curse. "Volod."

SIX

A Master Vampire living in the penthouse of the unique Hudson Hotel by Central Park. A hotel so unique that it was referred to merely as "The Hudson."

Hello? If someone says they're staying at the Hudson, they could just as well be on a houseboat on the river.

As we headed up toward Volod's city lair, I wondered if things could get any stranger than a Vampire in a penthouse.

Of course they could. This was New York City.

Arriving in Volod's personal elevator wasn't an option. Olivia, Angel, and Joshua were with me in the stairwell, taking the long way to get to Volod's lair. The three teamed up with me on this mission like they had throughout the Sprite fiasco and back during the Werewolf op.

Earlier today Joshua and I had continued interviewing other Sprites. Even using bits of the information from Negel, we hadn't been able to get any Sprite to talk.

A couple of the creepy beings had looked shocked, if not scared when they heard the Vampire's name, but still no one said anything. We'd been lucky with Negel.

Joshua's flail rocked at his side as we jogged the twenty-four flights of stairs to the penthouse of the Hudson. Shadow Shifters are as silent as Elves and Fae when they move, even when they're in human form.

I pushed long strands of my blue hair over my shoulder as I glanced behind me at Angel. She was incredibly quiet as she followed. Like me, she wore a form-fitting black leather fighting suit—only hers showed even more skin than mine did, which meant hers showed a lot of flesh.

The barbs on the whip at Angel's side had a dull look to them that didn't begin to betray their deadly knife-edged sharpness. Her beautiful features were set, a determined spark to her diamond-bright blue eyes, her blond corkscrew curls spilling over her shoulders like pale serpents.

Angel was a squirrel in Doppler form and as a human looked like a cover girl for a cheerleader magazine. A former Harvard graduate and NASA intern, Angel was one of the toughest Trackers I knew. She'd saved my butt more than once during the Werewolf op. Just goes to show you can't judge a Doppler by her human appearance or her animal form.

Olivia took up the rear. I winced every time I heard one of her shoes make a whisper of a sound. A former NYPD cop, she was pretty quiet for a human. But some beings have super-incredible hearing and I just hoped the Vampire's hearing wasn't *that* good that they'd hear the slight sounds of Olivia's running shoes.

"Fourteenth floor and ten to go." I looked at the number on the door as we made it from twelve to the next landing. "The fact that many hotels don't have a thirteenth floor has got to be one of the silliest superstitions humans have."

"Humans have lots of silly superstitions." Angel's voice was deceptively innocent and sweet and I glanced at her again. "And Brownies looooove to play up to them."

I grinned as we hit another landing. "If humans knew that Brownies are behind just about every superstition or haunting, then they would really flip."

Brownies are Fae and some of the most devious creatures known to paranorm kind. I dislike them as much as I dislike Sprites. But they can be amusing at times—when they aren't being malicious. Like Sprites, they too often take up valuable investigative time with mindless pranks and stunts.

"Not all humans believe in that crap." Olivia might not be what anyone would consider slender, but she was in such great shape she wasn't breathing hard. "Don't even go there."

"Keep your traps shut," Joshua grumbled. Angel flipped him off. I grinned. "The bastards may have lookouts."

Joshua stopped on landing twenty and I came just short of running into him. I took his flail automatically as he handed it to me. The full weight of it caught me by surprise and I almost dropped it. Thank goodness I'm Drow and not simply human because the thing was so heavy that I wouldn't have had the strength to hold it otherwise.

"Going ahead to scout." Joshua shifted—sort of melted away—and then I watched as a large shadow drifted up the stairs. Sometimes he blended with the stairwell shadows, sometimes not. And then he was gone.

Angel reached my side and gave me her whip. "Ouch," I said as one of its barbs dug into my palm and blood formed where the small cut was.

"Sorry, Nyx," she said just before she transformed

into a blond squirrel, jumped onto the railing and darted along it to cover the last few flights.

"What am I?" I muttered as I hurried up the stairs. "A coatrack?" As I moved I hooked Angel's whip on my weapons belt next to my right dragon-clawed dagger and gripped Joshua's flail in my left hand. The blackness of the metal was dark against my pale amethyst skin.

Within seconds I was up the last four flights and reached the penthouse, Olivia right behind me. A strange yet familiar odor that I couldn't identify cloyed the air. I frowned. Why couldn't I place the odor? So familiar . . .

Joshua and Angel were nowhere to be seen. As a Shadow Shifter, it was a given that Joshua had slipped beneath the door and into the Vampire's lair. But squirrels . . . I looked up at the low ceiling. Dust was slightly disturbed on an air vent. That explained Angel's disappearance.

"Like we talked about, wait here," I said to Olivia. "I know you don't think Vampires are dangerous because of the pukes at the Pit, but I think we have more to worry about than anyone realizes."

She scowled and I cut her off before she could say a word. "Don't come in, no matter what." I grasped the handle. "Your job is to shoot anything that exits this door. And make sure it's through the heart."

"Just get your purple ass in there," she muttered as she positioned herself to the side of the stairwell door, her Sig held in a two-fisted grip and pointed upward.

I called to my air element and felt its reassuring embrace as it cloaked me and my weapons so that I was invisible. Most paranorms can still see me when I use a glamour too, but Vampires are different.

Vampires aren't born paranorms, they were once human and in some ways they have human weaknesses. So to them I'm invisible when I draw a glamour. Thank goodness for that favor.

When in a glamour, it's almost like I'm a chameleon. I blend with whatever I'm around, no matter what it is. It's a better analogy than comparing me to the Invisible Woman.

With my free hand I tested the doorknob to the penthouse's emergency exit. Locked. Joshua must not have been able to unlock it for me. I needed to be cautious because someone could be on the other side and see the door open. I might be invisible to them, but they'd know something was up. A door being opened invisibly was bound to draw attention.

First I reached out with my senses, using my air element to search the area close to the door. It was clear.

I focused on the lock and used a small amount of my air element to unlock it and cushioned the mechanism so that the sound wouldn't be heard. I used the same element to buffer any squeak the hinges might make.

Olivia couldn't see me anymore but I looked at her over my shoulder before I slipped inside. Her features were set and grim. Her New York Mets sweat jacket was open and I shook my head as I looked at her T-shirt. It showed a Vampire playing a video game, with the words

Vampires have no life

Well, that's true.

The smell of Vampire was strong as I eased through the doorway. Modern classic design greeted me. But more than that, startled me.

Stark white walls with black accent walls towered to the vaulted ceiling. Muted city lights came through opaque drapes on the floor-to-ceiling windows.

Touches of red, like splashes of blood, were scattered on dead-white furniture. Crimson pillows were arranged on white sofa cushions and I noticed hints of red in every one of the black-and-white paintings arranged on the walls. An enormous flat-screen TV was built into the wall. And I mean enormous. Go-to-the-movies enormous.

Voices echoed in the large room, words bouncing from one wall to another like the hollowness of a Ping-Pong ball. I caught my breath as I settled the flail and barbed whip against the wall, keeping them cloaked in an air-glamour. Joshua and Angel should be able to see them—wherever they were.

I eased behind a potted black tree. The white pot was as high as my waist and the tree itself about seven feet high. The tree was naked of any leaves and would have been worthless cover if I hadn't shrouded myself in a glamour.

My gaze narrowed at Volod and another Vampire as they strolled into the room. Volod's black shoes sank into the rich white carpet as he walked with his casual yet arrogant movements.

Dressed in a black button-down shirt and tailored black slacks, Volod looked like any one of New York's elite aristocrats—just a lot paler. He was outfitted from head to toe in Gucci, Ferragamo, and Versace. Obviously I have a well-trained eye for the finer things.

The other Vampire's white turtleneck sweater against the deadly white of his skin did nothing for his complexion. Except make him look more dead. Is that possible? The fact that he wore Levi's and Nikes as opposed to Volod's designer clothing might have indicated he was some kind of underling if it wasn't for the arrogant way he carried himself.

I peered at them through the branches of the naked tree. It seemed bright in the room compared to the night sky barely visible through a slim part in the sheer drapes.

Despite my glamour, a tingling sense of danger rippled up my spine as I studied the two Vampires.

Volod picked up a smooth black statue of a nude female and trailed his white hand down the statue's curves. I swept my gaze around the room. Joshua might be one of the many shadows, and as a squirrel, Angel could be just about anywhere.

I reached out with my senses, using my air power to guide me. I found, but still couldn't distinguish, Joshua on the other side of the room. In another second I felt Angel's presence beneath one of the sofas.

Vampires have extraordinary senses but I didn't think they were able to sense Joshua and Angel like I could.

"Do you truly think that bunch of garbage can do it?" the second Vampire said as he tossed a crimson pillow on the floor and settled back in an oversized white chair. His skin was nearly as pale as his seat. "Can we put faith in the stupid creatures?"

Volod set the black statue on a glass table and the thumping sound caused me to flinch. The irritation on Volod's angular features sent that creepy sensation up my spine again. "Questioning me, Danut?"

Danut didn't seem bothered by Volod's glare. Danut shook out his long black hair that gleamed in the light. "If they complete their mission is it wise to give them the *permanent* ability, brother?" It shouldn't have surprised me that he and Volod were brothers. The resemblance was clear to me now.

Volod didn't bother to answer Danut's question. "As long as the Night Trackers remain ignorant, nothing will stop the Sprites from getting the information."

I caught my breath as thoughts spun through my mind. What was so important that he would be afraid of the Trackers finding out? I had a feeling that it had to be dangerous, whatever it was.

The Master Vampire turned to one of the windows and pushed aside the flowing sheer curtain. He studied the glittering Manhattan skyline through crystal-clear windows. The city's skyline seemed almost close enough to grasp each light in my hand.

"I have given the creatures what they need to accomplish this task and this task only," Volod said.

Danut said, "It was brilliant that you gave the Sprites the ability to escape the elemental magic containment as only Vampires can."

So many questions ran through my mind that I had to set them aside to concentrate on what was being said.

Danut grinned, baring his fangs. "The Trackers have no idea what will happen tonight at the Paranorm Center or what we have planned for the future."

Tonight. Something is going down tonight. I gritted my teeth, torn between listening to the two Vampires and rushing to the Paranorm Center to stop whatever they had planned.

Volod continued, "Tonight the Sprites will gain the archives which will give me the control we desire. Tobath has assured me only three Sprites know who the information is for. Once we get what we seek, we dispose of those Sprites, including Tobath, and no one will suspect us."

"We assume a Sprite can keep a secret," Danut said. "I hope we are right."

Volod shrugged without comment.

Disbelief at what the Vampires had said caused me to

shift my body backward. The Sprites in the detention center. How could we have not thought of that? I'd have bet my last Drow-mined diamond that the Vampires had intended to have the Sprites caught so that the creeps could go after something in the archives.

Not to mention there had been so much Sprite activity on such large scales that it had kept us from cracking down on the increased number of Vampire attacks.

I clenched my hand around the hilt of my sheathed dagger. Just like we'd thought, the Sprite mischief hadn't been random. But the realization that Vampires were behind it all made my skin feel tight.

"We have played the part far too long." Volod slammed his palms on the windowsill. He bent at his waist as he braced his hands. "Today the council meeting only confirmed that they have no regard for us. Having information on us and our movements, our vulnerabilities, is too much. They crossed the line. More important than any of that, however, is we must be free to do what we did for centuries."

My heart beat faster, my breathing grew heavier, my palms becoming sticky as I digested what I was hearing. What ability had the Vampires given to Sprites to break free of their cells and to get past the guards?

The Master Vampire straightened and then went still.

At once I knew he was searching for me with his mind, his senses.

Volod had felt the strong shift in my emotions.

"You think you can enter a Master Vampire's domain and not be found out?" He looked in my direction.

My heart thundered harder but I maintained my glamour. In a rush I sought out my elements with my mind and senses. I could use water from the pipes behind the walls, fire from the stove in the kitchen, and of course I had air.

In the flash of a moment it took me to reach for my elements, his hand shot up.

Invisible power slammed into me. I bit my lip to keep from crying out as the force of his power sent me skidding on my side on the carpet. The blast burned through my chest. Was my suit melting? It felt like the leather was sinking through my skin.

Shock tore through me at the strength he'd been able to use against me. I rolled with the momentum of the power as it shoved me toward one of the floor-to-ceiling windows. My concentration on my glamour failed and I could be seen again.

With a shout and cry, I flipped my body into a crouch, drew one of my dragon-clawed daggers, and faced Volod. Shards of pain raked my lungs as I dragged in harsh breaths of air.

"Tracker." Volod tilted his head and studied me, his hand still outstretched. He looked at me as if not concerned at all. "The strange one. The Drow female."

"This creature is a Tracker?" Danut laughed, obviously not feeling threatened by me either. "A purple woman?"

Give me a moment and I'll show you purple when I shove your—

"What are you going to do with her?" Danut asked, looking at his brother in a lazy, bored way. "Fun and games?"

Volod's black gaze held mine. "What do we do with all trash?" Volod splayed the fingers of his outstretched hand. "We dispose of it."

I surrounded myself with my air element, a thick cushion that would have protected me if I hadn't been so stupid and unprepared.

If I tried I couldn't have held back the dangerous white flash in my eyes. "Vampire scum."

I grasped the double-edged buckler from the front of my weapons belt and flung it at Volod's neck. My air element shoved the buckler faster than a human eye could see.

Volod wasn't human. Not for a very long time.

He caught the buckler right before the razor edge would have sliced into his throat.

In a blur he threw the buckler at me. I dodged it. The buckler sailed through the floor-to-ceiling window behind me. Glass shattered with a loud *crack*. Icy wind whipped inside the penthouse.

Danut shouted something. From the corner of my eye I saw Angel's barbed whip wrap around Danut's neck. Multiple lacerations. Blood streamed down his body. Blood splattered the white sofas. Angel could rip the Vampire's head from his body.

I didn't have time to dwell on it. My target was too powerful to allow myself to be distracted.

Faster than any Olympic Shifter sprinter, I bolted for Volod with my dagger. Blood rushed in my ears. My skin tingled. I'd carve his heart out.

Air cushioned me. Knowledge that I was protected gave me more strength.

My gaze was focused on the Vampire's grim expression. His bared fangs. A red glint in his black eyes. His pale raised hand as he faced his palm out to me.

I gripped my dagger. I was protected. Volod wouldn't be able to hurt me this time.

Five feet. Three feet—

An even more powerful invisible blast slammed into me.

It was as if I had no protection at all buffering me.

Breath rushed from my chest. Did my lungs collapse?

Fire. My body was on fire. Burning more, even more than the last time.

My concentration on my air element shattered. All elements.

The power flung my body backward.

No control. I had no control.

My back and head hit one of the massive windows.

Glass shattered as I was slammed against it hard enough to break the thickness of it.

Shards sliced my skin and dug into my flesh as I sailed through the window.

I screamed as my body started to drop.

Twenty-four stories.

SEVEN

One long scream tore from my throat, vanishing in the cold night air as I fell through the window.

I dropped. Breath left me in a rush.

My mind felt stuck. My heart was going to explode.

Automatically I gathered my air element around me.

Wrapped myself in a cushion of air.

As my body hurtled to the ground, I prayed that my magic would absorb shock from the fall. Protect me from pain.

I prayed that I would survive.

A strong presence shot by.

Joshua?

I had felt a shadow form brush my arm.

Had he been shoved out the window, too?

The street.

My body was about to meet asphalt.

The air element wouldn't be enough.

I squeezed my eyes shut.

And slammed against something hard.

Something that grunted.

It took a moment to realize I hadn't hit the pavement.

Strong arms surrounded me and I opened my eyes.

Joshua. Joshua had caught me.

Somehow he had reached the street before me and had been ready to catch me.

"Bloody Vampires." He was looking up at the window I'd been thrown from, anger on his strong features. He carried me into the darkness beside the hotel. "You don't want them to be seeing you alive."

"How did you do that?" I was still catching my breath as he looked at me and set me on my feet.

"Shadows fly when they need to." His gaze searched the night around us.

My heart still raced as fast as I'd been falling and I struggled to catch my breath. My body ached from the blasts of the Master Vampire's power and the shards of glass that had dug into my flesh. I would heal fast, but right now the injuries hurt like the Underworld.

"The impact should have slammed us both against the asphalt," I said, but then my senses came back to me and my chest tightened. "Olivia. We need to make sure she's all right."

"I will get her." He scowled as he looked around us, searching the night for any Vampires that might have been out. "I do not see Angel."

My buckler had sailed through the window and had to be here somewhere. "Angel had her whip around one of the vamps," I said as I called to my buckler. The weapon came straight to me. I caught the buckler and returned it to the front of my weapons belt.

Joshua gave a short nod. "I'll get them both." He melded into shadow and disappeared into darkness.

My chest ached with concern for Olivia and Angel. Especially Olivia since she wasn't a paranorm. I don't know how she managed to talk me into letting her come on this mission.

Well . . . it was almost impossible to keep Olivia

from doing anything she put her mind to. She could hold her own. She had to be okay.

I pulled my phone from my belt and pressed the speed dial number I used the most. Phone to my ear, I shot through the night, running the short distance to Central Park.

Rodán answered at once. "Nyx."

"We need as many Trackers as we can get at the Paranorm Center." My breath was short, remnants of the terror of the fall and my concern for Olivia and Angel. "Hurry."

"What has happened?" Rodán's rich voice flowed over me and would have been calming if I wasn't so intent on my mission.

"The Sprites." Glass dug into my flesh with every movement as I ran. "The Vamps planned it all. Got the Sprites to intentionally be caught so that somehow they can break out of their cells to get something."

"What do they want?" Rodán's tone was as always smooth, even.

"Something in the archives," I said. "The Vampires are behind it and the Sprites are involved. Something serious enough to throw me out a window."

"All we can spare will be there." The line went dead.

I shoved the phone back into its sheath on my weapons belt and sped to the Alice in Wonderland unbirthday party sculptures. I came to a full stop.

While I performed the ritual to get the door beneath the toadstool to open, my skin crawled. I almost shouted out loud my frustration when the ritual didn't work the first time. After the second time I'd said the idiotic chant while walking counterclockwise, the door finally opened.

My air element hid me as I called to it and created a glamour so that I was invisible. Vampires, Witches, and anything born human couldn't see through my glamour, but a lot of paranorms could. I was still working to perfect my glamour so that no being could see me. Developing better concentration and mind control would get me there.

I had no idea what to expect once I reached the great hall that led to the archives.

Torches flared to life as I hurried down the winding stairway. I heard nothing as I made my way. Not a whisper of sound from below.

When I reached the entryway with the five arches, I pressed myself against the wall of stone. I peered into the hallway that led to the council chambers and the archives.

Nothing looked wrong. Everything appeared normal.

The great hall was noiseless. Dryads slept in their wooden pillars, their eyes closed, breathing deep and even. Talk about asleep on the job.

After their major screw-up with the Metamorphs, it was a wonder the Dryads had been kept on as sentries. At least they'd hired Shadow Shifters as additional security. Not that Dryads could be called security as far as I was concerned.

So much shadow lingered in the hall that I had no idea what was shadow and what was a Shadow Shifter guard. But I could sense them.

Sprites . . . I couldn't detect their presences.

I definitely didn't think they were in their cells anymore after what Volod and his brother had said. They had probably escaped, doing whatever it was that the Master Vampire had arranged for them to do.

It was true that Vampires couldn't be held by paranorm cells. If Volod had somehow given the ability to the Sprites, they would have gotten past the Shadow

Shifter guards using their glamours. Their glamours are so strong that they can hide even from paranorms. The glamours would shield their presences once they had escaped with the power the Vampires had somehow given them. The guards would never expect any of the detainees to escape the elemental-magically-treated cells.

Shadows started to drift and Dryads blinked their eyes.

"Tracker." A Dryad's deep voice boomed from a column created from ancient wood. The Dryad had probably lived in the tree for countless centuries in Otherworld before she chose to serve at the Paranorm Center in New York City. "Leave. You have not the right to be here during this night hour."

I stepped under the archway and kept my voice low hoping she'd do the same. "Sprites may have escaped the cells and have broken into the archives."

A shadow rose and the form of a tall man appeared. Scars marred his face that could not be called handsome and his mouth was a fierce slash as he scowled at me. It was the kind of scowl that made a person want to take a step back. I didn't.

"Zeke, bid this Tracker to leave before I bespell her," the Dryad said.

Other shadows rose around Zeke as he spoke, the shadows all forming into large, tall, muscular men. "No being has passed by," Zeke said. "Nor is it remotely possible."

He and now the other Shadow Shifters blocked my way and I wanted to shout at them.

"Shut up and get to the archives." By the way Zeke narrowed his eyes, my words didn't gain me any favor and I wished I could take them back. "No one can see

Sprites when they've pulled a glamour. Their glamours are too strong."

Every word I spoke tumbled out as I continued in one long rush. "We're wasting time. They could find whatever it is they're trying to gain to take to the Vampires if they haven't already."

"Vampires?" The scary-looking scarred man studied me. "Vampires have not been a threat for well over a century. Sprites, never."

I wanted to jump up and down like a frustrated child. If I could get past the twenty or so males who'd appeared, I would have. They were an impenetrable wall. "Volod, the Master Vampire, is behind it." I swept my gaze over the male Shadow Shifters and met the eyes of several of the female Dryads in their wooden columns.

"He has some kind of plan," I continued, "and is the reason the Sprites are here. The Vampires intentionally had the Sprites create mischief so that they would be captured and brought here. The Vamps have somehow given the Sprites the ability to escape the cells tonight."

The scarred Shadow Shifter looked at me one second longer, then looked at the other men and tilted his head in the direction where the archives are kept. "Go," he said.

The men dissolved into shadow and a blanket of black flowed over the stone floor toward the archives.

Scarred man didn't look like he was going to let me by. I wasn't about to mess with him anymore. I jumped and grabbed the stone archway above me. My movements were fast, a blur as I swung over his head. I backflipped, tucking myself into a ball, then landed on my feet behind him.

I bolted too fast for him to reach, much less stop me.

"Get the PTF up here!" I shouted as I ran. "We're going to need them!"

The train of words being passed from one Dryad to the next was a strong whisper as the order was sent to the detention center and the Doppler guards.

In a fraction of a moment I'd caught up with the blanket of shadows. I leapt, stretched myself out as if flying. I sailed over them before flipping forward and landing in a crouch eight feet in front of them—right up to the archive doors.

The massive doors were closed. They appeared as heavy, thick, and solid as the council chamber doors were. I heard no sounds.

Shadow Shifters rose behind me as I grabbed an ancient ring on one of the doors. When I pulled on it, the door wasn't locked like it should have been.

A blast of noise met my ears and chaos met my eyes the moment I slipped inside.

No Sprites could be seen, but the glamour-concealed Sprites shouted and yelled in wicked glee and malicious laughter.

Paper flew everywhere. Old parchments and papyrus littered the floor and desks. All of it was ripped, shredded, crumpled. Ancient yellowed and new white sheets of paper were scattered and torn, too. Small pieces rained from the ceiling like a continuous pour of confetti.

Balls of paper sailed through the air. I watched a piece of paper crumple into a ball by invisible hands. The ball shot straight toward me. I blocked it with my forearm before it could hit my face.

"Shit," said a Shadow Shifter that had risen at my side. I didn't see any others of his kind. "How are we going to get these creatures if we cannot see them?" he said in a thick English accent.

"Be creative." I had to follow my own advice and figure out a way to see the Sprites.

With my air element, I sent swirls of paper around the area where the crumpled ball came from that had been aimed at me. In the whirlwind of torn paper, I made out the shape of an invisible being and heard him shout in surprise.

I grasped my buckler and flung it into the middle of the mini paper storm. A shriek and a Sprite appeared, the buckler having cut his leg. He shrieked again, dropped off the desk, and onto the floor. Blood dribbled on the paper around him.

My shot in the dark had the exact reaction I'd been hoping for. An injured Sprite was a visible Sprite.

Shouts echoed through the room. Shadow Shifters rose, tracking the sounds the Sprites were making. One by one the Shadow Shifters took the Sprites down. Just like the one I'd taken care of at the Statue of Liberty, these Sprites couldn't maintain a glamour when another being touched them.

Torches flared to life on every wall and the room was filled with light. I continued to use my air element to track down more Sprites and attacked each one I found.

Several Night Trackers arrived and some guarded the door so that any remaining invisible Sprites couldn't escape.

Dopplers from the PTF showed up and started counting the Sprites we caught. They weren't positive, but it looked like all thirty-plus had gotten out of the detention center and we needed to make sure none escaped with whatever information the Vampires had been looking for.

Elemental-magically-treated cuffs didn't work on most of the Sprites, but did on some. Apparently the Vampire "gift" wore off after a certain amount of time. The Sprites still able to escape the cuffs had to be physically held onto by Shadow Shifters, Dopplers, and Trackers so that they couldn't use a glamour again.

In the meantime, I was prepared to fight any Vampires that might come to finish the job the Sprites had attempted to accomplish. No Vamps so far.

Joshua and Angel came up beside me. "How's Olivia?" I asked before either of them could speak. "Where is she? Is she all right?"

"Spitting angry that we left her behind and wouldn't tell her where we were going." Joshua looked amused which told me Olivia was perfectly fine. "Don't you teach your humans any better than to charge into a Vampire lair?"

I narrowed my eyes. "What happened?"

"Ignore him." Angel rolled her eyes at Joshua. "I got to Olivia before the Vamps could. She never had a chance to go into the penthouse. We were halfway down the stairwell when we met up with Joshua."

"Olivia can hold her own," I said, "but I'm not so sure against a couple of angry Vampires."

Angel had a thoughtful expression. "Vamps have not been a threat to the paranorm world for longer than some of us can remember. What do you think is going on?"

I looked around us as the chaotic scene wound down. "I'm not sure about anything right now."

My adrenaline rush was starting to fade. I felt the ache at the back of my head and the cuts on my skin stung. I glanced down at the drying blood streaking my arms and fighting suit and the bits of glass.

"Avanna." The magical Elvin word cleansed my clothing and skin when I said it. Even the small bits of

glass disappeared. Unfortunately it didn't repair my skin, but when I shifted back to my human form the transformation would take care of it.

"Do you think they got what they came for?" Angel pushed a corkscrew curl out of her eyes. "Whatever the Vampires wanted?"

"I don't know." I looked at the contained Sprites and frowned. "Where's the Sprite I captured at the Statue of Liberty? I think his name is Ordox."

"Over there." Joshua nodded to one corner of the room.

"Good," I said.

Angel looked at two PTF agents wrestling with a couple of Sprites and called out, "Any Sprites left in lockup? Is everyone accounted for?"

Gary, the Doppler that Joshua and I had met earlier in the day, glanced at us. "All are gone from detention."

"That means Negel is out, too," I said to myself. "Have you seen the one called Negel?" I asked Gary.

The PTF agent with Gary said, "We've counted all of the Sprites once. Four are missing, unless our count is off, Negel is one of them." He grabbed a chart from another PTF agent and looked at it. "Tock, Zith, and Ecknep are the other three."

"I think I remember them." I fixed my buckler to my belt again. "We've got to get those last four. And fast."

"Let's get searching." Angel glanced up at Joshua who nodded and they both started out to look for the missing Sprites.

"They've been tampered with, the paranorm archives." A frantic-looking elderly Doppler archive-keeper with half-moon glasses came rushing up to me. "Messed with, all of them."

I censored myself and thought, "Just look around us.

No kidding they've been tampered with," but I didn't say it aloud.

"Some of the most important ones." The skinny archive-keeper lowered her voice as she hissed the "s" sound in every one of her sentences. She had to be a snake Doppler. Her words were so low that it was obvious she didn't want anyone else to hear. "They are accounted for, each piece, but they have been disturbed."

Her statement and the mess around us made me want to laugh. "Otherworld to archive-keeper," I thought to myself, "I don't think each piece could possibly be accounted for."

"These." She dragged my attention back to her by the panic in her high voice. "All of these have been rifled through." She held up a thick folder filled with yellowing paper, her bony thin knuckles white. "They are not even and neat as we always keep our filed papers. And an inkwell was spilled on the folder."

The folder was labeled with thick blood-red runes that I didn't recognize. I wrinkled my brow. "There's no ink on it."

"It is a special ink that copies and does not leave a residue. Look at the papers inside." Her face was flushed now, almost as red as the runes on the cover. The archive-keeper shoved the folder into my hands. "See the imprint on each one? The imprints are deep enough to see that someone was copying information from the file using magic ink."

My stomach churned as I looked at the first paper. "Oh, no," I said, my words slow as if my tongue had thickened.

"The weaknesses of every paranorm being." Her eyes looked huge as she said what I already knew from my first glance. She added, "I read this when we archived it."

Hairs on my arms rose and my skin prickled as if needles jabbed my skin as I flipped through the yellowing pages. "Everything about every paranorm being is in this folder. Every single one." My head spun as I saw my own name and my own version of kryptonite laid out in detail. "Notes, drawings, pictures."

"Yes." She nodded, the movement and her expression frantic and the hissing sound of every "s" becoming louder and louder. "Even the location of every paranorm's lair or home. Every secret hideaway and where each paranorm originated from. Those locations the council has found and keeps monitored."

"Shush." My heart pounded hard enough to hurt my chest. "No one can know about this. Including the fact that you know anything about it."

"My apologies," she said with more than a little fear in her voice. "We keep it closely guarded."

"Apparently not." I scowled. "I can't believe this information is allowed to exist in such an accessible place. None of this should ever have been logged. It's too dangerous."

I shook my head hard enough that my blue hair fell across my face and I shoved it out of the way with my free hand. Then I looked at her. "You weren't supposed to read this, were you?" I asked, knowing it was the truth before I even said it.

She swallowed. "N-no."

I waved the folder at her. "The fact that you have any knowledge about the contents of this folder means you could be in danger."

Her brown eyes widened and she brought her hand to her frail chest. "Danger?"

She had to know how serious this was so I wasn't about to spare her any fear. She *should* be afraid. "You have information that some would kill for," I said, trying to keep anger out of my voice. "Don't tell anyone, do you understand? I'll take care of it with the right people."

The archive-keeper nodded so frantically that her half-moon glasses fell from their perch on her thin nose. The glasses dangled at the end of the beaded chain that kept them from dropping on the floor.

"What is your name?" I said.

"Dolores," she said in a shaky voice.

"Well, Dolores, you'd better keep your mouth shut from this point on." My gaze shot around the room as I spoke.

My skin chilled and went hot and chilled again. I looked at the Dopplers, Shadow Shifters, and Trackers who were each holding onto one of the Sprites. The creatures all had to be accounted for with the missing four located. Every one of them. Had to.

I clutched the thick file in my hands and ran toward the PTF agent from the detention center, Gary. "Were the Sprites recounted?"

"We found one of the missing Sprites, the one called Tock." He looked stern, angry, frustrated. "We're still searching for the last three."

Panic seized me and I shouted to the team Olivia and I'd had this past fall in the Catskills for our Werewolf case. The case had been a dangerous one that led to a virus that had the potential to wipe out all paranorms.

One member of our team was Ice. Almost intimidating in height and build, the white-blond Shifter's blue eyes sparked like sunlight on snow when he was angry. Or when he was being an ass, which was most of the time. He was such an ass I wondered if he ever changed into a white mule.

When all three reached me, I kept my voice down,

explained the situation—what the archive-keeper had discovered.

"Every paranorm race's weaknesses?" Angel looked almost as much in shock as I was. "They collected and retained that information here?"

I clenched the file folder. "The Sprites were to obtain it for the Vampires."

"Vampires." Joshua fisted his hands at his sides. "I think we have underestimated the bastards these many years since the Rebellion."

I had underestimated them. I'd thought of Vampires as nothing but lowlife scum ever since I came from Other-world and met my first Vampire. Whiny, waxy-faced creeps.

Volod had shown me a side I didn't know existed. I'd seen it in his eyes. Hard. Cruel. Cunning.

Ice growled, his voice a deep rumble like it was when he was in his jaguar form.

"Volod." I started to run for the door. "We need to find him, *now*."

EIGHT

Before heading to the Hudson Hotel, Joshua shifted into a dark shadow that blended into the patches of darkness in the Paranorm Center. He vanished in the night after we left the center through the unbirthday party sculpture.

Angel shrank, her pert blond cheerleader looks transforming into that of a blond squirrel before she scampered over the grass behind Joshua.

At the same time, Ice shifted into a pure white falcon. He gave a piercing cry as he darted toward the Hudson.

I ran.

We gathered in the darkness of the hotel before slipping inside and going the back way again to the Vampire lair. I used a glamour, Angel the squirrel darted beneath lounge chairs and curtains. Ice shifted into a tiny white mouse and scurried behind Angel.

Once I'd opened the door to the stairwell, we hurried in an all-out run—or flight considering Ice shifted again to his falcon form. We couldn't reach the Vampire's penthouse fast enough as far as I was concerned. We had to get to the Sprites before they gave the information on paranorm weaknesses to the Vampires.

I came to an abrupt stop when I reached the top of the penthouse *Exit* landing. Ice settled on a stair railing and ruffled his feathers. Joshua's shadow became still in front of me. Angel the squirrel crouched by my feet.

The exit door from the stairwell into the penthouse was already open.

It was only a crack, but it was open. And I'd bet Joshua hadn't left it that way. Cold air blew from inside the penthouse, likely from the broken windows.

That same almost-familiar odor hung in the air that I had noticed the last time I'd stood in this spot. Not just Vampire, but . . . Bless it. Why couldn't I identify the smell?

It couldn't be a good thing that the door was open. Maybe the Vampires opened it the last time we were here, searching for us. It could even be a trap.

Thankfully the hinges didn't squeak as I pushed it and let Joshua enter as shadow. When he didn't raise an alarm, Angel passed through as a squirrel. Ice seemed to melt as he landed on the floor and shifted from a white falcon into a small white mouse again before scampering inside.

I pulled a glamour around myself as well as drawing one of my dragon-clawed daggers. The hilt was firm, familiar in my grip. We spread apart to sweep the area but I already knew we were in the right location as soon as we entered the Vampire's living room.

In that moment I knew the Vampires were gone.

And I knew what that cloying smell was that I hadn't been able to identify. It had been faint remnants of burnt sugar. The smell was all but overpowering now.

Lying on the floor was the body of a decapitated Sprite.

Blood spattered the white carpet. My stomach churned. The Sprite's head was in one corner, its bulbous eyes staring into infinity.

Joshua rose to stand beside me. "I'll check the other

rooms." He stared at the dead Sprite. "My gut tells me no Vampires are here, but I will search. It's too close to sunrise and this location has been compromised."

"The Sprites got the information to the Vampires." My voice was nearly a whisper as the horror of it hit me. "They must have." Angel walked across the carpet and I looked at her. "They have it, Angel. I'm sure of it. Every paranorm races' weakness."

"Bloody hell." Joshua faded into a pool of shadow again and I stared blankly at the shadow as he traveled into the next room and vanished.

When my gaze met hers again, Angel's blue eyes seemed almost black as she spoke. "They could blackmail all paranorms if they have what we think they do."

"Those bastards will die before they can use the information," Ice said with his teeth bared.

I let loose with a string of Drow curse words, worse than anything even Ice could say.

Ice made a growling noise as he approached. "They killed the one who could give us more information."

A gurgling cough came from behind one of the plants that was in an enormous pot. The other Trackers and I had our weapons out and ready.

An ugly face with bulbous eyes appeared. The Sprite crept around the pot, then braced his back up against the white pottery.

Ecknep. One of the missing Sprites and one I'd interviewed at the detention center.

He had slashes through his blood-soaked rags. Blood seeped from a gash on his chest and his teeth were stained with red as he opened his mouth and gave a sound of ironic laughter before he coughed.

"They killed Zith. Left me for dead." Pain crossed

Ecknep's features and I wasn't sure if it was for the other Sprite or because of his wounds.

"We had a deal with them," Ecknep said and seemed to shiver from cold air coming in through the broken window. "But they thought we double-crossed them and set them up for Trackers to find. They said that you, Purple Lady, and others were here, and working with us."

What Ecknep didn't know was that before Volod had known we were in the room, we'd heard him say that he was going to kill the Sprites who knew of the operation. So Ecknep and the others had already been targeted for death by Volod.

Angel approached Ecknep and examined him. "His wounds look mortal." She glanced at us before she turned back to the Sprite. "There's nothing we can do. He doesn't have long."

"Now that they killed my friend and did this to me, I don't care, I will tell you." Bitterness was in his voice. "Gave them secrets," he said with another choke and a cough before laughing again. "Secrets that might give them complete control of the paranorm world. In turn the Sprites were to have freedom and power, too."

Ice stepped forward, his face a mask of fury, looking like he was going to beat the nearly dead Sprite.

"Stop." I signaled Ice to back off. "You're talking about the file of paranorm weaknesses."

"That was nothing," Ecknep said in obvious pain. "Tried to bargain with them on what else we had. Look at me . . . it didn't work. They were crazed with anger . . . monsters . . . ruthless monsters. We could have given them more. So much more."

He wheezed in a deep breath before letting it out.

"We didn't give them everything. Tobath wanted to hold back . . . glad he did."

"More than paranorm weaknesses?" I flexed my fingers around the hilt of my dagger. "What do you mean?"

"I don't know why I am telling you." Ecknep tipped his head back against the large planter like he was resting and looked at me. "You Trackers treat all Sprites like troll dung. You have no respect for my people."

I couldn't argue with him. That's how all Trackers felt about Sprites. Malicious troublemakers.

"You'll tell me because you hate the Vampires," I said. "They killed your friend and they tried to kill you. We need to stop them from hurting others. What do you have? Tell me."

Ecknep didn't seem to hear. "Before they could kill me, I said to them, 'You fools. You don't believe me. Do you really think I will give you such information now. I will tell you and you will only kill me'?"

The Sprite wheezed and coughed. "I tried to make a deal to save my life. There is no dealing with them . . . monsters . . . they are monsters." Ecknep's voice was a wet rasp before he coughed up more blood. "I told him, 'We Sprites aren't so stupid to completely trust you Vampires.' "

Ecknep's eyes were starting to go opaque and I knew he wouldn't be around much longer. "They tortured me after I told them that we had held something back." He laughed, a strange sound between a cough and a burp.

"What did you give him?" I asked slowly. "And what did you keep?"

"Almost everything went to the Vampires." The Sprite was speaking at a lower pitch now. "We found something else in the center. Knew this was even better than what we had promised to get them from the files."

He coughed and coughed, and I didn't think he was going to be able to get anything else out but he did. "We knew it would please the Vampires when we gave them the other information that we copied from the archives." His slack features tightened into anger before relaxing again. "But then they betrayed us.

"Volod tortured me himself." More pain flashed across Ecknep's face and he gritted his teeth. "For spite . . . told them what we had. Said they would never get it for what they did to us." The Sprite's face went whiter with his pain. "He left me to die when he had to travel to another sanctuary because the sun will soon rise."

He was right. I could sense it was almost sunrise. I would need privacy to shift.

"Almost everything includes what? Tell me." I was losing patience.

"All of the papers in the file we gave to them." The Sprite tried to laugh but it came out as a cough. "Something very special. Very, very special. Something we didn't plan for."

"What papers? What file?" I instinctively wanted to grab the Sprite by the throat and make him tell me all he knew *now*.

"Yessss." Ecknep coughed again. There wasn't much life left in him, his features so white, nearly bloodless.

He didn't answer my question. Despite the obvious pain the Sprite was in, he grinned again. "But Volod doesn't have it, we do. You might be able to get it, Tracker, but you will have to deal with . . ."

Ecknep's voice trailed off and his body went slack. All life left his large cunning eyes.

"Damn." Angel crossed the floor to where I stood. "We have to track down that other Sprite in a hurry and find out what was given to the Vampires, and what was hidden from them."

I rubbed my forehead with my thumb and forefinger. What had the Sprite been talking about? Joshua returned to the room shaking his head, indicating he hadn't found anything.

Prickles ran along my spine and I raised my head very slowly. Another being was in the room. One with a glamour so strong that other paranorms couldn't see him.

But I could sense him.

Without looking in the direction of the being, I sheathed my dragon-clawed dagger, then unholstered my Kahr 9mm. I made subtle signals to the three other Trackers to spread out behind me.

I grasped the handgun in a two-fisted grip and swung it in the direction of the invisible being. "I know you're there and I can track any move you make."

A small gasp came from the direction I had my barrel pointed at. "These three other Trackers in the room know you're here now, too. You'd better show yourself."

I chambered a round.

A slight shimmer to the air and then another Sprite appeared. Only this one was very much alive.

"Negel." I narrowed my gaze as he raised his head and I got a good look at the puny Sprite. "Sure had me fooled. You're into this further than you led us to believe."

With his boot, Joshua pushed the Sprite onto the white carpet that was scored with blood. Negel landed facefirst. Some of the blood from the carpet now stained his face.

He got to his knees, his expression pleading. "I came to stop them. I snuck out of the cell after you questioned me. I tried to catch up with Ecknep and Zith to see about stopping them. After confronting them in the detention center, I knew just when they were going to the Vampire apartment and I was going to head them off and try and stop them."

Negel looked to the other Trackers, then back to me. "Followed them here. They met with Tobath first. Just as they arrived I tried to convince them not to turn the information over to the Vampires. They said it was too late for that. They would not go against the orders of Tobath.

"I followed them inside in glamour. Just as Ecknep said, the Vampires were crazed." Negel's cheeks seemed more mottled as he spoke, as if it was making him agitated. "I have never seen such anger. They were convinced we double-crossed them. I think when they finished torturing Ecknep they finally believed that the Trackers were not in with us, but by that time it was too late for him."

Negel wrung his hands over and over as if he was washing them. "The Vampires were all too big, too strong, too powerful. I did not know what to do."

"What do the Sprites now have that they held back from the Vampires?" I asked.

"I thought it was a different operation." Negel looked down and shook his head. "I thought we were just there to create havoc for the fun of it. You know, like we are known for." He avoided looking at me. "I found out in the archive room it is much more than that. So I tried to stop them at the center, and then just outside, but I failed."

He did meet my gaze then. "This is not what my people do. We do not harm people. We made a deal with the Vampires that can harm other beings. I knew nothing of the real operation, I swear to you."

His big Adam's apple bobbed as he swallowed. "We were intentionally in the detention center. We thought we were there, as I said, for fun. Apparently, Tobath wanted a number of us to be arrested. Creating the chaos around the city would get us arrested together."

He swallowed again before continuing. "We kept the chaos going for a while because Tobath believed as long as we were going to be arrested, we might as well make it memorable, thus the Statue of Liberty painting party and the Nathan's hot dog deposit among other things.

"Tonight we escaped from the cuffs and holding cells with the magic the Vampires provided for our release," Negel said. "Only Ecknep and Zith knew the real mission. They were to copy the pages of paranormal weakness and then escape.

"The rest of us Sprites," Negel went on, "were a diversion. Tobath wanted it to look like we were just making mischief." Negel shook his head. "By copying rather than stealing the documents, Tobath figured no one would ever know what was done.

"I confronted Ecknep and Zith," Negel continued, "when I saw them making copies and they told me of the plan. As I told you, I then followed them out. The rest you know." Negel sighed. "And unfortunately the information was delivered to the Vampires."

"This Sprite is full of shit. He didn't answer your question on what Ecknep was holding back." Ice scowled and kicked the little Sprite. "He was here to deliver the goods to the Vampires." Ice leaned down and grasped the tuft of hair on Negel's head. The Sprite screamed. "Weren't you?" Ice asked in a cold voice.

"I knew nothing of the operation until tonight," Negel said. "I would never have gone along with such a destructive plan. Never."

Despite myself I felt sorry for the pitiful creature. I'd always been tough with Sprites. Sprites were malicious creeps. But Negel seemed different than the others I'd roughed up.

"Stop it." I glared at Ice before crouching in front of Negel. "You need to tell us everything you know."

He wiped his nose with the back of his hand. "It is not much, but I will tell you what I am able to. Just do not send me to the detention center, please."

I held my hand out to Negel and helped him to his feet. Joshua raised his eyebrows, Ice scowled deeper, and Angel tilted her head a little as they watched me.

"So that we can talk, I'm going to take you to my office and keep you there for a while before you go to the detention center." I pulled out elemental-magic-treated handcuffs. "In the meantime, I want to make sure you don't escape."

"I will not try to get away, I promise you." Negel shook his head with fervor. "I am worried for our people. I want to help."

"Are those going to work?" Angel pointed to the elemental-treated cuffs.

My skin started to tingle. The sun would be up soon.

"I'm banking on the Vampires' power over the Sprites fading because they've had to go to ground to prepare for sunrise." I looked at Negel. "And the Vampires did say the ability was temporary." The cuffs snapped into place and stayed when I slipped them on the Sprite's wrists. I made sure they were secure and he didn't have the ability to slip out of them.

"Looks like you were right," Angel said. "The Vampire magic, or whatever you call it, must have worn off."

"I have a visit to make," I said to Negel, "and then I will see you in a couple of hours."

Negel looked up at Ice and Joshua with fear as the two big males glared at him.

"Don't worry." Angel frowned at Joshua and Ice. "I'll get you there in one piece, Negel, if that's what Nyx wants."

"That's what I want." I watched as Angel took the Sprite by the arm and left in the direction of the stairwell door.

My skin was tingling more and more. I needed to call Rodán but I would start shifting soon and I didn't want an audience.

"Wait for me," I said and left Joshua and Ice behind as I jogged to one of the Vampire's penthouse bathrooms to shift.

After I closed the bathroom door I stared at myself in the huge floor-to-ceiling mirrored wall across from the black marble vanity and double sinks. My skin started tingling more.

I shrugged, then rolled my shoulders working on loosening up for the transformation. My cobalt blue hair framed my face. I ran my fingers along my cheek, over the pale amethyst of my skin.

As the tingling started in earnest, I moved into position. I didn't normally watch the shift in my body in a mirror, but today I did.

When I shift I always move as slow and as graceful as a cat as I lean into every stretch. My sapphire eyes stay the same shade but my pale amethyst skin fades into ivory.

From the roots of my hair down to the ends, black flows like ink over blue silk until my hair is black with blue highlights.

My small fangs retract and my muscles and bone

shift from my enhanced Drow form back into my more delicate-looking human form.

The back of my head no longer hurt and I watched as cuts in my skin healed.

When I was fully changed, I cleansed myself again with the word "*Avanna*." I pushed my hair over my shoulders and headed out to meet up with Ice and Joshua.

The two males stopped speaking when I walked out of the bathroom. I knew they'd been talking about what I'd done—had the Sprite taken to my personal office rather than to the detention center—and they didn't approve. Well, they'd just have to get over it.

I pulled my cell phone out of my weapons belt and pressed the speed dial number for Rodán. To say we had a lot to talk about was like saying the Statue of Liberty needed a new paint job after yesterday's fiasco.

"Get over here." Rodán's normally calm, sensual voice was anything but and it startled me when he answered. He sounded urgent in a way I'd never heard him sound before. His tone was almost hard. He never spoke that way to me. Never.

He needed to know that something big was going down. "I have to tell you—"

"To my office," he cut me off. "Now."

NINE

It didn't take me long to get to the Pit at a dead run across Central Park.

There wasn't a line when I walked into the Pit. I greeted Fred, the muscle-bound but sweet Doppler who was a golden retriever in his animal form, and Matthew's best friend.

"Hey, Nyx." Fred stepped back and for once he didn't smile. Instead his square features were set in a worried expression. "Rodán sounded kinda . . . different when he said to make sure you get to the back right away. I've never heard him sound like that."

"I'm sure everything is fine." So sue me. I lied. I didn't want Fred to be concerned. He had a tendency to dwell on worst-case scenarios.

I reached up and kissed his cheek and got a shy smile out of the big blond Doppler.

Because it was morning, the club was relatively quiet, the band packed up and gone, and most of the patrons had left. I walked past tables around the dance floor, the air still, the fans above motionless. Odors of various paranorms were not as overwhelming as usual.

My stomach tightened as I neared the fog-shrouded hidden entrance to the passageway that led to Rodán's dungeon. For Rodán to sound so urgent to me, and to Fred too, meant that whatever it was had to be bad.

Scents of rain and moist earth greeted me as I passed through the fog. Torches were bracketed along the hallway, the smell of pitch and smoke only faint in here.

I made it down the passageway to the black arched doorway straight out of a medieval dungeon. To the right of the doorway was a more modern-looking oblong pad. I placed my hand on the spongy pad and it sifted through various colors until it matched the sapphire blue of my eyes.

The pad even flashed white for a moment, matching the flash in my eyes. That flash usually meant danger to whoever was on the other side of my dragon-clawed dagger.

The door swung open without a whisper of sound. My stomach tightened a little more as I walked through.

Rodán wasn't in the room. Odd. He always greeted me. The fact that Rodán wasn't there to meet me caused my heart rate to quicken. Something had to be wrong. Desperately wrong.

I went to the right and stepped through another fog-shrouded wall and onto a landing. The chill air caused goose bumps to rise on my skin and I rubbed my arms as I started down the winding stone steps to his sanctuary.

When I reached the den, my eyes widened and my lips parted. Rodán wasn't here either. The surreal feeling it gave me was unexpected. I sucked in a breath of wisteria-scented air from the plant that crawled across the earthen walls. The rich loam smell of the walls always reminded me of the home I'd grown up in, the underground realm of the Dark Elves.

Sometimes the scents made me a little homesick. For some reason today was one of those days.

I looked around at the perfectly arranged den with thick tomes and smaller books arranged so that not a one was the slightest bit out of place. I'd never had the chance to really take in his den. I was always too busy discussing our latest case or traumatic event with him in this room. Fun and lightheartedness was for his chamber above. His den was not the place for any of that.

Upstairs Rodán had cases filled with unusual collectibles from various races including a Faerie cone as well as a tooled leather Abatwa quiver filled with arrows. The quiver and arrows had been a gift from the queen of the rare beings. An underground Troll club took up one entire wall above short glass cases filled with more trinkets in his chamber above.

But here, in Rodán's den, books of all sizes and shapes took up almost every bit of shelf space and there were but a few trinkets. I trailed my fingers along the beautiful polished wood of his huge desk. All wood in the room from the desk to the chairs to the shelves were created from wood the Dryads had provided Rodán.

I ran my fingers along my collar as I wondered what payment the Dryads had required of Rodán or if it had been gifted. I would normally have doubted the latter. Dryads aren't known for their generosity.

But in Rodán's case . . . I suspected he had power far greater than I could imagine. He served the Great Guardian and that in itself was a big deal. That had to be the most frustrating job in the Otherworlds—trying to get a straight answer out of the GG and not just a bunch of riddles. Or trying to decipher her riddles.

No one truly knew that much about Rodán, even me, and I'd been so close to him for over two years now. He was powerful enough that it was possible the Dryads had hoped to gain favor with him.

An inkwell, with an iridescent green Faerie plume tipping an ink pen, was on his spotless desk next to a tray of neatly stacked parchment that I could see beneath a single file folder.

The folder obviously didn't belong. It was worn and looked like it had been through many hands. Words were on it in red and I moved closer to see what was written across it.

I cocked my head and a squirming sensation started wriggling in my stomach when I saw that the writing was actually red runes like the ones that had been on the file folder I'd seen earlier. These runes were different, but it didn't matter.

Something was wrong here. I could sense it with everything I had.

"Nyx." Rodán's voice from behind me startled me so much that I knocked over the inkwell.

"Bless it." I felt frantic as I looked over my shoulder at his stern face, then tried to right the well and figure out how to clean the mess.

"Avanna." Rodán said the word that cleared away the mess.

I felt ridiculous for a moment. I should have thought of that. And since when did I feel frantic or worried because of Rodán? The sensations threw me off and for the first time since those early days after I met him, I wasn't sure how to act around him.

He offered me a strained smile as he gripped my shoulders in his long-fingered hands and gave me a light kiss on the cheek. He had moved with the litheness and speed of the Light Elves and was seated behind his desk before I had a chance to absorb anything.

I lowered myself into a chair in front of his desk and met his crystal-green eyes.

Hands down he was the most beautiful male specimen I had ever known—not just the Light Elves, but every other race known to human- and paranormkind.

Even now with his stern expression he was gorgeous. White-blond hair fell around his shoulders and his pointed ears peeked through the silken strands that I'd run my fingers through so many times when we were lovers.

Considering the sternness of Rodán's gaze and the tension in his beautiful body, not to mention the fact that I was dating Adam, I had no business thinking of Rodán in any way but from a professional standpoint.

Sure. See Rodán in only a professional light? As if that was ever going to be easy.

"Tell me everything that happened last night," he said in a demanding voice. It wasn't a request.

I couldn't help a frown. Since when had he talked with me this way? "Excuse me?" I leaned forward. "What happened to 'hello' and maybe even 'please'?"

Rodán closed his eyes, hiding the beautiful crystal green of them. When he opened his eyes his features were still tense but I didn't feel like it was directed at me any longer.

"My apologies, Nyx." Rodán gave a deep sigh, something he never did. "The developments in tonight's events have gone beyond what knowledge you may have." He indicated with a nod that he wanted me to talk. "Tell me what happened tonight and about anything you learned."

I leaned forward in my chair. "The Sprites gave the Vampires information regarding all races of paranorm beings. Weaknesses and locations of every known home, hideaway, or lair." Frustration shot through me when Rodán's expression remained the same. "Everything, Rodán."

"You are certain the Vampires obtained this information?" he said.

"Yes." I pushed my hair out of my face as it swung over my shoulder when I leaned even closer. "We found a dying Sprite who told us," I said. "Then we discovered a Sprite who'd been hiding in glamour and had watched the whole thing. That Sprite told us they gave it all to the Vampires who double-crossed them."

Rodán closed his eyes for a moment which threw me off. He looked like he was holding back emotions he wanted to set free.

He opened his eyes and met my gaze. "Then it is worse than you know."

A cold, clammy feeling crept over my skin. "What can be worse than Vampires being given that kind of intelligence?"

"The council—" Rodán looked like he was fighting off anger as he broke off. Rodán never showed his true emotions. The fact that he was now made my insides ball up and tighten.

Rodán grasped the worn folder from the tray and didn't even seem to notice the papers that had been beneath it sliding out all over his desk. He handed me the folder. I felt as if it might burn my hands when I took it from him.

"The council deemed it important to keep this." Rodán gestured for me to open the folder.

My sense that something was wrong was so great that my hands trembled as I looked at the red runes. Slowly, I turned back the much-handled cover of the folder. When I realized what it was, my heart raced and fear made me almost dizzy.

"The Werewolf case we solved." My whisper was hoarse and I was surprised he had even heard me when he nodded. "It looks like everything on creating the virus is here. All the notes, memos, diagrams, photos, research . . . everything."

"Yes," Rodán said. "Everything."

"The council kept all of the documents from the case," I said slowly. It was in black and white yet I had a hard time believing something so incredibly stupid had been done. "Every bit of this information was supposed to be destroyed."

"You are correct," he said. "It *was* to be destroyed, but they believed there was good reason it should not be."

I glanced back at the file and started flipping through the contents, feeling more and more sick. My stomach churned with the turn of every bit of research that had been done by an insane scientist bent on wiping out Werewolves and then all of the paranorm population.

When I came to a page labeled SERUM at the top, horror rose in my throat like acid.

"The formula for the virus that attacks the mutated gene that all paranorms share." I jerked my head up and stared at Rodán. "If the Vampires have this and manage to find a way to reproduce the serum, they could infect every single paranorm. All of us could die."

"Yes." Rodán's jaw tightened.

I went on as more thoughts sped through my mind. "It would be possible that they could blackmail us and control the paranorm population."

"Yes," Rodán said. "That is possible."

So many questions continued to race through my head. "The Vampires. Why would they do something that would hurt them, too? They're paranorms."

Rodán steepled his fingers. "If you read the detail there, you will see that Vampires would be safe."

Confusion made me blink. "What are you talking about?"

"Vampires were once human, before they were 'turned.'" Rodán's gaze didn't waver from mine. "Due to that fact, Vampires do not share the mutated gene that all true paranorms have in common. Witches, Necromancers, and Zombies were once human and do not carry the gene as well."

I shuddered at the word "Zombies."

"The Vampires could hold us hostage to their demands," I said. "But why would the Sprites be so stupid as to give the Vampires information that could kill others of their kind?" Nothing was computing.

"I think I just answered my own question," I said as I glanced back at the folder. "Sprites are stupid to begin with. This is just additional evidence to add to the rest."

"Do not be so quick to judge an entire race of beings, Nyx." Rodán spoke to me in the formal tongue of the Light Elves, his statement surprising me into looking from the file to him again.

Before I could respond, Rodán reverted and no longer spoke with formality or in that language. "There is more to this than a formula for the serum."

I turned my attention from Rodán and started flipping pages of the file. Toward the back I found pages separate from the rest. They were faint, in a messy scrawl that was difficult to read.

Rather than decipher the pages, I held them up and met Rodán's gaze. "What are these? Why are they separate from the rest of the pages in the folder?"

"That is the reason why this entire disaster is more than a simple formula for a serum," he said.

My throat felt constricted as I repeated a sentiment

I'd had earlier. "What could be worse?" I really should have shut my mouth.

"The council kept a vial of the scientist's serum," Rodán said as for a brief moment I was too in shock to move, to say anything. "And we do not know its current location."

"What?" I stood so fast I dropped the folder and all of its contents spewed out and scattered across the hardwood floor. I was beyond incredulous. *"The council kept a vial of the serum?"*

Rodán gestured for me to sit but I was so angry I stayed on my feet. "How could you let this happen, Rodán?"

"I was not informed." Rodán held out his hand, his palm up. The papers that had been spread out all over his floor slid back into the folder. The file rose in the air, then went to him and settled on his palm. "I learned of it last night after the archives had been broken into."

"How could you not have known?" My knees didn't want to hold me up and I sat. Hard. "Didn't the almighty Great Guardian deem to inform you?" I asked, fury in my voice.

Rodán raised his hand. "Nyx." His tone was a warning not to push it with my comments about the Great Guardian.

I pushed it anyway. I hated the GG's riddles, her holding back when we needed help. Like when she didn't give us more Night Trackers when she could have during the time we Trackers were being wiped out by Demons. And now, this?

"We've got to get it back," I said. "Now. Before they use it against us."

"The council's cleanup team found additional serum and the antiserum in the scientist's lab." He gestured toward what I was holding. "Those pages are the details on the ongoing experiment and effectiveness of the anti-serum," he said. "But no formula for the antiserum was recovered."

"Antiserum?" Everything we had been talking about was spinning in my mind like crazy. "They made an anti-serum?"

"We really don't know why," Rodán said. "Perhaps Johnson believed he needed it in case the serum had some effect on humans after all. Unfortunately the small vial in that safe was the only existing antiserum."

"I can't believe this." I was almost too stunned to speak. "I just can't believe it," I said again.

"Dr. Warner Burke is one of the most respected sci-entists in the field of biological warfare." Rodán tapped the folder with his index finger. "The serum and antise-rum, along with all of the notes, were to be given to him tomorrow. From that information, he was to develop the formula for the antiserum so that there would be more than the single vial."

"That's the stupidest thing I've heard yet." I tossed the handwritten pages onto Rodán's desk. "If the serum was disposed of and every page of that file had been de-stroyed like they were supposed to be, we wouldn't need to develop a formula for an antiserum."

"Agreed in part." Rodán gathered up the pages I'd tossed on his desk, this time by hand, not by magic. "What the council maintains is that there could be a pos-sibility the serum could show up one day. Had the scien-tist entrusted someone with the information . . . they felt they had to try to develop more of the antiserum on the chance that happened."

"The scientist and all of the junior scientists were ei-ther wiped out or imprisoned," I said.

"Were they?" Rodán didn't look like he was judging

me, more like he wanted me to think through the situation.

"We thought so—"

"Important words, Nyx," Rodán said. "You thought. Not that you knew, but thought."

"You're right." I rubbed my palms on my slacks. "We assumed and that was a stupid thing to do."

But then my anger resurfaced. "It was insane to not have guarded the serum better. The archives? Are they out of their minds? The archives are no place for serums that could wipe out the entire paranorm world."

"Apparently it had been guarded in a different place all of this time," Rodán said. "As I said, the council maintains that it all was to be transferred tomorrow."

"Then why was it in the archives?" I would really have liked to have a few words with those responsible. Better yet, a little sparring with me against the entire bunch of brainless idiots at once.

"The serum had only been at the archives for twelve hours." Rodán kept his expression calm. "The records having been stolen was a 'freak of timing' as the council members say."

"I'll freak-of-timing them," I said and clenched my teeth.

Rodán continued. "The Sprite break-in for the paranorm weaknesses was coincidental to the information on the serum and vial of serum being there. A horrible coincidence, and now we believe it is all in the hands of the Vampires."

"Idiots." I ground my teeth. "And why on earth was the weakness of every paranorm in such an accessible location?" I continued. "It's pure lunacy, stupidity . . . bunch of idiots. It's all beyond reason." I shook my head as I spewed the words.

"What is done is done," Rodán said. "Now we must fix it."

"Fix it?" I pushed both hands through my hair, shoving it out of my face. "We have to assume the Vampires have the entire file of paranorm weaknesses, a serum which can destroy the paranorm world, *and* they have the only known antiserum to exist." I shook my head. "As Olivia would put it, we are so screwed."

Rodán used his calm, soothing voice on me. "I need your entire focus now."

"The Sprites." A thought occurred to me. "They said they held something back from the Vampires." I frowned and said, more to myself than to Rodán, "Could it have been the serum and the antiserum?"

Rodán said, "It is a possibility."

"And that would mean the Sprites have the serum," I said. "We have to find out."

I didn't realize I'd been sitting on the edge of my seat, my hands clenching the armrests in a death grip. I forced myself to settle back in my chair. My fingers ached from grasping the chair's arms so tightly.

"What if the Sprites make some kind of deal and give the serum and antiserum to the Vampires?" Heat balled up inside me—anger, concern, fear. Emotions were attacking me all at once. "Or what if the Sprites try to use it themselves?"

"It takes a minuscule amount of the serum." Rodán's words had me sitting straight up in my chair again. "According to further research performed by paranorm scientists, the virus incubates for forty eight hours once it is injected into a paranorm being."

He paused as I held my breath for his next words. "Then it can spread throughout the rest of the species like a windstorm."

The enormity of his words had my head spinning but I grasped onto the first thought that came to mind. "What about the antiserum?"

"It takes an even smaller amount," he said, "to cure the virus as long as the person injected with the virus is the one receiving the antiserum."

"The antiserum needs to be administered before the incubation period is up, or about forty-eight hours after exposure, according to the scientists' recovered documents," I said as I spoke my thoughts aloud, putting together pieces of what was said and what had been left unsaid. "And then it's completely unstoppable."

Rodán moved the folder from in front of him and placed it back with the papers that had slipped out of the tray on his desk.

"The Sprite we captured at the scene was taken to my office for questioning," I said.

"Excellent." Rodán stood and I knew it was time for me to go. "We can't afford to waste any time."

"Okay." I took a deep breath. "I think I know where to start."

TEN

"I can't believe you brought a Sprite here." Olivia had her hands on her hips and glared at me when I walked into the office.

I'd known I was in trouble when I saw what was on her bright orange T-shirt.

IF YOU CAN READ THIS YOU'RE WITHIN ROUNDHOUSE KICK RANGE

"Technically, I brought him in," Angel said from behind Olivia.

I hoped Olivia couldn't tell Angel was trying to hide a smile or the Doppler might get to experience a roundhouse from a former NYPD SWAT team officer who had a third degree black belt in karate. Olivia might not be a paranorm but she could kick major ass.

Angel didn't get to experience Olivia's roundhouse kick, but she did get Olivia's glare. "When I want to hear something from you, Perky, then I'll dial your number," Olivia said. "Otherwise shut up."

The Doppler Tracker bit her lower lip and I knew she was about to burst into a fit of laughter. Angel apparently valued her life, though, and managed to hold back.

Olivia clenched her jaw as she looked at Negel who was cuffed to one of the chairs in front of my desk. He was either asleep or knocked out. I had a feeling it was the latter.

I tilted my head. I'd never seen a Sprite in the daylight. It didn't do anything for his complexion.

"We can't interrogate him if he's not conscious," I said.

"Forget the Sprite." Olivia cut her furious gaze to me again. "Not only did all of you ditch me last night, and you won't tell me where you were, but you also allowed this thing to be brought into *our* office."

"Sorry." I winced.

Olivia used her hands as she spoke, which was a sure sign I should consider running away. "Where did you, Ice, Joshua, and Perky here go last night after you decided to take flying lessons out a Vampire's window?" She narrowed her gaze. "No bullshit."

"After the Sprites." I walked past Olivia to my desk and dropped my handbag on the credenza. "We found out that the Vampires were behind all of the chaos—they worked out some kind of deal with the Sprites." I cocked my head toward Negel. "That's what he's here for. To help us fill in the blanks. And there are a lot of blanks."

Olivia's exotic features were set as she crossed her arms over her generous chest and leaned her hip against her desk. "Explain."

"I've got to go." Angel gave her brightest, dingiest smile so that she looked like a brainless wonder. No one would ever have guessed that she was the farthest thing from a bubblehead that you could get. "I have an appointment for a pedicure."

"You do that, Perky." Olivia waved her hand toward the door. "Just remember that you bring another one of these *things* in here and I'm going to shave every one of your curls off and toss them into the Hudson."

I walked toward the door and opened it. Angel winked at Olivia, then shifted, her body vanishing as she transformed into a blond squirrel. One of Olivia's erasers almost hit Angel's little squirrel butt as she darted out the door.

Fae bells jangled as I let the door close and it was just me, Olivia, and a pitiful ugly and unconscious Sprite who might not have long to live if Olivia got her hands on him.

Before Olivia could say anything else after she tossed a rubber band on her desk, I got the first words out. "Something really bad has gone down. We have to talk."

Olivia crossed her arms over her chest but now she looked more concerned than angry. "All of it. Now."

With a nod I walked to my desk and leaned against it, facing Olivia. I brushed a few of Kali's blue hairs from my slacks. She'd only shredded a third of my new panties but had walked through my closet and rubbed up against some of my clothes, leaving blue cat hair on a good portion of my slacks and skirts.

I took a deep breath, then let the words out in a rush. "The Vampires not only have the lists of paranorm races' weaknesses, but they now have the scientist's notes from the Werewolf case."

Olivia stared at me with a stunned expression. "You'd better start explaining. Don't you dare hold anything back, including why you ditched me last night."

I closed my eyes, trying to figure out how I was going to explain everything without telling her about the Paranorm Center. Damn the council for not allowing us to tell humans.

When I thought I could get the story out without breaking my vow, I opened my eyes and met Olivia's gaze.

"No bullshit," she said. "Not one word. I know you're

holding back and you have been for a long time. I'm not putting up with it a moment longer." She pointed to the door. "See that sign? That's my name up there with yours. It's not going to be there anymore if you keep anything from me. *Anything.*"

I rubbed both hands through my hair in a frustrated motion, like I had earlier. "You're right. You should have been told everything from the beginning. The Paranorm Council should never have forced us to withhold any information from you." So much for not breaking my vow.

Olivia blinked before she slowly said, "Paranorm Council? What in the hell are you talking about?"

"I'm sorry, Olivia." I began to pace the length of our office as I started to tell her all that I'd been holding back. "The council makes Peacekeepers take an oath that we never speak of them, never disclose the location of the Paranorm Center."

I continued, "Any paranorm being who learns about the center has their memories altered so that they will not remember it. Anyone who is not a Peacekeeper, guard, or in some form of what you Earth Otherworld beings call 'management' can't know about the center."

Olivia stared at me with incredulity. "I have been risking my ass day after day for two years for you paranorms and you have the audacity to hold back this kind of information from me? I seem to remember Rodán making *me* a Tracker, so human or not, I should have been in on this a long time ago."

I started to speak but I clamped my mouth shut when she started a full-blown rant.

"Adam and I are good enough to *die* for you paranorms," she said, her voice rising. "But we're not good enough to be given all of the facts."

Olivia's eyes were so dark they were like pools of black ink. Her silken brown features had taken on a reddish hue. I'd never seen Olivia so angry in the two years we'd been partners.

"You're right." I held my hands up, surrendering, placating, anything to get her to calm down. "I'm breaking my vow to the council and I don't care. I should have talked with Rodán about it. Maybe he could have swayed the council, but I didn't even try."

"How could you not try to get the stupid ruling changed?" Olivia clenched her fists. "After everything we've been through."

"You're right," I said again. "I was so conflicted. But now I'm going to tell you everything."

And I did. I told her every little thing all the way back to the time when I'd first been taken to the council and sworn in as a Peacekeeper.

"You do know you're going to have to explain all of this to Adam, right?" Olivia said when I finished. "You can't hold this back."

"I agree, he's laid his life out as well." I sighed. "There were so many times I wanted to tell you both, but the rules of no disclosure to humans held me back." I held up my hand to ask her to hear me through.

"But everything you're saying is correct," I went on. "I know I can trust you and I can trust him. And there are times you need to know things, like in this case. I just want him to understand."

"If you explain it that way, he should understand," she said, still frowning. "I guess I understand where you're coming from. Thanks for finally trusting me." She gave me a long, hard look. "You *know* I would never let you down."

"I know you never would," I said. "And I won't hold

anything back from you again." I held one hand to my heart like humans do when they make a promise—whether they plan to keep it or not. I planned to keep mine. "Promise."

"What about that thing?" Olivia pointed to something behind me.

I stared at Negel who had remained unconscious during my and Olivia's heart-to-heart. His big head drooped and drool ran down one side of his ugly face. His eyes were closed, his body relaxed as he sagged against his bonds.

Kali jumped onto my desk from out of nowhere. The blue Persian stared at the Sprite before she arched her back and hissed.

"If you don't like the company, then you can leave," I told my cat.

"Why don't you visit Nyx's underwear drawer while you're at it," Olivia said as Kali stalked toward our backroom.

"Stay away from my panties," I called after the cat, then glared at Olivia. "She's already shredded most of the new ones I bought. At Victoria's Secret I found some really cute—"

"I don't need to know about your panty drawer," Olivia said.

She walked up to the little Sprite and clapped her hands in front of his face. "Wake up, Dog Food."

At the sound of the clap, the Sprite jerked his head up, his big eyes going wide.

"That's enough." I frowned at Olivia. "Negel is going to tell us what he knows." I looked to Negel. "And that had better be a lot."

"Sprites stink." Olivia wrinkled her nose. "The whole place smells like something burned."

"Are we going to interrogate him or smell him?" I said.

She propped her hands on her hips and looked down at Negel. "Apparently both."

His huge Adam's apple bobbed. "I will tell you what I know."

"Start from the beginning." I braced my hands on my thighs and leaned close to him. "I want to know every single thing you can possibly think of that has to do with this whole mess. Like the fact the Sprites might have the serum and antiserum to a deadly virus."

"What are you talking about, Nyx?" Olivia said with shock on her face.

I felt almost frantic as I filled her in on what Rodán told me about the serum and antiserum. I held back only the information that I didn't want the Sprite to overhear.

When I'd finished telling Olivia what she needed to know, I turned to the Sprite. "We have to find out from Negel exactly where this serum is, if they have it." I glared at him. "And why he didn't tell us last night."

Negel flushed red.

"First, do the Sprites have the serum?" I asked.

Negel lowered his head. His ears flopped forward. "Tobath has it."

"Tobath has it?" I repeated what Negel said.

He nodded, ears flopping.

The Sprite looked a little green. "Remember that when he was tortured Ecknep told the Vampires about it just for spite. He just didn't tell you what 'it' was. He taunted them with the fact that the Sprites had the serum and antiserum and they would not get it."

Negel continued, "Ecknep told the Vampires they should not have killed Zith and treated him that way. Told them that they lost a great prize because of that . . . As if the Vampires could not figure out how to get it from us."

"Great." I put my hands on my hips and looked at the ceiling. "Can't cut us a break, GG, can you."

Negel continued and I looked back at him as he spoke. "That's why Ecknep laughed even as he died. The Vampires didn't get everything." Negel frowned, the skin on his forehead becoming lumpy lines. "That was idiocy. Now the Vampires will come after my people to find the actual serum."

I cocked my head. "What's worse? Sprites having the serum or Vampires?"

"Vampires are intelligent." Olivia's nose wrinkled in concentration. "Sprites aren't."

Negel looked affronted. "We are so. Intelligent."

Olivia seemed not to have heard him. "Sprites might get careless and break the whole vial of the stuff. Vampires probably have steadier hands."

"Vampires are evil." Negel raised his chin. "Sprites are not."

"That depends on your interpretation of the word 'evil,'" Olivia said in a dry tone.

"Now tell us the rest," I said. "I want to know more about this Tobath, too."

"It is not much more than I told you, but I will tell you all that I do know," Negel said. "I fear for my people. I fear for my wife and sons."

From Olivia's expression, she was having the same experience I'd had earlier—She'd never thought about a Sprite having a family.

"You fear for your people and family, yet you give the Vampires the kind of information that was in those documents?" Olivia looked ready to give *him* a roundhouse.

"I told Miss Tracker that I did not know about the operation. If I did I would not have gone along with it." Negel blinked, his eyelids covering his huge eyes for a moment. "I tried to stop them when I learned of it."

Olivia leaned against her desk again and crossed her arms over her chest. "You sure did a crappy job of that."

Negel hung his huge head.

I snapped my fingers beneath his nose. "We don't have time for you two to mess around like this. Keep talking."

Negel raised his head. Was he ever ugly.

"Tobath is a self-appointed leader over our five Sprite clans." Negel's expression showed a twinge of almost terror and a flash of hate before his expression slid back into his current fear of Olivia and me. "He has many followers now who act as his guards and his army."

"Sprites hate authority," Olivia said, echoing what I had in the detention center. And they definitely don't like responsibility."

"That was true before Tobath," Negel said. "Our clans are our families and extended families. We argue, fight, but no single Sprite had ever led us."

I braced my hands on the back of the chair beside Negel and he had to turn his head to look at me. "Why now? Why this Sprite? What makes him different?"

"You should very well know since you are a halfling of the same race," Negel said. "Tobath's mother mated with a Drow warrior."

My eyes widened. "Tobath is half Drow?" The thought of remotely being related to one of the slimy creeps made my skin crawl.

"That explains a lot." Olivia looked at me. "Does he have purple skin?"

I moved the chair so that I was directly in front of

Negel. I kept my hand braced on the back of the chair. "What does he look like? Drow or Sprite? Or does he shift at sunrise and sunset?"

"His skin is gray, like dirty dishwater," Negel said. "He is very ugly and his ears are more pointed than other Sprites' ears. With those exceptions he looks like all of our kind."

"All Sprites are ugly," Olivia said. "What's different about that?"

Negel looked insulted. "My race is not ugly."

Olivia smirked. "Says you."

"Our females are quite beautiful," Negel said, his nose in the air.

"Suuuuure," Olivia said.

Come to think of it, I'd never seen a female Sprite.

I thought about Tobath again and his reign over these Sprites. "Drow males are often arrogant and ambitious."

"That is Tobath." Negel nodded. "Arrogant, ambitious, and evil."

"Not all Dark Elves are evil." I directed my scowl at him. "Most aren't."

"What I want to know is how one of those Drow dudes went after a Sprite." Olivia gave an almost over-the-top shudder.

I held up my hands. "I *don't* want to know."

No way in all of the Underworlds did I want to find out if I was related to this Tobath, either.

"What I do want to know," I said as I brought my attention totally to Negel, "is how he managed to make a small army for himself from a bunch of Sprites who don't like authority."

"Intimidation," Negel said. "Fear."

"Wash the windows and be a little clearer, why don't you?" Olivia said.

"It was like rolling a booger in the dirt," Negel said.

Olivia made a face.

I grimaced.

He went on. "It starts out with one grain of dirt and collects more as it rolls."

I had a feeling part of Negel's childhood involved rolling boogers in the dirt for entertainment. I didn't want to know more details about that activity.

"How do booger rolling and Sprite dictatorship relate?" Olivia asked.

"Tobath recruited a group of childhood friends," Negel said. "He may have threatened them or their families. The first followers gained more followers because of similar threats. Then more and more . . . Tobath controls most of the five clans now."

"You said 'most.' " I gripped the back of a chair. "Tell me about the others."

"Remember what I told you about my brother, Penrod. He organized us. We are but a small group and we meet in private." Negel said the words in a whisper, like one of Tobath's followers might be somewhere in the room.

"Don't worry." I pointed to the doorway. "Nothing cloaked or otherwise can pass through that doorway without permission. It's heavily warded and Fae bells sound a warning if any being tries to come in. You're safe."

Negel licked his thick lips. His tongue was purple. "One thing we have learned is that Tobath has great might, but lacks in reason and to some extent intelligence."

Olivia snorted. "Sprites and intelligence? An oxymoron."

Negel actually looked hurt, then ignored her and spoke

to me. "We have a secret way of communicating and the males meet when we go hunting for our clans," Negel said.

"Hunting as in rooting through trash barrels?" Olivia said.

"Enough." I frowned at her. "Keep interrupting and we'll never get anything out of him."

Olivia shrugged. "I wonder how much, if any of this, is the truth."

"I want what is good for my people." Negel had a note of pleading in his voice. "Nothing more."

"Go on." I ignored Olivia. "You go hunting with other Sprites and then what?"

"We discuss ways to rid ourselves of Tobath." Negel sighed. "Thus far we have failed."

"Color me surprised," Olivia said. "So why did you get in on all this hot dog stuffing and statue painting?"

"Most Sprites thought that it was just fun and harmless play. Penrod and our little group went along with it to appear loyal to Tobath." Negel grimaced. "We didn't know it was a much larger scheme of Tobath's.

"But then I spoke with one in our group who is close enough in rank to Tobath that he overhears things." Negel licked his lips again. "Through him we learned that Tobath had approached the Vampires. He believes we need protection from other races and especially from you." He tilted his head indicating it was me he was talking about. "You and all other Trackers."

Negel went on as I considered what he had said. "Tobath and Volod made a pact. Ecknep and Zith told me before we broke out of the cell that our adventures around the city were part of the Vampire plan. Most of us were to distract Trackers by performing mischief and to allow ourselves to be caught and taken to the paranorm jails," Negel said.

"And they would give you the temporary ability to escape," I said and he looked surprised. "Once you brought something to them from the archives, they would give all Sprites the permanent power to escape paranorm jails."

I waved him off when he started to speak. "We know about the file of paranorm weaknesses."

"Yes." He nodded. "And Ecknep told me just that night of the mission. I honestly did not know before that. Ecknep said that Vampires want to rule all paranorms. The information would allow them this ability."

"The Sprites copied an entire folder relating to a case the Trackers handled." I gripped the back of the chair tighter. "The case that involves the serum that could wipe out every paranorm being with the exception of anything close to being human."

"I—I—" Negel looked from me to Olivia and back.

"How did you find out this file exists?" I was still furious it had been kept by the Paranorm Council.

"After they told me of the plan, Ecknep and Zith said I could come with them. Just the three of us got into the archives first," Negel said. "Tobath wanted them to have time to copy what the Vampires needed before the other Sprites created chaos to cover our tracks."

"And . . ." Olivia gestured for him to continue.

"There was a safe," Negel said. "Ecknep is—was— Tobath's most dedicated follower. He said that whatever was in that safe must be important."

Negel continued. "Ecknep and Zith broke into the safe and quickly read and copied everything. I heard them. They said the Vampires would be in even greater debt to the Sprites if we gave him that information and the two vials they found as well. At that point I pleaded with them to leave it all."

"Maybe we can obtain the vial more easily from the Sprites," I said. "It might be harder to get it from Vampires."

She nodded slowly. "Okay, Dog Food, where's Tobath's hideout?"

"Sprites never tell any beings where we live." Negel shook his head, ears flopping. "It would put all Sprites in danger."

"I'll danger your ass." Olivia rested her hand on her Sig Sauer in her side holster. "Starting with a bullet right—"

"Olivia." I cut her off. "Negel is going to tell us where Tobath is without you shooting him in the butt."

She moved her hand away from her handgun and folded her arms across her chest again. "He damned well better."

"I will go myself." Negel tried to stand, obviously forgetting for a moment that he was cuffed to a chair. The chair legs squeaked on the ceramic tile. He thumped back in his seat. "It is better if I sneak in and get the serum from Tobath."

"That's not going to happen." I walked around the chair I'd been holding onto and sat on the cushioned seat. "You're going to tell us exactly where we can find Tobath."

Negel shook his head and didn't say anything.

"Only my team will know." I braced my forearms on my thighs. "We'll go in covertly. I promise you that we will not tell anyone where the Sprites live." Well, I'd tell Rodán, but that was a given.

"I do not think . . ." Negel squirmed in his seat. Olivia had her Sig out, resting in her palm. "How many of you?" he asked.

We had him.

"Five including Olivia and me," I said.

"She's human, she would not survive." Negel glanced at Olivia and seemed to reconsider his comment. He would probably not be opposed to that considering their stellar new relationship. He looked back to me, obviously ignoring Olivia now. "You promised. I will tell you."

The Fae bells jingled as the door opened and we all turned our heads. Adam walked in. I stood and smiled until I glanced at Olivia whose expression said, *You'd better come clean with him or I will.*

"Of course I'll tell him." I wasn't looking forward to it, but I would. "I was planning on it."

"Tell me what?" Adam reached me, settled his hand on my shoulder and brushed his mouth over mine. I let his coffee and leather scent wash over me. "Does it involve any alone time?" he murmured.

I wanted to melt at his sexy smile. "No, but we can make up for it with some time together later."

He smiled back at me, then frowned. I wondered if he could read minds now. Rodán did say that all human liaisons to the paranorm had some kind of latent psychic talent.

So far Adam's talent seemed to be sensing when I needed him or if I was going into a dangerous assignment or I was in some kind of trouble. He didn't know anything about his latent psychic talent and I wasn't going to say anything—yet, anyway.

I saw that his frown wasn't directed at me and I looked over my shoulder at Negel.

Adam cocked one eyebrow at me. I loved how he did that. "You brought one of those here?"

"You get the prize for the 'Most Observant Detective

of the Year Award,' " Olivia said. "A true student of the obvious."

He grinned at Olivia. "Don't you have some rubber bands to load?"

"Don't tempt me." She picked up a large eraser. "I'll start with the big guns."

Adam laughed and raised his hands. "Peace." To me he said, "So tell me about your guest."

"Meet Negel." I gestured to the Sprite. "Negel, this is Detective Adam Boyd."

"Another human." Negel looked perplexed. "I will not tell you the location with him in this place."

"His gun is bigger than Olivia's," I said with a shrug.

Negel slumped in his seat. "You promised."

"Detective Boyd is on my team, too." I'd just neglected to mention it earlier.

Adam shoved his hands in the pockets of his worn brown leather bomber jacket. "Location of what?"

"The Sprite lair," Olivia said.

"It is not a lair." Negel sniffed and raised his chin high. "It is home to our clans."

She smirked again. "A.K.A. lair."

"Children. Listen up." I was tempted to roll my eyes. "Every moment that goes by gives Tobath more time to do something with the serum."

"Like drop the vial," Olivia said.

Adam started to speak and I raised my hand to indicate I wanted him to hush. "I'll give you a complete rundown later. Right now we need Negel to give us the exact location that the Sprites call home."

Negel's thick lips tightened into a firm line as if he wasn't going to tell us after all. Smart move for him when he started speaking. "Abandoned sewers."

"Should have known your lair is in the sewers." Olivia wrinkled her nose. "No wonder Sprites stink."

"Home." Negel shot back. "It is our home. You may think sewers stink, but we are incapable of sensing certain human odors. Sewers are one of the odors. It is the perfect spot. No one comes there bothering us."

"Wish there was a way of us not having to smell you," Olivia said.

"Where in the abandoned sewers?" I asked.

"We recently relocated to Hell's Kitchen." He sighed. "Under the post office, Radio City Station."

Adam, Olivia, and I looked at one another.

"You have your lair under that post office?" Olivia burst out laughing. "Gives a whole new meaning to 'going postal.'"

Negel slumped, dejected.

"Tell us everything we need to know to get in and out of there without anyone getting hurt, maimed, or killed," I said.

Negel told us which manhole cover was closest to Tobath's stronghold. It was a separate location than that of the clan Tobath had been raised in.

I was still trying to avoid thoughts about how a Sprite and a Drow warrior managed to get together, much less thinking about growing up in a clan in the sewers and then moving into Hell's Kitchen sewers.

It was still referred to as Hell's Kitchen, but the area in Manhattan was now also referred to as Clinton or Midtown West. As far as Sprites were concerned, the old name from the days of mobsters and gangs seemed to be more appropriate.

I studied the Sprite. "Give me something I can use. Like how I can find Tobath and his grunts."

Negel licked his lips again. Not attractive. "Every night he assembles his force at midnight in the same place," Negel said. "It is very secret and very new. New enough that it is not even on the list of paranorm weaknesses and known locations. I checked the documents when Ecknep copied the information."

"Details," Olivia said.

The Sprite told us what I hoped was the exact location of the meeting, under a tenement on Fifty-forth Street.

When we'd gotten all I thought we could out of Negel, I said, "I'll call the PTF. They can take you back to the detention center. My team will be in place at Tobath's meeting location by midnight."

"You are not going to free me?" Negel asked, his bulbous eyes wide.

"Are you kidding?" Olivia laughed. An evil laugh. She was good at them. "Let loose the best source of information we have?"

"I will meet with you anytime you wish to." Negel gave me a pleading look. "Anytime. I promise. I will help you get the serum and antiserum."

For the first time since I'd met Sprites in New York City, I didn't think of them as nothing but slime. There was something about Negel that caused me to see Sprites as beings with families, friends. Beings with real emotions. Yesterday, I never thought that possible.

"I wish I could." I studied the Sprite. "But we need your help and I can't risk letting you go."

"I promise." I thought Negel would be on his knees, hands clasped as he begged if he wasn't cuffed. "I will be here when you tell me to and I will guide you to the meeting place."

"Sorry." I shook my head but still felt bad at the dejected look on his face. "I trust you to take us to Tobath, yes. But I need to make sure we can reach you. That's why we need you here."

"You can call me on my cell phone," he said.

Collectively, Adam, Olivia, and I dropped our jaws.

The three of us looked at the rags he was wearing to see how he could possibly be carrying a phone. Olivia and Adam both seemed to be at a loss for words. The bigger surprise was Olivia not having something to say.

"It is quite small," Negel said. "Easy to hide from the PTF."

"Okay . . . Um, what's your number?" Strange as it was, we might as well get all of the information we could. I retrieved my phone out of my handbag on my desk. "I'll put you in my contacts."

The whole idea of a Sprite having a cell phone seemed a little bit on the surreal side of life. Negel slowly said his phone number and I entered it on my own phone.

"A Metro New York area code." Olivia had found her tongue. I thought she'd lost the ability to speak for a few moments there. "How the hell does a Sprite get a cell phone? Where does he get the bill?"

"Phones with prepaid minutes." Negel shrugged. "Then we—we obtain cards with more minutes."

We nodded like it was totally normal.

"We'll save that for after, Negel." I dashed his hopes again. "For now you stay with us."

He sighed. A big sigh that was a show of resignation. "I will stay. I will help you. Then you will let me go to my wife and sons."

"Yes." I gave him a little smile. "I promise. No matter what happens, when we get the serum and antiserum, you are free."

"Thank you," he said in a polite tone.

A polite Sprite. Who'd have thought?

My thoughts turned to the Werewolves, where everything ultimately started.

"I think we should call Dmitri Beketov." Still holding my phone, I got up from the seat in front of Negel and walked around my desk. "After everything they went through, the Werewolves would probably like to know the serum is on the loose again."

"You're on your own with that one, girl," Olivia said. "I've got better things to do than be around a pissed-off alpha Were."

I dialed Beketov's phone number. My call could go straight to a generic voice mail telling me to leave my number. The Werewolves could be hunting in the Catskills for all I knew, out of cell phone range.

The Werewolf answered, "Beketov."

"Dmitri, this is Nyx Ciar." A shiver trailed my spine as I thought about the case we'd solved for the Werewolves. It was an experience I never wanted to go through again. Yet here we were facing the same threat, only with cunning Vampires instead of an insane scientist.

"Yes," Beketov said, as friendly as ever. Not.

"About that virus that the scientist developed." How did one tell an alpha Werewolf that a serum for a virus was on the loose . . . a virus that was developed to wipe out his people and had almost been injected into his own son?

"What about it?" His tone was harsh and I had the mental image of his body going rigid with anger. His son had been kidnapped by the scientist who had developed the serum.

"The documents weren't destroyed." I rubbed my temples with my fingertips as I heard his harsh intake of breath. I wasn't ready to tell him some of the serum it-self still existed. "The New York Vampires have the doc-uments, including the formula."

Beketov let out a long string of curse words. "Two hours and I will reach your office."

He severed the connection before I could get a word out.

I wondered if calling him had been such a smart idea after all.

ELEVEN

Adam walked with me up to my apartment above Olivia's and my PI office which was located on 104th and Central Park West. I leaned my head on his shoulder as we walked, simply enjoying being close to him.

"Amazing how tenants of the building don't even know your PI office is there," Adam said as we made our way toward my apartment.

"Just you and Olivia." I straightened and looked up at him. "Every other norm doesn't have a clue. No other norm has even been in the office but you two. Our magic wards are too strong."

It only took a bit of my air element to unlock the door to my apartment when Adam and I reached it. I never carried a key.

I loved my apartment. Partly because it was mine and away from the Drow Realm belowground in Otherworld. Partly because of the views. Partly because it was pretty.

I'm a princess. I like pretty things.

Just because I'm a warrior doesn't mean I'm not feminine.

As soon as the door closed I was in Adam's arms. His kiss was intense yet sweet. He kissed me like I was the most precious thing to him on this Earth Otherworld. In any Otherworld.

He tasted of mint and I loved to breathe in his wonderful scent of leather and coffee. Leather from his worn bomber jacket and I suspected coffee because of the Starbucks he always hit on the way to work.

When he drew away he pressed his lips against my forehead.

I stepped back and held both of his hands in mine. "Come on." I began to lead him to the kitchen. "I need to feed Her Highness before I have to go panty shopping again."

Adam brought me toward him and rubbed his hands down my hips and across the curves of my rear. "She didn't get the leopard ones or the black with the red lace, did she?"

I laughed and reached up to whisper in his ear. "I hid them since they're your favorites."

He grinned and I led him across the hardwood floor through the arched entryway into the spacious kitchen. Brown marble countertops, cherrywood cabinets, and stainless steel appliances made it a beautiful space.

Considering I don't cook, my Shifter maid, Dahlia, didn't have a whole lot of cleaning to do in that particular room of the house. Still, she made the appliances shine and the cabinets glow just like the beautiful hardwood floor.

Kali's crystal champagne saucer sparkled on the countertop beneath the track lighting. I grabbed a can of Kali's favorite cat food out of the walk-in pantry, opened it, and spooned some onto the dish before snapping a plastic lid on the can and putting it into the fridge.

"A sprig of catnip and you've got a queenly meal," Adam said.

"Hmmm . . ." I tilted my head in mock seriousness. "Maybe that's the key to getting into her good favor."

"I'll help you shop for the catnip." Adam leaned against the center island, his hands in his bomber jacket, his ankles crossed. He wore brown athletic shoes and Levi's and a chocolate brown shirt beneath his bomber jacket. Delicious. He gave me his adorable boyish smile. "So where is Kali?"

"Once we're out of her way she'll come out," I said.

"I've always meant to ask you how Kali gets from your apartment to the office," he said.

I shrugged. "I swear that cat has magic. I never have been able to figure it out."

"She's not very sociable, is she?" he asked with a smile.

I put my finger to my lips. "Shhh. She'll hear you. Your Looney Tunes boxers might end up being her next favorite thing to shred."

The corner of Adam's mouth quirked. "When you get a chance, tell Kali I think she is the most beautiful cat I have ever seen."

I giggled, then clapped my hand over my mouth. Where did that come from? I never giggled. Certainly never in front of anyone.

"I liked that." Adam pushed away from the kitchen island and reached me. He brushed a strand of hair from my eyes. "You sounded cute."

"Cute?" I tried not to let another giggle escape. What was wrong with me? "I don't think cute is a word that anyone has ever associated with me before."

"I do." He put his hands on my hips and placed his forehead against mine. "Yes, you're beautiful, sexy, intelligent, tough, kickass, driven to do what it takes to bring down the bad guys. You feel you have to be tough, all of the time . . . But there's a side of you that you try to hide. You don't have to hide who you are. Feel comfortable being you."

His tone was gentle and I swallowed, unable to say anything. Was I that transparent?

"I see through all of that, Nyx. You have a soft side that you cover up like you are afraid to come off looking weak somehow." He started swaying, as if we were dancing, his hands resting on my hips as he guided me, his body flush to mine. "You care more deeply for both norms and paranorms than you show. You want to save everyone and it hurts you when you can't."

"I'm not sure how I feel about you nailing me like that." Heat made its way through my body. "You're right, I don't want to look weak. I had to fight to be tough growing up around Drow male warriors."

He cupped the back of my head and pressed my face against his T-shirt. "Caring about others and showing emotion is not a weakness. It's a virtue. You can be yourself and still be effective," he said. "You don't have to be the tough woman, especially with me, Nyx."

"Sometimes I get tired of being like a paranorm version of Wonder Woman." I sighed. "Sometimes I just want to be a girl. I feel like I have to do everything on my own, that it's weak to ask for help." I tilted my head up. "I can't believe I'm telling you all of this."

"I like that you can admit the things you struggle with." He ran his fingers through the length of my hair and I shivered. "I like this vulnerable side of you."

I met his eyes. "I grew up in a world where any sign of weakness would have made me lose all credibility, everything I fought for. I still feel that I have to constantly prove myself.

"Sometimes I want a hug when things are tough," I went on. "Just a hug before I go back to being Nyx, PI and Night Tracker."

"What you do for an occupation does not define who you are." Adam continued stroking my hair. "You're good at being a Tracker because you're doing something you believe in. You're making a difference by protecting those who can't protect themselves.

"But there's more to you than that. Who you are is a wonderful person who is brave, sensitive, intelligent, strong, funny, fun, crazy, sweet, tough, beautiful inside and out, and caring. Those are the qualities I think that define you. Those are the qualities I love."

"I've never had anyone say something so wonderful to me." I suddenly felt shy, something that was almost an alien feeling. "I don't know what to say."

Adam hugged me then tickled me under my arm as he held me close. He surprised me, catching me so completely off guard that I started to giggle.

"Ticklish, huh?" he said as he did it to me even more.

"Don't." I couldn't stop laughing as I tried to get out of his hold. "Please."

"Since you said please." He stopped and I sank against him, exhausted from laughing so hard. "Now I know exactly what to do to get you to do what I want."

"Ha." I gave a pretend frown as I looked up at him. "I have handcuffs and I'm not afraid to use them."

"Promises," he said and heat eased through me, hot and liquid.

I cleared my throat. "I'd better put Kali's food down before I get in serious trouble with Her Highness."

Adam released me long enough to set the crystal dish on the floor beside the refrigerator.

I led Adam back out into the living room. My interior

designer had furnished the room in white with cobalt blue accents.

Thoughts of the Vampire's penthouse and its white sofas and splashes of red came to my mind.

"What are you supposed to tell me, Nyx?" Adam brought me down with him on the couch and we faced each other.

Oh. I'd managed to forget that little topic.

Here goes. "I haven't been totally up front with you and Olivia." I felt like squirming in my seat when he tilted his head. I hoped he wasn't thinking about the major mistake I'd made right before we started dating.

He propped his elbow on the back of the sofa. It was hard to read anything in his brown eyes. "Tell me."

It wasn't a demand, just a request for me to continue. Having grown up with dominant Drow warriors and subservient Drow females, I know the difference quite well.

One of the reasons I hadn't fit into the world of the Dark Elves was because I was raised by my human mother to never bow down to any male. My father, the king, indulged mother. Despite the fact his age was over two thousand years old, he was too much in love to care about centuries-old conventions.

And he spoiled me, indulging me in everything I wanted to do. I am the only female Drow warrior from the world I grew up in. I wasn't ready to share all of that with Adam. Yet.

"Come on." Adam's voice coaxed my attention back to him. "It's nothing I can't handle."

"You can handle it." I rubbed one of his hands with mine. "You just might not like it."

When he frowned, I decided to let everything fly. I shared with him about the Paranorm Center, the Paranorm Council, and my oath. Then I told him what the

Sprites had stolen and what we believed was given to the Vampires, and everything in between.

Adam took my hands in his when I was finished. "You were doing what you thought was right by following the council request."

"You're sure taking it better than Olivia did." I shook my head. "I think she was right, though, that after an almost two-year partnership I should have told her a long time before now."

"Like I said, everyone has their secrets," Adam said. "Everyone is entitled to them."

"Have any secrets you'd like to share?" I gave him a teasing smile. "Detective Boyd is bound to have a few tucked away."

"I have a few fantasies." He leaned close to me. "They all involve you in one way or another."

"Are those secrets you want to share with me?" I whispered before Adam encircled me in his strong arms and settled me in his lap.

His answer was a kiss. Soft and sweet again, then a little more intense. "One day," he murmured against my lips, "I'll tell you everything.

"Remember the waterfall and the pool in the Catskills?" He moved his mouth to my ear.

I shivered from the contact and from the memory. "It was amazing."

"You were so beautiful in the moonlight." Adam brought his mouth to mine and bit my lip. "But then you're always so beautiful."

A moan rose up in me as he kissed his way down my neck and brushed his lips over the hollow of my throat. "I—oh . . ." A pool of honey was what it felt like. I was drowning in a pool of sweetness and desire.

He kissed his way down the V of my blouse to the button between my breasts, causing me to gasp. I caught my breath and moaned as he ran his tongue in slow circles around one of my nipples, then gasped as he sucked my other nipple through my shirt.

Adam pulled my blouse out of my slacks and I slid my hands into his hair as he unbuttoned my blouse and revealed my belly. My heart was pounding faster and faster. His fingers felt strong and masterful as he moved his hands down my legs to my feet. He slipped off one of my heels and then the next, leaving my feet bare.

When he circled my belly button with his tongue I clenched my fists tighter in his hair. He nipped my belly, a playful bite that set me on an erotic edge that I knew I might just tumble over.

"What happened to mild-mannered Detective Boyd?" My voice was strained from trying not to give into this desire that on some level scared me.

"He just left the building." Adam's warm brown eyes met mine as he knelt on a rug on the hardwood floor. He reached for the button of my slacks and the button easily came undone. He unzipped my slacks slow enough to drive me crazy.

Adam grasped the waistband of my slacks and I moved so that he could slide them down my thighs. He tossed them to the side and gave me his adorable sexy grin when he looked at my panties. I was wearing his favorite leopard print panties and a matching bra.

Most Drow females don't wear anything beneath their clothes—well, they often don't even wear clothing. But I love the sensual feel of satins and silks against my skin and I love the way they make me feel sexy beneath whatever I might be wearing.

He pushed my blouse over my shoulders and it dropped to the crooks of my elbows before he helped me take it off the rest of the way.

"You know how much I love these." He tossed my blouse over his shoulder before bringing his hands to my breasts and rubbed his thumbs over my nipples.

I tilted my head back and rested my upper body on the couch on my elbows and forearms. He pulled my bra beneath my breasts and I closed my eyes. A moan rolled out from me as his warm mouth settled on one of my nipples. He moved his lips to my other nipple and sucked it, too.

He rose to his feet and looked down at me with intensity and desire. More than that was in his brown eyes, but I wasn't sure of the depths of his feelings for me. I knew how I felt about him.

Adam shrugged off his bomber jacket and let it drop on the floor, followed by his T-shirt. I loved to see him like this. Muscular, toned, sexy.

When he unzipped his Levi's I saw his Looney Tunes boxers, this time Bugs Bunny.

"It's hard to be serious when you show me your cartoon characters first." I had to try really hard not to giggle again. He had me on a roll tonight.

He kicked off one of his shoes, then the next, before taking off his socks. He smiled and started to push his jeans and boxers down. "I have more to show you."

"Nice." I said. "It's been too long." Twenty-four hours without him was too long as far as I was concerned.

Adam hooked his thumbs in the sides of his Levi's and pushed them down past his knees before kicking them off.

When he had settled me on the couch he positioned me and moved between my thighs. I cried out at the wonderful feel of him inside me. He kept his pace slow, steady.

The feel of him alone could have made me climax. The combination of him taking me and sucking my nipples pushed me to an orgasm that was so wonderful I couldn't have made sense of anything right then.

I just felt, didn't think.

Adam murmured something but my mind was fuzzy from my orgasm, warmth making its way through me from the very roots of my hair down to my toes.

Adam continued to thrust inside me. My orgasm continued and I didn't want it to stop. He had braced his hands on the couch to either side of me and stared into my eyes as he pumped his hips harder and harder.

I borrowed a little static from the air with my command of the fire element, then sent it through him.

Adam raised his head and shouted before he pressed himself to me. I smiled. I loved to hear him when he climaxed, loved the throb of him coming inside me.

He was trying to catch his breath as he looked down at me. His dark hair was damp from sweat and his body coated in perspiration. Then he adjusted himself so that we were now facing one another on the couch.

Adam hooked his leg over my thigh and I loved the closeness we shared. I was still amazed at everything I shared with him in the kitchen, how I had opened up.

A feeling of peace yet exhilaration filled me. How wonderful it was to have someone who cared for me just for me. Not as a freak, not as a sex object. But someone who I opened up to and who cared about me.

I brushed strands of sweaty hair from Adam's brow, then kissed him, before he wrapped his arms around me and held me tightly to him.

TWELVE

"Why are we meeting with Rodán tonight?" Nadia set her plate on the surface of what made do as a coffee table. She'd eaten some kind of fish as usual, being a Siren and all of that. "Do you know what's up?"

Like every night, most of the Trackers gathered in the corner of the Pit where we hung out before leaving to track down the bad guys.

I'd finally come to the point where I could sit with all of the other Trackers and not feel overwhelmingly sad because Caprice was gone. One of our fellow Trackers and one of my closest friends, Caprice had been murdered by Demons not that long ago.

I took my last bite of my favorite meal—a char-grilled hamburger. "Rodán is going to fill everyone in on the latest developments in the Sprite case."

"So what are the new developments?" Lawan, a Siamese cat Doppler from Thailand, scooted next to me on the overstuffed black leather sofa I was sitting on. "Can you give us a hint?"

I brandished my tiny red sword with one green olive left on it from my dry martini. "You expect me to steal Rodán's spotlight?" I ate the last olive and tossed the mini sword onto a cocktail napkin. "No way."

"Let's go." Angel stopped behind our sofa and braced her hands on the back of it. "We're being summoned."

I wiped my hands on a paper napkin and left it on the plate for one of Hector's busboys to pick up with the rest of the empty plates and glasses in our corner.

When I got to my feet to head to the conference room, Mandisa brushed by me in a wake of spices and pepper. Mandisa was a new Tracker, an Abatwa Fae from South Africa. She hadn't been friendly to any one of us since coming to Manhattan.

I really didn't know if I wanted to be the one to invite her for a girls' day at the spa. The quiver of poison-tipped arrows and the bow slung across her back was intimidating enough, much less her height and presence.

Ice made one of his smartass remarks to Mandisa as she passed him and entered the conference room. It was a wonder she didn't skewer him with one of her poisonous arrows.

Olivia came up beside me. She had no love for Ice, but the jury was still out concerning the Abatwa Fae as far as she was concerned. I checked out tonight's T-shirt and grimaced.

MARY HAD A LITTLE LAMB
I ATE IT WITH MINT SAUCE

"Don't let Tracey see your T-shirt." I nudged Olivia with my elbow as I nodded toward the Romanian Fae, a Sânziană. Sânziene were known for their gentle sides and that included a love for animals.

Too late. Tracey had already glanced at Olivia's shirt. The Sânziană put her hands on her hips. "That's not funny, human."

Olivia was clearly holding back a laugh. "Then I won't tell you about the time—"

I jerked Olivia by the arm and just about dragged her into the conference room while giving Tracey an apologetic look. Polished Dryad wood gleamed in the low lighting. The room was huge, able to accommodate all of the Peacekeepers—including Healers, Gatekeepers, and Soothsayers—at standing room only.

It had been a very long time since that had come to pass, all of the Manhattan Peacekeepers together at once, and I really didn't want to see everyone forced to be there again. It would mean something really bad was about to go down.

Twenty-three Trackers, which included Olivia, along with Ondrej—the Were from Beketov's pack—seated ourselves around a huge Dryad-wood oval conference table big enough to seat twenty-six. We always left the chair at the head of the table for Rodán even though he rarely, if ever, sat.

Our group included four Dopplers: Angel, Kelly, Robert, and Lawan. We had five Shifters: Meryl, Hades, Ice, Gentry, and Nakano. Five Weres were Trackers: Phyllis, Max, Dave, Carlos, and Rich. Joshua was our only Shadow Shifter, and Olivia the only norm.

Where it got fun was the six different types of Fae who helped make up the rest of the Night Trackers: Mandisa, an Abatwa Fae; Tracey, Romanian Fae—a Sânziană; Fere, Tuatha—winged Fae warrior; Nancy, a Pixie; Bronwyn, a Nymph; Nadia, a Siren.

I of course was the only representative of the Elves, unless you counted Rodán, but he was our Proctor, not a Tracker. He was also over all of the Healers, Soothsayers, and Gatekeepers.

Murmurs came from the Trackers, everything from

speculation about tonight's meeting to who was going to win the women's paranorm ice skating competition to the paranorm biathlon.

The room went silent as Rodán made his entrance. His white-blond hair fell around his shoulders like cream silk, striking against his golden features and grass-green robe. Rodán was beyond classically handsome. He was in a class all by himself.

"Nyx, Joshua, Angel, Ice, and Olivia have taken on the Sprite case," Rodán said. "It goes far deeper than anyone expected."

"If the word 'deep' can be associated with Vampires," Angel said. "With the exception of them going to ground when the sun comes up."

Lawan frowned. "I thought we were talking about Sprites. What do Vampires have to do with them?"

"Everything," I said. "Vampires have been putting the Sprites up to all the chaos and mischief they've been doing."

"Vampires have never been a threat," Tracey said. "They're nothing but creeps."

"They've just allowed us become complacent." Angel twirled one of her curls around her finger in an absent motion. "And it's worked. We haven't seen them as a threat since the late eighteen hundreds when most of the Vampire clans were wiped out in the Paranorm Rebellion."

"Volod, the New York Master Vampire, is furious that Vampires have been again denied a seat on the Paranorm Council," I said.

"The Vampires are not true paranorms." Ice snorted. "They don't belong on the council or in any position of leadership."

Born human but with paranormal abilities, Witches,

Necromancers, and Vampires were considered to not be true paranorms. At least by all other paranorms.

Rodán met and held the gaze of each Tracker in the room, one at a time, as he spoke. He shared with the Trackers everything I had relayed to him earlier, plus information he'd learned from his various sources.

"Rodán's voice was low as always and as soothing as still water. Beneath that calmness laid a fierceness that I believed few had experienced.

But I sensed something I'd never felt from Rodán before. Almost as if he felt . . . fear. Fear for all the paranorm world.

Maybe that scared me more than anything, because Rodán never showed fear of any kind. It fired me up to respond with how ominous this situation could get.

"Everyone here needs to understand something," I said. "Volod is evil and he appears to be out for revenge." I looked to each Tracker as I spoke. "He has a lust for power. History has told us repeatedly, both in the paranorm world and the world of the norms, how dangerous one crazed leader with a lust for power can be if he actually has it."

The thought of the kind of crazed leader Volod could be made my gut tighten. "We have some indication that Volod might be that type. Right now he does not have the power. Our concern and mission is to recover something which might give it to him."

"Nyx is right," Rodán said. "Let's focus on our mission and our plan as a team. "We have the Sprite in the detaining room. Nyx and her special team will follow the Sprite."

He looked to each one of the other Trackers he wanted to add to my team as he named them. "Mandisa, Kelly, Nadia, and Lawan, you will join the team tonight. Nyx is your leader and you will follow her instruction."

Rodán gave orders to the roving Trackers who would take the place of those who were being taken from their territory.

When he was finished, Rodán said, "Nyx, you and your team will stay here to lay your plans." He gestured toward the door. "The rest of you, track well."

Rodán settled into the chair at the head of the table.

"We thoroughly interrogated Negel, the Sprite we took into custody," I said as I got down to business. "We believe it is best to have him attempt to talk his people into releasing the serum."

"What's the plan?" Lawan asked.

"It's relatively simple," I said. "Negel will take our team to the abandoned sewers of Hell's Kitchen. Once we're there he'll lead us to the latest location where the Sprite leader is holding his little get-togethers."

"What do we do then?" Nadia's long red hair gleamed as it lay against her black leather fighting suit.

"I'll go in first." I pushed my chair away from the table and stood so that I could look at each of them more easily. "I plan to observe Negel present his case to his people, and specifically Tobath, that they need to return the serums."

"Do you think this can be done without a small war amongst the Sprites?" Nadia asked.

"Negel believes this can be done peacefully," I said. "He believes when they consider the ramifications of this serum in the hands of the Vampires, they will turn it over." I pursed my lips before I continued. "I'm not so sure."

"Sprites peaceable?" Ice snorted. "The whole of them aren't worth our time except to retrieve this serum."

I could have defended Negel, but it would have taken

time away from the meeting and we needed to get to the Sprite lair.

"One Sprite in particular, their self-appointed leader, Tobath, set out to make a deal with the Vampires," I said, "but the bargaining chip was never going to be the destruction of paranorms. As Negel said to me, no Sprite in his right mind will give an instrument of complete destruction to the Vampires. My question, is, is Tobath in his right mind?"

"Right mind?" Kelly snorted. "What Sprite is ever in his right mind?"

Their comments about the Sprites made me realize just how poorly we'd treated them throughout the centuries. It wouldn't be easy to change that feeling amongst many paranorms.

I went on, "So, we give Negel his chance to talk reason with his people. If he fails, you'll be called in to take control."

"Why don't we just rush the place and recover the serums without Negel's sales pitch?" Joshua said.

Lawan tapped one finger on the table. "These Sprites, even in large numbers, are no match for a small force of us."

"Because of time we have had to act quickly," I responded. "We do not have the advantage of reconnaissance. We simply don't know if the Sprites have the serum in this location or not."

I frowned. "If we rush the place and potentially kill some Sprites, it will escalate the situation and could result in them becoming more vengeful with the serum. Or we might kill the only Sprites who know of the location of the serum."

"What do you know of their leader? This Tobath," Nadia asked.

"We do not know much about this Tobath." Other than the fact he was half Drow, but I wasn't going to share that fact unless it became important. Didn't see how it could, but being Drow myself I didn't want to be related to that Sprite in any way. I continued, "However, we do know that he does desire power and respect more than any other Sprite we have seen before."

"Respect and Sprites," Kelly said. "Those are two words I never expected to hear together."

"We have had no reason to focus on Sprites other than their mischief. They have been, for the most part, harmless," I said.

"Harmless?" Kelly replied. "Are we talking about the same beings here?"

Kelly was going to drive me nuts. I was thankful when Rodán said, "That is enough interruption." Kelly shut up.

"Tobath is simply an unknown to us," I said. "We will soon find out if he's even sane in a short while. Our mission is not to destroy and punish the Sprites. It is to recover the serum."

"How will we know when the time is right?" Lawan asked.

I settled my hand on my right dagger out of habit. "Ice will give you a signal. You then rush the place and listen to my orders."

"How do you know this Sprite will do what you in-structed him to?" Joshua said.

"I have spent enough time with Negel and I have no reason to believe he will not do so. Again, while Negel tries to negotiate with Tobath, I will observe," I said. "You and Ice will back me on the inside." I gave each of them a nod as I spoke.

Ondrej said, "I'm going in with you."

"Ice can shift into mouse form and Joshua slip in as shadow, so they are the best candidates to accompany me," I said. "We need Trackers and other reinforcement surrounding the area on the outside. You'll be on that team."

Ondrej frowned, but didn't say anything else.

I pushed my cobalt-blue hair over my shoulder before I drew one of my dragon-clawed daggers. "As I told you, if the leader won't turn it over, we as a team will descend on the Sprites and take control."

"We should do that from the start," Ondrej said. "Why waste time?"

"I'm hoping we can settle this with a simple show of force and negotiation," I said. "We will do whatever the situation calls for, however. If it becomes a battle, so be it. We will get the serums one way or another."

I watched each of my team members who looked serious, considering all that I had told them.

Rodán gave a nod of approval.

"As I'm sure you all realize, time is essential." I leaned forward with my forearms braced on the table. "We have every reason to believe that the Vampires are after this serum, as we are certain they know that it exists."

I took a deep breath. "There has never been a more urgent mission than to secure the serum, antiserum, and formula," I said. "You're all aware how much the paranorm world could depend on this."

THIRTEEN

In Hell's Kitchen I made my way from rooftop to roof-top.

I shivered. Not from the cold, but from a strange, ee-rie feeling that crept along my spine as we followed Negel. The little Sprite kept his promise and didn't use a glamour and didn't try to escape.

Negel had been told about the plan and we had worked out every detail we could with him.

The Sprite seemed so sincere about protecting his people as well as his brother, wife, and children. More and more I saw Negel as a person, a being with a life, a being who wasn't bent on making others miserable. Maybe it was a few that made the whole look bad. That had been the case for many races in virtually every known society.

While we trailed Negel I felt a little bad—just a little—that I hadn't exactly kept my promise. Well, I hadn't kept the one promise at all. Not only did I add Adam to the team, but had the four other Trackers and a Werewolf with me. But this was not only for our safety but for Negel's as well.

I doubted the Sprite had any idea of the number of Trackers as Angel bounded behind him as a squirrel,

Joshua followed as shadow, and Ice flew overhead in his white falcon form. Kelly was surprisingly quick for a stupid fluffy bunny rabbit and Lawan was graceful and elegant in her Siamese cat form.

Mandisa, an Abatwa, and Nadia, a Siren, were both Fae and as silent as the Elves. Of course I had taken on a glamour.

Ondrej stalked the night as a black wolf. Fury radiated from him and I was sure he was thinking about his dead brother. Maybe it hadn't been so smart to allow the Were on the team when Beketov had brought him to our office. I hoped Ondrej wouldn't start ripping out Sprite throats the moment we got into the chamber and took control.

What we planned to do was get in there, get the vials, and get out. No carnage, just the serum and antiserum. We had to make it fast because it wasn't just the Sprites we had to worry about. It was the Vampires.

Because they were humans, Olivia and Adam were probably the only beings who Negel could sense on our team. But both my partner and my lover were professionals and almost as invisible to the night as the Trackers were.

Our team would go in and wrap this up. It didn't take long for us to reach the location. Negel proved to be surprisingly strong when he lifted the heavy sewer manhole cover as if it were a penny he had just noticed and had picked up off the asphalt.

Negel climbed down into the manhole. My heart thumped as he closed it back over his head and I wondered if he was going to try to escape after all. When I saw the crack of darkness next to the lid that showed he hadn't closed it entirely, I breathed a little easier.

My team and I converged near the manhole. "I'll go

in first," I said as I spoke to my team. "Wait ten minutes, then follow, if you can keep yourself hidden from the Sprites. From what Negel told us, the area they're using is pretty craggy with plenty of hiding places.

"Here I go," I said, more to myself than anyone else, as I grimaced from the thought of going down into the sewer, abandoned or not.

When I moved the manhole cover aside, I imagine the smell the dank, musty-smelling place must have had. "Ugh." I thought about clothespins and wished I had one to put on my nose, like in human cartoons when the character didn't want to smell something.

I eased down the ladder, so happy that it was abandoned and I didn't have to work my way through the tunnel otherwise. No clothespins needed.

All I heard was the sound of a plopping noise in the distance, like large drops of water pinging into a pool. I clung to the ladder, closed my eyes, and used my earth element to search for Negel.

There. I located Negel with my element as well as sensed at least twenty other presences that I identified as Sprites. I glanced up where the squirrel, Angel, peered down at me. I indicated with my head the direction I was about to go, then her face disappeared.

I stepped down into the tunnel and started in the direction of the other beings I'd sensed. Because I'm Elvin, the only beings who could possibly hear me coming were other Elves. Other paranorm beings *sensing* me was another thing altogether. Being Drow and having lived belowground in Otherworld made it easy for me to see ahead in the darkness.

I'd traveled about seventy-five yards when I finally came to a junction where sewage from other tunnels would have fed into it. It was abandoned but I still grimaced at the thought of what I would have had to walk through if the Sprites were any more disgusting than I'd always thought them to be.

In one wall at the junction was a crude opening carved out of stone and earth. Dim light came from the hole which was as high as my head and I couldn't see over it. But I could sense the Sprites. Thank goodness for Elvin stealth—I needed it as I reached with my hands, grasped the edge of the jagged wall, and pulled myself up.

I rested my forearms on the rough opening as I took in everything below.

For a Sprite, Tobath wasn't bad-looking compared to other Sprites. His Drow half made him taller than other Sprites, not so knobby, his eyes not so bulbous, and his face a little more Drow-looking than Sprite-like.

It was easy to tell he was the leader because he was the biggest, most intimidating Sprite there. Not to mention it was his booming voice that filled the Sprite-made cave below.

Like Negel had said, Tobath's coloring was the color of dirty dishwater. Instead of a blond shock of hair like each of the rest of the Sprites, his was black. Leather metal-studded straps crisscrossed his bare chest and he didn't wear rags. His pants were black and looked new. Two swords were strapped to his back.

To either side of Tobath stood what I assumed to be his lieutenants. Both were armed with large swords and had weapons belts with sheathed daggers. It was obvious they didn't have the discipline or bearing of true warriors as they watched with clear interest while Tobath interrogated Negel.

I took a quick inventory of the room. The chamber was walled by dirt and rock, obviously crudely made. Two other entrances/exits were on other sides of the room.

Around the chamber torches burned at the tops of long poles that had been shoved into the dirt.

It smelled of pitch, dirt, and old sewage as well as the Sprite smell of burnt sugar. Which meant it wasn't fun to take a breath in that place.

My attention swung back to Tobath. On the dirt and stone floor in front of him sat a red box that was about the size of a shoebox.

It was a shoebox. Prada, four-inch heels, size seven.

I glanced down at Ice in his mouse form and assumed Joshua was one of the shadows. "I'm pretty sure the box is there, between Negel and the Sprite leader."

Ice bobbed his little mouse head once and I felt the brush of something against me that I assumed was Joshua.

I used my earth element to tell me the exact location of the openings in relation to the one I was at. "Ice, let the others know that there are two additional entrances," I said. "Have them break up into teams and let's get this place surrounded."

The mouse turned, morphed into a white falcon, and flew back into the sewer.

As Tobath spoke to the Sprites gathered around him, I raised myself further into the opening by my arms. I eased my body into the cavern and moved into a depression in the earth that must have been created by a removed boulder. I studied the leader and Negel while I pressed myself as far into the darkness as I could.

"Tell me, Negel." Tobath's features were set in an angry expression. But then as ugly as he was, maybe that was his permanent expression. "Where have you been? Why are Ecknep and Zith dead while you went missing? We found them in Volod's penthouse lair. Did the Vampires capture you, torture you to tell our secrets?"

I thought Negel did an admirable job of holding onto

his composure considering he was probably one-third the size of Tobath.

"I remained hidden while the Vampires killed Zith and tortured Ecknep to his death." Negel shifted on his feet but otherwise didn't show how nervous he probably was. "Volod and his minion never saw me."

He added with a sad expression, "I could not help our brothers. I had to remain hidden to bring you back information. To have attempted anything on my own with the Vampires would have been suicide."

Tobath gave Negel a stare that would have made a New York City cabbie shake, and those guys had seen everything. "What information do you have for me?" Tobath said.

"As soon as Zith gave Volod both folders of information, the Vampire killed our brother," Negel said. "Before he did so, he asked if anyone other than Zith and Ecknep had witnessed our taking the file on the virus. Zith lied and said no. Volod said he didn't want any witnesses and he cut Zith's throat."

Negel hurried on. "Ecknep started to cloak himself in a glamour but the Vampire named Danut grabbed him by the neck."

I felt a moment's brief surprise that Angel's whip hadn't beheaded Volod's brother earlier in the night.

Negel took a deep breath and continued. "Before Danut could kill Ecknep, our brother told the Vampire what fools they were because we had discovered something far greater than the papers on weaknesses. After being tortured, Ecknep told them that we possessed the serum and they would never get it. They will be after the serum, Tobath. I know it."

"He mentioned the serum?" Tobath narrowed his eyes. "What then?"

"They continued to torture him about where you are located. He lied about this meeting location, but they will figure out where we are at some point." I was a good thirty feet away, but I saw Negel's large Adam's apple bob. "They tried over and over again to make Ecknep talk about your location, but he wouldn't." Negel lowered his head. "In this respect he was faithful to our brotherhood from the beginning to the end."

"And what of you?" Tobath's voice was harsh enough that Negel jerked his head up. "Did you turn traitor and tell the Vampires?"

"No, oh no." Negel shook his head and his big ears flopped. "But now they know of it. The Vampires are ruthless. They will find it and take it from us."

Tobath laughed. "We have hidden ourselves well here."

"They are ruthless," Negel repeated. "When we copied the papers, I saw in them that Vampires are immune to the virus because they were once human." Panic edged Negel's words. "They will destroy us and the paranormal world if they get the serum. We cannot win."

"They will never get it." Tobath scowled at Negel. "The Vampires will honor their promise to us. I will ensure they do."

If they killed your emissaries, then why do you think they'll honor their promises, I thought. This half-Drow, half-Sprite was operating on an empty ore cart for a head.

"The Trackers know about it." Negel licked his lips as Tobath's gray features took on a charcoal hue. "I saw them come after the Vampires left."

Tobath clenched and unclenched his fists. "You told Trackers?"

"No." The pitch of Negel's voice rose. "I watched them talk with Ecknep before he died. Then one of the Trackers used a phone. I heard her talk with her leader, then—then—" I could sense Negel was starting to panic. "When she was finished she told the other Trackers that their leader knew about the copied folder, too."

Good on-the-spot thinking, Negel.

Tobath growled. It was not a pleasant sound.

"But the serum." Negel was beginning to look as panicked as I sensed him to be. "They know about it. They will come for it."

"Then we will be ready for them," Tobath said. "They will bargain with us."

"This is not what we planned." Negel's ears flopped as he shook his head again. "We made a deal with evil and that evil double-crossed us."

"Are you questioning me, Negel?" Tobath spoke very slowly, his anger sounding more controlled than he looked.

I sensed Negel's desire to look to see if I was in the chamber with him, but he managed to not give in and to continue talking with Tobath. "Giving the Vampires information about all of the paranorms was bad for us. Keeping the serum that can destroy almost all paranorms is genocide. Do you understand, genocide?"

"We will use it to our advantage." Tobath seemed to expand in size, like Kali did when her hair rose on end right before she attacked an unseen foe. "Being in control of the serum protects us, you worthless *hundoff.*"

"From what?" Negel raised his hands at his sides. "We as a race have been fine for millennia after millennia."

I winced at the brazen way the little Sprite was talking with the self-appointed leader. This was not going to go well for Negel. I'd have to show myself soon, before Negel managed to get himself killed.

Negel appeared to know he was getting nowhere with Tobath and he turned to plead his case to the other Sprites. "Do you understand what this means to all of us, our families, our paranorm world? We have to turn it in," Negel continued without pause, but a murmur of voices from other Sprites started traveling around the chamber. "The Trackers will take us down or the Vampires will. We cannot win."

Anger on Tobath's face told me that he sensed Negel was reaching some of the Sprites. Tobath drew one of the swords strapped to his back and raised it. "You smell of a traitor, Negel."

He gave a nod to the lieutenant on his right. "Get the *hundoff*. I will deal with him."

"This is a mistake," Negel said as two male Sprites grabbed Negel by his arms and dragged him closer to Tobath. "A huge mistake. You can't let this happen."

My cue.

"Stop." I had my hand on my buckler as I stepped out of the depression in the wall. "You're surrounded by Trackers. You can't escape." I said my words with slow deliberation. "We didn't come to hurt anyone and we don't want a fight. We came for the serum and the antiserum. You *will* give it to us."

Tobath looked like he might explode with rage. "Traitor, you led the Trackers here," he shouted as he brought his sword down on Negel.

I flung my buckler. It reached Tobath's sword before the blade could sever Negel's head from his neck.

Tobath's sword was jerked from his hand by the force I'd put in throwing the buckler.

A stunned look crossed the large Sprite's face as his sword clattered across the stone floor of the chamber.

The buckler returned to my hand and I replaced it at the front of my belt in a fast movement. "Where are the serum and antiserum?" I asked even though I was sure it was in the shoebox near his feet.

"It's there!" A high-pitched voice shouted from the back of the room. "The red box. Don't kill us, please."

"Grab him." Tobath pointed at the Sprite who had spoken up. "He is a traitor, too."

Then Tobath bared his pointed yellow teeth and drew his other sword. "Get the Tracker," he said to the lieutenant on his left. "I will take care of this one."

Tobath stared at Negel who started struggling to get away from the two Sprites holding him.

The lieutenant looked at Tobath. Looked at Negel. Looked at Tobath again.

"Now," Tobath said in a roar as he glared at the lieutenant.

The lieutenant stepped forward and raised his sword.

And swung it at Tobath.

Tobath's ugly gray face froze into an expression of complete shock.

Blood splattered Sprites and the chamber.

Tobath's head rolled across the floor.

His body crumpled forward, landing on his second sword.

The chamber went completely quiet.

My own surprise at Tobath's execution caused me to hesitate just as I started to walk away from the wall.

At the same time my senses went on full alert. Something beyond Tobath's execution was desperately wrong. I felt a presence . . . something that didn't belong.

"Negel should be our leader." The lieutenant who'd slain Tobath straightened and swept his gaze around the room. "He speaks sense. I do not wish this terrible serum to be unleashed on any paranorm. It would mean our deaths as well. Our people are not evil."

Murmurs started in the chamber like an ocean wave, then shouts echoed in the chamber like the wave crashing, followed by cheers that rose up into an almost deafening crescendo.

"Negel," they started to chant over and over. "Negel should lead us."

I looked around me, trying to see what was bothering my senses so much, while I still tried to keep track of what was going on with Negel.

The two Sprites holding Negel stepped away from him and Negel let his arms fall to his sides as he looked around the chamber.

For a moment confusion was on Negel's face as he stared at the Sprites cheering for him. Then he straightened and he wore an expression that showed a strength and bearing I would never have guessed Negel possessed. He actually wasn't bad-looking for a Sprite.

The room quieted when Negel raised his hands in a motion that meant he wanted to speak.

"We are a brotherhood." Negel cleared his throat. "Sprites have never had a leader and we do not need one now."

"But you *will* have a leader." A deep male voice rang out and I jerked my head in the direction it came from.

Volod.

He smiled and his fangs glinted in the dim lighting. "And that leader will be me."

FOURTEEN

"Not only will I be your leader, but I will be so much more." Volod casually walked across the chamber from one of the entrances.

Icy prickles erupted all over my skin. I couldn't believe I hadn't known it was Volod who had set off my senses. Immediately I drew a glamour around myself, hoping the Master Vampire hadn't noticed me. If I was lucky, he hadn't been there long enough to have seen me earlier.

Maybe all the nooks and crannies impaired my ability. More so, the fact that they're dead. It's easy to sense the living. It's not so easy to get a read on the dead.

"It is simple." The Master Vampire's smile was disarming, charismatic. He had an expression of confidence, like a man who knew his orders would be carried out without question. "With the serum I will control everything. I will easily control every paranorm being that exists."

My heart thudded as I stared at Volod. The Vampire's presence almost overpowered the room. His expression was one of confident arrogance.

As Volod strode toward Negel and the box, power rippled not only from his presence but from his bearing. The flex of his muscles through his snug polo shirt, the broadness of his shoulders, his athletic build.

Volod came within twenty feet of Negel before he stopped, but didn't seem to see the beheaded Tobath who was blocked by some of the other Sprites.

"You Sprites wanted to be a part of my reign. You started your service strong to me. I wanted to make sure Sprites were held above other paranorm beings, but I didn't like that you chose to hold back a prize."

"None of our brotherhood wants to be under your rule anyway." Negel's expression was firm, his big eyes hooded. "We will not bow to you."

The Vampire shrugged. "It makes no difference what you say or believe at this point. What matters is that we have the documentation, the formula, and now you will hand me the serum."

How did Volod know about the serum? Supposedly Ecknep had only alluded to the fact that something was held back from the Vampires.

Not only did we have a Master Vampire to deal with, but we had an incredibly charismatic evil Vampire who could easily take in those around him without having to put much effort into it.

So not good.

I sensed Joshua as shadow beside me and I wondered where my other team members were. How had Volod made it in here without my team getting word to me? There had to be Vampires at the entrances that my team members were having to deal with or they would be here.

Vampires began walking into the chamber through the exits to the right and left of me.

I caught my breath.

Two. Six. Nine. Thirteen. Seventeen. Twenty-three. Twenty-nine. Thirty-three.

Thirty-four Vampires, including Volod.

Now that I had focused on the dead I could sense all of the Vampires in the chamber. Could feel the undead like falling into a crude oil slick and being coated with oily filth.

My mind raced. All of these years had passed . . . well over a hundred Earth Otherworld years . . . and it was thought the Vampires had lost the desire for power.

Apparently not.

As a group of beings we had become complacent and had taken the Vampires' defeat to mean we didn't have to deal with them anymore. Volod was proving that wrong. Oh, so wrong.

I swept my gaze across the room, taking in each Vampire male and female. I didn't doubt that we had an incredible fight on our hands.

We weren't even sure what we were up against. What powers did the Vampires still have that we thought were gone with the Master Vampires who had been destroyed? A hundred-plus years might seem like a lot to those who lived in the Earth Otherworld, but to beings from my Otherworld, that amount of time was nothing. Not even a drop of water.

Whatever the case, I had a feeling we needed more backup than we'd originally thought. I touched the cell phone on my weapons belt and without looking, pressed the speed dial number for Rodán.

Nothing. I sensed nothing.

No signal in the sewers.

No additional backup at hand.

I gathered my elements to me. This time I'd be ready for Volod. I had plenty of air; I could control and use water from nearby water mains; fire from the torches around the room was at my bidding; and perhaps most importantly of all, I had no shortage of earth at hand. I also had the element of surprise because Volod thought I had died when he threw me out his penthouse window. At least I hoped he wasn't aware of my presence.

For the most part, the Vampires didn't wear black like in human movies. These Vampires wore anything from jeans to slacks to dress suits, gowns, and tuxedos. In Volod's case he wore black Dockers and a polo shirt like he had the time I'd seen him at the Paranorm Center. I had the weird image of Volod playing a nighttime game of polo and had to mentally shake it out of my head.

"How did you find us?" one of the lieutenants shouted as he drew out a dagger. "This location is not on the list of known brotherhood meeting places."

A bored expression crossed Volod's face. "I have no time for interruptions."

Volod held out his hand. Invisible power slammed into the Sprite. He was flung backward so hard, so fast that when he struck the wall his head exploded. Blood splattered Sprites nearby. Murmurs and shouts of fear erupted in the large chamber.

"I will answer your question." Volod spoke as if he hadn't just murdered the Sprite whose lifeless body he was staring at. Volod looked over his shoulder, gave a brief nod, before returning his gaze to the chamber. "It was extremely easy to find you."

From behind Volod two Vampires dragged in a bloody heap of rags. Make that thirty-six Vampires now. Not very good odds at all if my team didn't get here. They must have faced some opposition outside. I couldn't think of another reason why my team wasn't already in here.

The two new Vampires raised the pile of rags and I swallowed when I saw it wasn't a bunch of rags at all.

"It is Ordox," one of the Sprites shouted, and sounds of fear and horror moved through the room.

I clenched the hilt of one of my dragon-clawed daggers tight as I slowly recognized the Sprite. Yes, the bloody being was Ordox, the same Sprite whose nose I'd broken just a couple of nights ago at the Statue of Liberty.

Ordox's eyes were swollen shut, which was a feat considering how huge and bulbous Sprites' eyes are. His thick lips were split, his nose impossibly flatter than when I'd broken it. Even his tuft of hair was covered with blood.

"The list that you Sprites obtained for us." Volod said with a casual smile, "has all of your other locations. All we had to do was search them one by one and then we found this worthless trash who led us to this toilet you call home."

Volod's eyebrows narrowed as he continued. "You Sprites held back from me—the serum and the antiserum. Did you really think I would not find out?"

The pity I felt for Ordox should have surprised me, but it didn't. After getting to know Negel in the short amount of time I'd spent with him, it was easy to see Ordox as just another being. Unfortunately, this Sprite was one of those malicious, nasty beings who make his whole race look bad.

I concentrated on my elemental magic. My powers surged through me and waited for me to set them free. An almost nervous, anxious feeling that made me a little jittery.

Volod tossed Ordox onto the floor in front of him. The Sprite landed with a thud and moaned, but didn't move.

"So you survived." The Master Vampire looked at me as if bored. "Did you enjoy your flight out of my window?"

Shock coursed through me. Volod had seen through my glamour. Did my emotions reveal me again?

"Did you not think I knew you were standing there, Purple One?" He bared his fangs at me. "You thought to hide yourself when I made my presence known. You cannot hide from me."

I straightened, reining in my power. "You won't get the serum."

Volod laughed. "You could not defend yourself against two Vampires. What makes you think you could possibly stop us now?"

"We will." I clenched my jaws before adding, "You're not a match for me or the other Trackers."

A flash of impatience crossed Volod's face as he dismissed me and turned to Negel. "The serum, please."

"No." Considering what we had all just witnessed, Negel showed even more strength than I'd ever thought him capable of. It might have been stupidity instead, but I was going with the former. "You will not take it from us."

"Get out of here, Volod." I stepped out from the shadows, gripping my dagger. "Trackers have you surrounded." A thought that I hoped was true. What if the Vampires had totally disabled my team before getting into the chamber? I had a hard time believing that was possible. "Even if you were to find it, you won't be able to get the serum past us."

"We will take it now," Volod said in a calm arrogant tone that had me grinding my teeth. "Attempt to stop us and I'll finish the job I started in my penthouse."

The Master Vampire made it clear he was ignoring me, that he found me a mere nuisance. He raised his hand, his palm facing Negel.

My heart raced and blood pounded in my veins.

I shot my power through the earth with all the elemental strength I had.

The floor of the chamber bucked beneath Volod's feet.

Shouts echoed in the room as dirt began raining from the chamber's ceiling coating everyone there.

The Master Vampire stumbled backward.

My earth element gripped me as if I was encased in it while the element strained for me to set it free.

I did.

The room bucked harder. More screams. More yells. More dirt falling from the ceiling and sliding down the wall.

The other Vampires struggled to stay on their feet.

Volod turned his scowl on me just as I used my earth element to open a fissure where he stood.

He shouted as he dropped.

At my command an entire wall slid and pounded down on Volod, burying him in the huge crack in the chamber's dirt and rock floor.

"It is she who caused this to happen." Danut's voice came from my right. "That blue-haired bitch violated one of our sanctuaries."

I cut my gaze to him to see him raise his hand, his palm facing me. I had just enough time to throw up an air shield to block the power he shot toward me.

Danut's own power rebounded and slammed into him. He fell on the chamber floor and skidded across it before hitting his back against a wall.

Vampires descended on me, their mouths opened in fierce grimaces showing their brutal fangs.

Adrenaline rushed through me, feeding my power over the elements.

But I didn't know if it would be enough to fend off the nine Vampires charging me.

Where was my team?

I drew both of my dragon-clawed daggers. I felt the dangerous white flash in my eyes.

With a warrior yell, I charged the closest Vampire, catching him off guard. One stroke made a clean slice across his throat, severing his head from his neck.

I rammed my other dagger through the heart of a second Vampire.

More Vampires came at me. Blood pounded in my ears.

I called to my fire element and a wall of fire tore from the torches to either side of me and engulfed three Vampires. Unfortunately, fire won't kill Vampires. Their tissue regenerates within minutes. Take their heads or hearts—that's the only way to get rid of Vampires.

Angel's shout cut across the mayhem.

Reinforcements. Finally.

From my side vision I saw Angel wrap her barbed whip around a Vampire's neck. She jerked her whip and blood spurted from the Vampire as she yanked his head from his shoulders.

Olivia crouched behind a boulder and each of the shots from her Sig rang off the walls. Adam had her back and he was putting bullets into Vampires.

I had told them what to expect so they were using hollowpoints. One bullet in the heart could take out a Vampire by obliterating the organ. Adam and Olivia were tough, but they also knew they had some human limits. On cases like this they worked as a team, back to back.

The Werewolf, Ondrej, growled and snarled just

before he snapped his jaws on a Vampire's neck. With a ferocious jerk of his muzzle, Ondrej ripped out the Vamp's throat. The Vampire started healing at once. It was going to take more than a sore throat to bring a Vampire down. Ondrej never paused. He flung his body forward and drove the Vampire to the ground.

Joshua bellowed and swung his flail at another Vampire. The Vamp moved in a flash, just before his head could be smashed against a wall. Drago. The Vampire's eyes flashed with green flame as he dove for Joshua.

I started to go after Drago and help Joshua, but another Vampire came after me and I had to behead her.

Lawan gave a battle cry as she raised her Krabi, a sword from Thailand, her native country. Just as she swung, the Vampire she attacked shot a burst of power at her and knocked her onto the floor.

Sprites had joined the fight, throwing weapons and rocks at the Vampires.

More Vampires came after me. Ice morphed into his white jaguar form in midair before driving one of the Vamps to the floor and tearing into him.

Mandisa's poison-tipped arrows brought down two Vampires. They sprang to their feet and charged her. She planted one foot into the chest of one and sent him flying across the chamber. Then she grabbed an arrow from her quiver, rammed it into the other Vampire's heart and twisted it, grinding out the Vamp's heart. There was no growing that organ back.

A Vampire neared me. I forward-flipped through the air, using my air element to project myself on the opposite side of the Vampires after me. They were too surprised and too slow to stop me from beheading two more of them.

Kelly morphed into her bunny rabbit form, dodged

between the legs of a Vampire, then transformed back. She caught the Vampire totally off guard. When he turned, she jammed a wooden stake through his heart. Seeing a fluffy bunny rabbit in the midst of battle would have had me laughing if I wasn't trying to keep from getting killed.

I had to get that box. I looked for it, but two more Vampires came at me. I used my buckler to behead one.

I rammed my sword through the other, then saw that it was Chuck, one of the two Vampires from the Pit. I totally missed his heart and he snarled as he backhanded me and knocked me to the ground. My dragon-clawed dagger tore a jagged hole in Chuck's flesh as I jerked the weapon out at the same time I fell.

He started to heal at once. I surged to my feet, but before I could go after him, Lawan had engaged him in a fight.

Nadia's serpent swords flashed in the light as she swung them so fast they were a blur. She beheaded two Vamps at once.

Vampire bodies and heads littered the chamber's floor, but so did the bodies of dead Sprites.

In the blink of an eye that it took to take it all in, I was grateful that I didn't see any of my team members down, injured or otherwise.

Shouts and yells echoed through the chamber that was filled with dust and splattered with blood.

I grabbed hold of my fire element to fry another Vampire as I looked for the next one.

All of the remaining Vampires were rushing for the exits with such incredible speed that I barely saw them move.

The Vampires were gone before I could process what they were doing.

"The box!" a Sprite shouted.

I whirled to look at the spot where the box had been resting.

It was gone.

"No," I swung my gaze around the room.

My fear was confirmed when I looked toward the fissure I'd created and had buried Volod in, and saw that the dirt covering it had been blown away. The crack in the earth was wide, but there was no sign of the Master Vampire.

"I saw him take it," came the gravelly voice of one of the Sprites. "The Master. He grabbed the red box."

No. No. It can't be. The Vamps couldn't have taken the box.

But it was gone.

"We'll split into three groups and go after them from all exits." I pointed to each of them. "Kelly, Ice, Joshua. Take the exit to the left." They were gone as soon as I gave them their assignment.

I turned. "Lawan, Adam, Nadia, Ondrej. You get the right exit." The moment they took off, I faced the remaining members of the team and with a nod indicated the entrance I'd come through. "Mandisa and Olivia, you're with me."

I followed Olivia and Mandisa through the opening and jumped down into the abandoned sewer junction. I ran through the tunnels, toward the ladder I'd taken to get here, then hurried to climb up and to the street.

When we were out of the manhole, five Vampires were running in all directions, in a star pattern to throw us off.

Without my having to tell my team members what to do, they each went after a target. Mandisa gave a loud warrior cry before she used her bow and poison-tipped arrows to down one of the Vamps. It gave her enough time to reach him before he could disappear around one of the tall buildings surrounding us.

"I'll get this sonofabitch." Olivia squared off with her Sig and shot another Vampire, but that one kept running. "You get your Vampire ass back over here!" Olivia tore after him, taking shot after shot. Each hollowpoint bullet hit the Vampire and slowed him down, but didn't stop him because she hadn't been able to blow out his heart. I wished we would have brought the garlic guns and the mini-stake crossbows that had been located in Paranorm Center storage.

With one of my dragon-clawed daggers in my hand, I forward-flipped three times, then landed on the back of one Vampire who wore a sparkling red sequined evening gown. I drove her to the ground, tearing the front of her gown with a loud ripping sound, and hitting her face against the asphalt.

She screamed and hissed.

Before I had a chance to take my dagger and remove her head, she flipped over, throwing me off with a strength that surprised me.

My heart pounded as I skidded a few feet away on the asphalt, the small rocks and pebbles scraping my skin. I twisted and pushed myself into a crouch.

The Vampire bared her fangs. It was the blue-eyed Vamp who'd hissed at me at the Pit the night Drago and Chuck had been tossed. The Vamp's smell of old dirt and musty leaves was so strong that I knew she had to be at least as old as Volod, if not older.

As the Vampire leapt toward me, her fingernails became long dagger-tipped claws. She swiped her jagged nails across my bare belly.

Stinging fire burst in my gut and I let out a cry. Blood welled in the deep cuts she'd made in my flesh.

Anger surged through me. Now she'd pissed me off.

The Vampire grabbed my head between her hands and jerked me toward her at the same time she went for my throat with her fangs.

I smashed my fist into her mouth, slicing my hand on her fangs right before I head-butted her.

Stars sparked behind my eyes. I hadn't known Vampires had such hard skulls.

She screamed as she jerked my hand away from her mouth. Instead of looking stunned from the head-butt, she looked furious.

The Vampire grasped my arm in her incredibly strong clawed hands and went for my wrist with her fangs.

I ripped my other dagger from its sheath and swung it at her neck at the same time I jerked my arm out of her vice-like grip.

My blade only sliced halfway into her neck. Blood spurted. She shrieked and grabbed my weapon hand in both of hers and squeezed.

With amazing strength she threw me. My back slammed into a brick-walled building and my breath whooshed out of me. I slid down the wall and landed on my ass.

I scrambled to my feet. The Vampire was righting her half-severed head on her shoulders and I could see her flesh and skin start to knit back together again.

"No way." I stumbled to my feet, then rushed her. "I'm tired of playing."

"Who's playing, Drow bitch?" She had her claws waiting to score my skin.

But I dove for her feet. I wrapped my arms around her ankles while at the same time slamming my shoulder against her knees.

The crack of bone echoed in the dark night, along with the Vampire's cry.

I knocked her flat on her back, straddled her, and brought my dagger down in a high arc.

She was reaching for my face with her clawed hands and didn't notice the dagger until too late.

Her last scream pinged off the buildings' walls as her head rolled across the asphalt.

For a fight that had probably lasted a few minutes, it felt like it had taken an hour to do away with her.

I whipped my head around. In the distance I saw a Vampire running toward a motorcycle. He hopped on it, gunned the engine, and tore off through the night.

I ran after him.

FIFTEEN

Who'd have thought? A Vampire getaway vehicle that happened to be a motorcycle. Of course I'd felt the same way about the penthouse being non-Vampirish. All of my illusions shattered. Well, some of them.

I run faster than an earthbound cheetah, faster than most paranorm beings, faster than a motorcycle at seventy miles per hour. It's not so much running as it is gliding through the air and using my elements to push me, guide me.

So that the Vampire on the motorcycle couldn't see me in one of his rearview mirrors, I wrapped myself in an air glamour, making me invisible to him. This Vampire I didn't plan to take down. I intended to follow him to see where he might lead me. Maybe he'd go to whatever lair Volod was hanging out in.

I so wanted to get my hands on Volod. Actually, I'd have loved to get my hands on a wooden stake and drive it through his little heart.

The Vamp raced the motorcycle down Ninth Avenue, turning toward the Lincoln Tunnel. Great. Running in the tunnel wasn't exactly my idea of fun.

Streetlights passed by in a blur of red, green, yellow. Too many scents enveloped me, changing as fast as I was running. But I was able to identify the Vamp I followed.

If I knew where he was going I would have done my best to use the transference.

However, it would likely not be when running seventy miles per hour. My father had told me I was much too young to be able to do the transference—go from one point to another by concentrating on it—because I was not yet a century old. I'd proved him wrong during the Werewolf case.

Yes, it would come in handy now, if I only knew where we were going. But that was the point, to find out where we would end up. One used the transference when standing still, so it was pretty much a moot point. But it gave me something to think about as I ran. And ran. And ran.

The tunnel was not too bad to navigate. We were in Jersey. The Vampire found his way to I-280. He kept going. And going. And going. After a while I began to think he'd never stop and we'd end up in Chicago.

Finally, after almost an hour of running hard, we reached the area around Jenny Jump State Park and he slowed. He turned off into an isolated part of the hardwood forest thick with trees that were naked of their leaves.

Elves don't tire easily, but I have to admit that after that run I was hoping he would get to his destination soon. My breathing was a little heavier than normal and my skin a bit damp from perspiration.

The Vampire guided his motorcycle along a two-lane dirt road that led deep into a wooded area. The area was rich with the scents of a forest. At least we were going somewhere that smelled nice.

We traveled for some time, me jogging behind him

while still in my glamour. Dead leaves crunched beneath the motorcycle's wheels and winter's breath made it appear chillier here than it was in the city.

Now that we weren't going so fast, the stinging slashes on my belly made me wince and my hand ached from the Vampire's fangs ripping into my skin. I'd forgotten the injuries were there. They were already healing, but of course they wouldn't be completely gone until I shifted.

Eventually, through the trees I could make out what looked like a pyramid of smooth glass. Beams of moonlight peered through the surrounding trees and glimmered on the structure's surface. Around the glass pyramid was an imposing stone fence that seemed to go on forever in each direction.

I thought about calling Rodán but decided it was better to wait. When I got over that fence and into the fortress, I'd send Rodán and Olivia a text message to let them know I was all right and what I was up to.

Then as long as I maintained my glamour—which meant keeping my distance from Volod if he was there—I could do some exploration on my own and report back to Rodán when I had something to report.

The closer we came to the structure the more and more I was impressed with what was in front of us. Nothing but glass—make that mirrored glass—I couldn't see any wood or concrete or brick. Strange, but the surface didn't reflect the bare tree limbs along with evergreens that surrounded the compound.

Around the mirrored pyramid an enormous and very imposing stone fence ran the perimeter. At least twelve feet high, the fence also had rows of razor wire around the top. Each barb looked as sharp as a Drow diamond arrowhead. From the looks of it, this was probably some kind of compound.

I wondered if this location was on the Council's list of known Vampire lairs, then decided it probably wasn't. After what had happened, why would the Vampires go any place that paranorms knew about? I was sure it was a Vampire lair. Everything in my gut told me it was.

A set of huge iron gates creaked open as the Vamp on the motorcycle slowed to a crawl. I walked behind him, analyzing the layout of the compound, looking for entrances and other ways of getting into and out of this glass fortress.

I didn't like what I saw. Or couldn't see.

The massive structure was like an Egyptian pyramid made of glass. Its dark, sleek walls swept all the way from its high peak down to the ground, the glass meeting the earth. Nothing broke the surface of each wall within view. No windows, no doors, nothing. From where I was, the only thing one could see was glass, trees, and dark earth.

Leafless trees stood like a hundred ghostly sentinels around the compound, virtually hiding it from the sky. Then I thought of light reflecting off its surface during the daytime, which would produce a glare.

But as I studied the pyramid, I realized it wasn't reflecting the moonlight. The glass was *absorbing* it. As if the moon's rays were being sucked into a black hole.

Maybe that was why the compound wouldn't be on the Council's list of known Vampire lairs. There was no way it could be spotted.

The motorcycle rumbled as it came to a rolling stop to the right of the structure. I stood behind and the exhaust from the motorcycle made me wrinkle my nose but warmed me at the same time. The nighttime breeze caused my invisible hair to rise around my shoulders.

I put my hands on my hips and had the strong desire to tap the Vamp on the shoulder and tell him to get on with it. I'd had enough of chasing and waiting and I wanted to get to work.

The ground rumbled and shook beneath my feet. On the right the ground quivered and began to rise. A great door slowly opened the earth, a door about the length of two buses, nose to end.

As the motorcycle Vamp drove into the cavernous opening, I followed. The earth slanted down, down, down. We finally came to a concrete parking garage.

The motorcycle's headlight flashed across other vehicles and the engine's roar vibrated through the garage as the Vampire guided the machine into a parking space next to a couple of other motorcycles. He cut the engine and the light, leaving darkness and silence filling the garage.

Dim lights suddenly illuminated the garage and twelve nice vehicles shone beneath the low lighting. Fifteen counting the motorcycles, most of the vehicles costly. Parking spaces for plenty more cars lined the garage that went as wide as it went deep.

What kind of place was this? Maybe a whole bunch of Vamps all living together in a Vampiric commune. Or perhaps it housed a kind of Vampire intelligence operation. Maybe they even called it the VSA—Vampire Security Agency. Who knew?

Back in Manhattan, I had a sleek black Corvette. I found myself having car envy, though, when I spotted a beautiful red Ferrari. Nice. Part of the garage's residents also included a yellow Hummer, red Jeep Wrangler, silver Lexus, black Chevy Silverado extended-cab truck. And a charcoal Prius.

A Vamp driving an eco-friendly car? I pictured one of the Vampires taking the hybrid down the HOV lane, flying past other vehicles in the slow lanes, and I almost laughed at the image.

Although a Vampire driving a Silverado truck or a Jeep Wrangler seemed almost as absurd.

I still hadn't seen the face of the Vamp who I'd been chasing. He shoved his motorcycle keys into his front jeans pocket, adjusted his leather jacket, and walked toward the back of the garage. I started to follow but stopped when he came to an abrupt standstill.

The Vampire slowly turned and looked in my direction. Right. At. Me. I caught my breath. A creeping sensation rolled along my arms.

It was Drago, one of the two Vampires who had been kicked out of the Pit—the Vampire with green eyes. An intensity was in his eyes now as he stared where I was standing.

Drago couldn't see me, could he? No, it wasn't possible. He shouldn't be able to and really shouldn't have the ability to sense me either. Volod was a very powerful and very, very old Master Vampire and I had let my guard down around him at his penthouse. That was why he'd been able to sense me.

But this Vampire . . . he couldn't be a Master because Vampires had only one Master per clan, I thought. From his scent, I didn't think he could be as old as Volod, but his green eyes were mesmerizing. And dangerous. Very, very dangerous.

The Vampire's expression was cold as he continued to stare in my direction. My hand moved to one of my daggers. If Drago kept looking at me the way he was, I was afraid my glamour would drop. I don't know why, but I had the sudden urge to run—with nowhere to run to. A strong glamour requires no loss of concentration and limiting emotions such as fear.

The Vampire let his gaze slide from me to the rest of the garage. When he turned away and started walking again, I said a silent prayer and let out my breath in a slow exhale.

Drago's footsteps echoed in the otherwise silent garage. He had walked the length of a basketball court away from me by the time I felt even slightly more relaxed. I watched as he stepped off the concrete garage floor and onto a dirt path that took him through an archway and into a nightmare dark hallway.

The rapid beat of my heart didn't let up until Drago vanished from sight. I wanted to trail the Vampire, but I felt like I'd come too close to being discovered.

The dim lights in the garage shut off. I heard the huge door begin to close with a shudder and a groan.

A quick sweep of my gaze showed no other obvious exits than the one Drago had disappeared through. The idea of having possibly the only means of escape closed off was not appealing in the least. I needed to do a little reconnaissance and find entrances and exits to and from the compound before I managed to get myself trapped inside.

I ran as fast as I could, up, up, up, for the garage exit—it was closing much too fast. Moonlight was disappearing and complete darkness setting in as the huge door shuddered on its way down.

The garage door was less than two feet from the ground when I reached it. I dropped and rolled out from under it just before it slammed shut with a low rumble like thunder.

Loose soil along the edge of the garage door settled into place. Even the motorcycle's tracks were gone, erased as if never having existed at all.

When I got to my feet, I brushed dirt from my bare arms while looking around me. The mirrored structure towered above like a great smooth iceberg in the middle of the forest.

I walked toward the pyramid, planning to send a quick message to Rodán, then to Olivia. Rodán would be able to find my coordinates through the GPS on my phone, but in my message I would tell him to let me handle this part of the op.

If I wasn't back in touch within two hours, then he could send out the hunting dogs. So to speak. His backup were his Doppler bouncers whose animal forms were dogs of different types and varieties. Fortunately his bouncers had both brawn and brains.

But when I reached for my phone, I touched . . . nothing. I looked down. My cell was gone.

Where had I dropped it? I rubbed my temples. Rodán would have someone go to wherever the GPS signal led them, but who knew where that could be. I could have lost it in the fight with the female Vamp or somewhere along my run from Manhattan.

I glanced at the garage door. It could have come out of my belt when I dropped and rolled. I hurried back to the garage door and something glinted in the pale moonlight.

When I got there I saw that it was my phone—only it had been crushed beneath the door. Great. Just great. My XPhone had everything on it—all of my contacts, notes, everything. I hadn't remembered to back it up on my computer at the office this morning, either.

Maybe the GPS still worked. I glanced around. Just

me, the pyramid and the trees. The phone wasn't protected by my glamour because it was no longer on me, so I needed to get every piece.

The earth was soft beneath my knees as I knelt and tugged at pieces of my poor, smashed phone. It was wedged tight. I used a little of my earth elemental magic and the dirt shifted enough that I could drag out what remained of my cell.

Total pancake. No way could the GPS have survived, much less any of its memory. Still I stuffed the pieces into a pouch on my weapons belt, not wanting to leave any traces. So much for contacting Rodán or Olivia. I was on my own.

I turned back to the task I'd taken on and studied the glass structure before approaching it.

Despite my glamour, I felt naked as I started walking along the front glass wall. I stopped and placed my hands against the surface. The glass was cool. Of course, wrapped in a glamour, I couldn't be seen. I could see myself, just no norm or paranorm that had been born human had that ability.

What was it like from the inside of the pyramid looking out? Could every little detail of the forest be seen through all of that glass?

I used my air elemental to search the pyramid all the way to its peak at the same time I moved my palms along the entire length of the front of the structure. I frowned. By the time I'd reached the end, I hadn't felt a single seam in the glass to tell me where a door or even a window might be. My air elemental magic had found nothing, too.

The soft purr of a luxury car's engine met my ears. Maybe it was Volod. I unsheathed one of my daggers. As I ran back in the direction of the garage, I lightly ran the tip of the dagger along the same territory I'd just used my hands and air elemental on. Might as well— couldn't hurt.

Unfortunately, the point didn't pause in the slightest, not catching on any break that might have been a clue as to how to get in and out of that pyramid from the front.

The surface was perfect. As in Per-fect. Nothing. Absolutely *nothing* marred the surface of glass from as high as I could reach on down to where the glass met the earth.

Just as the gate creaked open, I reached the corner of the structure closest to the garage. I peered around the tree while headlights cut the darkness and I blinked the bright light away. When I glanced at the pyramid I saw that the glass absorbed the light from the vehicle's headlights, rather than reflecting it, just as I'd suspected. I looked back to see a Rolls-Royce, moonlight glinting on its "Spirit of Ecstasy" hood ornament.

Ground shuddered to my right and the huge garage door yawned open again. I made my way closer to the door and followed the car into the garage all the way to where it parked. I watched as the vehicle took up two parking spaces—apparently even Vampires can be pretentious.

A Vampire in a standard chauffeur suit got out of the driver's seat and walked back to open the rear passenger door. A big Vampire climbed out with something draped across his arms.

The Vampire wore a pained expression and the chauffeur took off his hat, held it to his heart, and bowed his head. It was then that I saw the sparkle of a red sequined dress beneath the coat lying across the big Vampire's arms. My stomach churned as I realized it was the Vampire I'd beheaded before coming to the compound.

Another Vampire slid out holding a black bowling ball bag. I looked away, not wanting to imagine what was in there in place of a bowling ball. I still pictured it in my mind despite myself.

The trio remained quiet with only the thump of the car doors breaking the silence. They headed in the same direction Drago had gone but the garage door didn't close.

With my enhanced hearing, in the distance I heard more engines, probably a couple of miles away. Soon more Vampires would be arriving at the fortress, apparently to convene after the night's events.

One of them no doubt would be Volod, proudly carrying the serum and the antiserum. That thought had me grinding my teeth.

During the time it took the next vehicles to make their way through the forest to the compound, I had left the garage and explored the length of the one side of the pyramid, again running my palms along the perfect surface.

The garage couldn't be the only entrance or exit, could it?

My air elemental magic still had me cloaked in a glamour and I peered around an evergreen close to the garage. I placed my hands on it, more to ground myself than any other reason.

Three more vehicles approached the gate, which opened and allowed them through before closing again. A BMW, a Cadillac, and just to shake things up, a beat-up old Toyota four-wheel drive truck complete with lift kit, roll bars, and running boards.

Heh. Vampires with style.

I eased closer to the open garage door, then followed the vehicles down into the parking garage again. I watched the truck and cars park. From out of the Caddy and the Toyota, Vampires carried lifeless bodies of their comrades or loved ones who had died in battle. The sight made my stomach queasy. Like with Sprites, I had never liked to think of Vampires as anything but lowlife scum.

Yet now I was fighting off feelings of pity for beings who were set on destroying the paranorm world.

That thought alone made the pity leave my mind and my stomach settled. I ground my teeth as I thought instead of all of the dead Sprites. None of them had deserved to die. Well, maybe a couple, but for the most part they were a race of beings living life as their kind had for centuries, perhaps millennia.

And I thought about what could happen to all paranorms if I didn't get the serum.

We could be extinguished. Every last one of us.

Research in the notes had confirmed all paranorms who weren't human had the mutated gene. Paranorms not susceptible to the virus included any being not born human, including Vampires, Necromancers, Witches and Sorcerers.

I am half human, but lucky me, I carry the mutated gene from my Drow side.

Several more vehicles returned, some bearing the Vampires' dead as well as those who still lived.

Considering Vampires are the undead, it wasn't easy to distinguish between those who still had their heads attached and hearts intact from those who didn't. Then I figured it really didn't matter.

In between arrivals I managed to search all four exterior walls of the pyramid physically and with my air elemental.

It was quiet for a while with no more vehicles approaching. The garage had closed, maybe for the last time that night, and I still hadn't found any other way into the pyramid.

The fact that I was stuck outside when I needed to be inside started to eat at me. I should have gone into the garage when the last vehicle had passed through.

A low hum told me another car was coming and I breathed a sigh of relief.

I waited and watched until a black Mercedes convertible rolled up to the black gates, then traveled up the driveway to where the garage had opened, its big mouth ready to swallow the car whole.

Good. Now I could follow whatever Vamp this was, and find my way in.

When we got down into the garage, the Mercedes parked in the closest spot, which had been left empty until now. That gave me pause and I stopped mid-stride.

A Vampire stepped out of the Mercedes, then reached in and drew out a red shoebox.

Volod.

SIXTEEN

I held my breath. Kept my emotions under control. The blood throbbing in my veins couldn't be slowed, though, and I prayed Volod couldn't hear it or sense me. Vampires are known to be able to hear human heartbeats but not paranorms. I was grateful for that.

Volod appeared preoccupied as he shut the door of the black Mercedes. He stopped and faced the garage entrance. I bit my lip hard enough that my tiny fangs pierced my bottom lip and I tasted blood.

The Master Vampire's head snapped in my direction and my entire body tensed as I fought to control my emotions. He sensed me. He might even be able to smell my blood.

For a long time he looked my way, then finally took his gaze from where I stood and slowly examined the garage, searching for whatever it was that had caused him to pause. When he saw nothing, he turned and strode in the same direction everyone else had. I found myself having to control my breathing and my flow of emotions.

My gut clenched. Volod had sensed me. If I followed him, he might actually discover me, so I didn't dare try. I gripped the hilt of one of my daggers and didn't move.

Maybe another vehicle would approach and I could follow them inside the compound.

The garage door started to close and my heart sank with it. I'd have to wait for another car. I bolted out, this time making it with no problem.

After it closed, the earth settled once again, leaving a perfect unmarred surface. Just like the pyramid—

I cut my gaze to the glass structure. I'd tried finding exits and entrances to the building . . . but I'd never tried to find one in the ground. The garage went deep, and Vampires were known to go to ground when they slept, so just maybe where they congregated was below the pyramid.

This time when I approached the building, I searched the ground with my earth element, sending out feelers of magic all the way around the structure. My magic found one, then two, then three, and finally a fourth.

Four underground entrances and exits, one on each side of the pyramid. How could I not have thought of that before? Yes, it made sense that their ways in and out of the place would be below, too.

I went to the one closest to me and knelt beside it. The earth was soft and loose beneath my palm as I brushed it away from the square of stone.

With my eyes closed, I used my earth magic to explore the entrance. Below the slab, stone steps went far below the ground. The earthen walls allowed me to gauge the dimensions and the distance to a door. But that's as far as I could go because the door was metal and the walls beyond were not made of earth.

The slab was thick and heavy but it moved easily when I pushed it aside.

It was dark. Drow Realm dark. Good thing I didn't need light.

I moved the stone back overhead, cutting off the moonlight. I jogged down the steps, which led me about thirty feet underground to the slanting earthen passageway that went even deeper into the earth. Roots dangled from the ceiling and crawled along the walls in the tunnel and the cool feel and the scent of earth reminded me of home.

The door was black and too perfect-looking to be in a dirt tunnel. Didn't even look dusty. But there was a strip of light beneath the door where it didn't quite meet the ground.

When I reached the metal door, I let my earth and air elements search it to make sure it was safe. After my experience in the Werewolf case, touching something I was unfamiliar with had me a little gun-shy.

My earth and air magic told me the door was fine. I reached out and placed my palm on the cool surface of the door.

It caught me by surprise when the door swung open without the slightest sound and I caught my breath. My heart pounded as the open doorway revealed a black marble foyer.

Blood seemed to rush faster through my veins causing a jittery sensation along my skin. The metal door frame was smooth as I gripped it and peered in.

An enormous chandelier was overhead, hundreds of teardrop crystals winking with brilliance. A black marble staircase swept up from the entrance as if the way I'd entered was the main doorway. The hum of many voices came from beyond the staircase and my stomach flipped.

From a hallway to my left I heard two individuals talking, the sounds coming closer and closer. The sensation in my belly worsened. I still couldn't be seen, but I had to get the door closed before they reached the foyer and suspected anything was wrong.

Thank goodness the door was just as silent closing as it had been opening. When I shut it, I was no longer looking at a black metal door, but a huge ornately carved wooden door.

Between that and the foyer and sweeping staircase, I felt a little like Alice must have felt in Wonderland. Where was the unbirthday party going to be held?

I backed up and my thigh hit an umbrella stand. It rattled on the black marble and almost fell before I caught it.

What Elvin grace?

"Did you hear that, Drago?" a female voice said. "I thought this was an unused part of the mansion."

Why did it have to be Drago? I sucked in my breath and flattened myself against a wall, as if that might help him from sensing or seeing me.

"Yes." The word was clipped. "No one should be at this entrance."

I called to my air element to wrap me even tighter in my glamour and held my breath as I inched along the wall to my right, as far from the doorway as I could get before Drago reached me.

He walked from the hallway to my right and I came to a complete stop. At his side, with her arm hooked through his, was a beautiful female Vampire, a blond who wore a halter top evening gown in ocean blue.

She didn't look the least bit concerned about the noise she'd heard, but Drago did. He studied the doorway, the umbrella stand and the surrounding area. His gaze passed by me as he made a slow perusal of the area. The sight of his green eyes made my skin itch.

"What, Drago?" The petite Vampire siren had a cute little pout that would have had Olivia rolling her eyes.

He looked at her, and she paused, her lips open in a perfect little "o" and she stared into his gaze. Maybe she was mesmerized by his green eyes.

"When I want you to know anything, Jennifer," he said in a low, icy voice, "I will tell you."

He looked away from her and she blinked. "Whatever you say, Master."

Master? Drago was a Master Vampire? No wonder he'd been close to sensing me. To be honest, I didn't think there were any other Masters left in New York City after the Rebellion. One Master Vampire was enough.

Drago took another look at the surrounding area, then started walking to the right of the marble staircase toward the hum of voices. Jennifer still clung to his arm, but she seemed more subdued than before.

Relief that he was gone and hadn't found me made the cramp in my stomach relax.

I needed to explore, to memorize the layout of this place before following the voices. The broad staircase ended at a balcony and then split off three ways. To the right and to the left were open hallways—the dark wood spindles revealing doors along each side, bedroom doors was my guess.

To the center was a spiraling staircase that went up to another floor and who knew beyond that. Maybe it went to the top of the pyramid itself.

I had hallways to the left and right of me, and more area behind the sweeping staircase.

The best place to start was probably wherever it was that Drago had gone and where I heard talking because likely that's where other Vampires were headed and where I would find Volod and the serum and antiserum. Or at least get some clue as to where he was holding it.

I touched my collar and rubbed one of the runes. I took a deep breath and followed Drago, which was the last thing I wanted to be doing right now. Trailing a Master Vampire into what was probably a nest of Vamps.

It didn't take me long to find Drago—and the hoard of Vamps. A shudder rippled through me as I took in the huge ballroom filled with Vampires.

I remained motionless even though I had the urge to start staking Vampires while at the same time having the strong desire to run.

Locating exits would be a start in case I had to do the latter. There were four total. The large entry I had just walked through, a set of white French doors, and two archways.

The French doors were across the expansive ballroom floor, directly in front of me. The two archways were on either side of the ballroom, one of which was a hallway and the other I couldn't tell. The archway with the hallway was on my right, the other archway was to my left.

The Vampires were my biggest concern right now. If any one of them could sense me, like Volod had, I might have a big problem. Fortunately all of the Vampires in the ballroom were busy chatting in small groups, including Drago.

Rich wood flooring warmed the room and the walls were painted indigo blue. Sconces with flickering candlelight were along each wall, giving the room subtle lighting. The décor was nineteenth century, which seemed odd considering this lair was in a mirrored pyramid. I'd half expected Egyptian furnishings, maybe a depiction of the Egyptian god Set and a statue of Anubis.

Forty-one Vampires were separated into several smaller groups. Four males, including Drago, stood in front of a huge fireplace that sent out heat across the room. Vampires are impervious to weather and temperature changes, so I guessed it was for effect. Maybe nostalgia for once-human beings.

Females clustered together on blue velvet parlor furniture to my right on the edge of the ballroom. A love seat, rocker, settee, and several armchairs. More small groups of Vampires were holding discussions around the ballroom.

A waiter served appetizers that looked like different kinds of bloody meat on the end of toothpicks that had colorful frilly tops. Gross. I preferred my meat char-burnt. Those little hors d'oeuvres were enough to turn my stomach.

Another waiter bore a tray of blood-red cocktails. I wanted to heave when I realized that he wasn't serving just synthetic blood cocktails—real blood was in the crystal glasses.

I shuddered and looked away. Unfortunately just about every Vampire was holding and drinking from one of the cocktail glasses, and eating the raw meat for appetizers.

Of the many groups gathered around the ballroom floor, I wasn't sure which one to eavesdrop on first. Drago and the males at the fireplace seemed as good a place as any to start, despite the fact I really didn't want to be anywhere near the Master.

I stayed where I was but mentally focused on the four Vampires. My air element helped bring their words to me, making it easy to hear them from across the room.

"Danut is missing," one of the Vampires said before he took a sip of his blood cocktail.

Drago frowned. "Perhaps he is simply running late as Volod was."

A Vampire turned his head a bit. It was Chuck. "I saw Danut go down," Chuck said. "But he got to his feet again."

"He's always one of the first to return," the fourth Vampire said.

"Give him time." Drago drew a cigar out of an inside pocket of his leather jacket. He leaned down and lit the end of the cigar in the fireplace, then put the cigar to his lips. He drew in a lungful, then sent puffs of smoke into Chuck's face. "Why didn't you back up Danut?"

"I was fighting one of the Trackers," Chuck said with a touch of nervousness in his voice that hadn't been there before. "That blue-haired Tracker. I was sure Danut had the Tracker he was fighting under control."

"He's Volod's brother," one of the other Vamps said. "If he's dead, so are you."

"Hey, man." Chuck swallowed. "Danut was on his feet and like I said, I was fighting another Tracker."

The other Vamp who'd spoken just shook his head, indicating that Chuck should have backed up Danut if he wanted to keep his life. Chuck looked as queasy as I felt at that moment.

A beautiful redheaded Vampire was speaking to the blond female who'd been with Drago. Luxurious red hair was swept up in a smooth chignon, complimenting the female's high cheekbones and her slender neck.

The redhead was pale like all Vampires, but it looked good on her, as if she was royalty who kept her fair skin always safe from the sun's rays. Her emerald green taffeta gown hugged her slim figure, clinging to her body from her breasts to her three-hundred-dollar sandals.

What caught my attention, though, was the anger in her voice. As I looked directly at her, her green eyes captured me. Like Drago's, her eyes were fierce, intense, and almost hypnotizing.

Perhaps she was related to Drago, but, whatever the case, she was stunning—and dangerous. It radiated from her in a heated blast.

The redhead had her hand on one hip and fury blazed from her red lips. "The blue-haired Tracker," the female Vampire said. "Chuck said she's the one who killed my cousin Teresa."

Considering I'd only killed one female Vampire tonight I knew exactly who she was talking about.

The blond, Jennifer, held her hand to her chest, horror on her features. "Teresa? She's gone, Elizabeth?"

"The Tracker will die." The redhead's words were so fierce they cut through me as if she'd struck me with a blade. "I will hunt her. I will find her. I will drain her of all of her blood. I will *kill* her."

"We both will, Letty." Drago startled me as he approached the redhead, hugged her, and placed a kiss on top of her head. "Tonight, we hunt. And we will feed."

Elizabeth didn't look any less angry, even when Drago added, "I hear that Elvin blood is a high like none other."

"My high will be from killing the bitch," Elizabeth said. If Vampires could have color in their cheeks from anger, then she did.

I swallowed, trying not to imagine myself as a Vampire main course and the Vampire getting a high from my blood.

The desire to back out of the room *now* was strong.

It went from strong to urgent as Volod strode in.

"Have a drink, Letty." Drago selected a glass from a serving tray as a waiter paused beside them. "It will make you feel better."

The redhead took the blood cocktail but the fury on her features never changed.

Vampires around the ballroom went silent as Volod went to the fireplace. The males who had been standing there bowed their heads, clearly a sign of respect, and stepped away, leaving Volod alone.

"The reason we are gathered together now." Volod raised the red shoebox so that everyone in the room could see and he gave a grim look of satisfaction. "Our mission is accomplished and we now have what we sought. If we need to, we will use it to obtain what is rightfully ours."

A kind of frenzied tension traveled throughout the ballroom. It was palpable, enough to make my skin crawl.

The redhead moved through the crowd that parted as she made her way forward to Volod's side. She ran her fingers along the box as he looked at her.

"We can return." The anger was gone from Elizabeth's eyes, replaced by a look of pleasure. "No being can stop us."

Volod brushed his lips over hers and smiled when he raised his head. "Not a single being can get in our way, my love."

She stepped aside and faced the other Vampires, enough distance between them to let him take center stage, but close enough that everyone would know that she was his—lover, wife, fiancé, girlfriend, mistress, whatever.

"The contents of this box will allow us to be who we truly are. We had heard stories about this serum and the

Werewolves. The Sprites had provided us papers with complete details on the power of the serum, but they held back on the serum itself. Now we have it." Volod's voice grew louder, an almost psychotic gleam to his eyes. "Now with this vial of serum, it will be as it should be, as it is meant to be. We will never be forced to live beneath paranorm rule again."

Volod set the box on an armchair beside the fireplace, close to him, before he straightened and addressed the crowd. "Instead of being ruled by those pitiful excuses for paranorms, Vampire kind shall reign over all of New York and beyond."

Cheers rose in the ballroom, the Vampires nearly going crazy with their enthusiasm. A chair was knocked over with a loud thump and it seemed as if the sconces rattled against the walls.

Their frenzied excitement was almost frightening. It twisted my insides with a true sense of fear that made me feel ill. Volod really was willing to use the serum.

Volod's features went solemn. "Too many of our brothers and sisters were lost to us tonight. We lost seventeen in the battle."

Gasps and looks of horror from Vampires in the room.

"Before we go any further, we will pay our respects to those who are no longer with us," Volod said.

Every Vampire in the room bowed his or her head, including Volod. After several excruciating minutes, Volod raised his head and started speaking again.

"I have debriefed those who have returned from battle." Volod's jaw was set. "Most of our kind have been accounted for, including those lost to us forever. My brother, Danut, is the only one we were unable to locate."

A sense of unease traveled through the ballroom. I spotted Chuck and his face looked paler than it had the first time I'd seen him.

"We will find Danut," Volod said. "And those who took him will be suitably disposed of."

Murmurs of agreement met my ears and I shivered from a chill that crept up my spine.

"Ever since the Rebellion, we have been forced to be subservient to paranorms." Volod's dark eyes grew darker yet, his features even angrier than they had been. "They forced us to feed on the blood of slaughtered animals and terminated us if we touched humans—if they caught us with one of those pitiful beings."

An angry rumble from those in the ballroom was loud enough I swore the floor was shaking.

Goose bumps prickled my skin. I rubbed my arms, all the time working to keep my emotions hidden and my glamour as strong as possible.

"Not only have we been forced to live under these conditions, but the Paranorm Council has never respected Vampire kind enough to invite a representative to the council itself," Volod said. "They will pay for that lack of respect."

The crowd grew louder as words of agreement were tossed out.

"Thanks to our efforts tonight and thanks to the sacrifice of too many of our brothers and sisters, the Paranorm Council will bow to *us*." Volod raised his voice, almost shouting the words. "More importantly, Night Trackers will bow to Vampire kind."

"Or die." Drago raised his glass. "The Night Trackers should die. All of them."

"Die, die, die," the chant rolled through the crowd. "Kill the Trackers, kill the Trackers."

"You are quite right, Drago." Volod smiled and bared his fangs.

My body went icy cold as Volod looked in my direction. "Yes. They shall die. And I know which Tracker to start with."

SEVENTEEN

I went completely rigid. Volod was looking right at me.

I gathered my elemental magic. Air and fire were at my bidding. I would roast the Vampires with fire. Their tissue would regenerate, but it would give me time to escape.

Volod's gaze didn't linger on me. He was slowly looking around the ballroom at all of the Vampires gathered around him.

I could have slid down the wall behind me and sat on the floor, I was so relieved. I was in a nest of vipers doing my best not to get bitten and injected with venom. Which was an appropriate analogy considering he held serum that was beyond any venom that could have been put into my veins.

"Originally we sought information to aid us in gaining back our rights as paranormal beings." Volod put his hands behind his back and paced in front of the anxious crowd as he spoke. "We enlisted the Sprites to aid us in obtaining that information. But we obtained so much more than we ever expected."

"Drago." Volod nodded to the other Master.

He stepped forward and handed Volod a thick folder with several sheets of paper sticking out haphazardly. I hadn't noticed Drago holding anything before, but when he went to stand at the sidelines again I saw a Vampire servant hand Drago a second folder.

"This in itself is power." Volod held up the papers now in his grasp. His fingers were long, slender, and pale against the brown folder. "The contents detail every paranorm race's weaknesses as well as their known locations."

Volod set the folder down beside the box as he continued without pause. "Our scientists and other experts will now be working on ways to use the weaknesses against the paranorms. We had other ideas planned for our research room, but now it will be put to great use testing for ourselves the content of these pages."

Gasps and sounds of wonder and excitement from the Vampires.

My stomach dropped.

"But fortune was even kinder to us." Volod's smile was charming, charismatic while at the same time he looked psychotic. Drago handed him the second folder. "The Sprites discovered something even better."

"What is it?" Jennifer said from the sidelines, like she couldn't contain herself. She was bouncing on the balls of her feet as it was.

Volod gave her a cool look before addressing the crowd again. He set the second folder on top of the red shoebox. "What does that folder of information and the contents of this box mean to us?"

It was like the ballroom held a collective breath as he paused.

"It is akin to what a nuclear bomb is to humans. What is in this box can shut down every paranorm being except those who were once human or those who remain human but have paranormal powers."

More cheers. More frenzied excitement that left me cold.

When the cheers stopped I frowned and tilted my head. I now heard noises on the other side of the archway to my left which led away from the large area we were in. The sounds were like muffled groans and wheels squeaking across carpet. My attention went back to Volod as soon as he started speaking again.

"We have it all now." Volod smiled, showing his fangs. *We* will rule *them*. We will have control in every way."

The cheers from the roomful of Vampires were louder, frantic.

"We have captured a few paranorms and will be gathering more," Volod said and I caught my breath. "We will use them in whatever ways we deem necessary, from experimentation to threats."

I held my hand to my mouth, holding back a shout of fear and hate. Where were the paranorms he had captured? I had to help them.

Then my gut clenched as I realized that might not be possible. Not yet. I couldn't let Volod know I was here. He and Drago had sensed something wasn't right, and if the paranorms escaped, that might make him suspicious. If he grew suspicious, then he might move the location of the lair they met in and we would have to work to locate them again.

I had to wait until I could come back with a team to go after the serum and antiserum, and to save the paranorms.

"We are free." Volod held his right arm out toward a doorway and made a "come here" gesture with his hand. "Free to feed from humans again, whenever we choose to."

The squeaking noises and muffled groans became louder. Horror shot through me as a cage filled with four human men and women were rolled into the ballroom. The wheels rumbled across the wood floor. The Vampires had blindfolded and gagged all of the norms and each was cuffed to a bar of the cage.

Vampires were nearly hysterical with excitement as they stared at the norms. The Vampires bared their fangs or licked their lips in anticipation.

"Never again will you be forced to drink that synthetic garbage served at the nightclubs and restaurants. Never again will you have to drink animal blood." Volod's voice rose higher over the noise of the crowd. "You will have plenty of fresh humans to hunt down and feed on."

I grew more ill by the moment as the Vampires applauded and stared at the norms with fangs bared, hunger in their eyes. Drool rolled from the corners of some Vampires' mouths.

Pain ached at the back of my own eyes. I wanted to cry for these humans. But Dark Elves have no tear ducts, and all I could do was cry inside.

"Vincent, Afina, Bogdan, Timothy, join me, please," Volod said, and four Vampires moved to the front of the room. "These humans are simply hors d'oeuvres for these who served me best tonight."

My own blood drained from my face as I looked at the poor norms as their blindfolds were removed. Horror was in their eyes as they saw the room full of Vampires.

I looked from the norms to Volod when he said, "The rest of you hunt well tonight!"

Hunt. Vampires were going to hunt norms again, a practice that had been banned after the Rebellion.

It was like the beasts of the Underworld had been

unleashed. I barely had enough time to press myself into a corner of the ballroom where I wouldn't get trampled in the mad rush of Vampires going on the hunt.

I wanted to take my buckler and my daggers and start killing Vampires. I wanted to destroy them all and set the norms free and save any who would be hunted down tonight.

As much as every fiber of my being wanted to do it, I couldn't. Fighting off forty-one Vampires, including Master Vampires Volod and Drago, would be suicide and I would be of no use to anyone, paranorms and norms alike.

The fact that I couldn't help these norms made me beyond ill.

I forced myself to block out what was about to happen and turn my attention to Volod and the box.

Volod and the box were gone.

Panic made my heart beat faster.

My gaze searched the ballroom. Not here.

He hadn't passed me to get to the stairs and I hadn't seen the French doors open. He had to have gone through one of the two archways. Because the norms had been brought through one, I was betting that Volod had gone through the archway that led down the hallway on my right.

With my glamour wrapped tight around me, I dodged Vampires who still hadn't left the ballroom, and I made it to the hallway. At the same time I did my best to ignore what I knew would be happening to those norms.

As I entered the hallway, I wondered where the norms had been kept. And where Volod was keeping the paranorms.

I blocked out everything now but the need to find

Volod and the serum and antiserum, along with the folder of information from the scientists.

In addition, I wanted to locate the information on paranorm weaknesses and known locations and hoped everything was in the same place. If I could find where Volod ended up stashing them, I could take it all and end the mess paranorms were now in.

I walked down the hallway with walls painted forest green and a black marble floor. No décor was on the walls beyond wall sconces for the dim lighting.

The hallway was long with six doorways along its length. All of the doors were closed. I used my senses and my elements to search. My air element told me the first four doors were to bedrooms, all of which were empty.

The fifth—

My heart began to pound and I wanted to run right then. Volod and Drago were behind that door. Both of the Vampires had the ability to sense me, at least to some extent. With them in the same room together, I might not have a chance to make it out of there. To remain in total glamour I had to control my emotions. I was still working on it. Obviously I hadn't perfected it.

Still I paused to the side of the door and closed my eyes. I guided my air element so that it would bring back any information I could use. It was an office and Volod and Drago were the only two Vampires in the room.

"Is it safe, Volod?" Drago said in a firm yet respectful tone. "No one can find it?"

"Of course." A chair squeaked and I pictured Volod leaning back in an office chair. "Not even you shall know of its whereabouts. I alone will see to its safety."

I could almost see Drago frown. "Do you not think another of our kind should know where it is hidden?"

"Such as you?" Volod asked and I couldn't read his tone at all. "Do you believe I should share with you what I have done with our prize?"

"Yes." Had to give Drago credit. He didn't hesitate. "I think it prudent that at least one other should have that information."

"I do not—"

Volod stopped speaking. Through my air magic I could picture his sudden stop and that he was looking at the door, sensing me again.

My heart was going crazy. I couldn't let him find me.

Keeping my glamour tight around me, I turned and ran. I bolted back down the hall to the ballroom, too fast for him to possibly discover that I'd been there.

Well behind me I heard the door open, followed by Drago's, "What is it?" and Volod's reply, "Nothing. It is nothing," before the door closed again.

I made a point of ignoring the four Vampires and what they were doing to the humans in the ballroom as I passed them and made it to the stairs. It took a lot of pretending that nothing was wrong just to make myself go on. I am a protector by nature and to see innocents hurt or worse, and to be unable to help them, was almost impossible to bear.

The only thing left for me to do here, the only thing I felt I could do, was find out where the paranorms, and possibly more norms, were being held.

It was like being in some kind of maze or rat trap as I jogged around the area where I'd first come in. A library, study, parlor, sitting room, and the enormous ballroom were on that level.

After I checked those rooms out, I located another doorway, this one leading down a level where I found a huge kitchen where several Vampire cooks were busy at work. I started to wonder why Vampires would need such a large kitchen when all they did was drink blood, then decided I really didn't want to know why.

Next I came to a very large infirmary with a doctor and two nurses but no patients. Why would Vampires who could regenerate need any kind of hospital? It wasn't like their heads could be reattached. Missing Vampire hearts couldn't be replaced with a Jarvik artificial heart. I hoped.

Maybe it had something to do with a Vampire's weakness other than the two everyone knows about. Maybe they could treat holy water and garlic sickness, and cross burns.

Once I left the infirmary I found a set of locked double doors. I sent my air element in to search for me at the same time I peered through the clouded glass in the doors. It was empty of Vampires but appeared to be a scientific research center.

After our last case, anything to do with scientists— even Vampire scientists, maybe especially Vampire scientists—hit too close to home. My skin crawled and I just wanted to get away from there.

Later. I could bring a team in and we'd take care of anything that might need to be done.

Another set of stairs down brought me to catacombs. It was a nest of passages with rooms and recesses, coffins in every nook and cranny.

I shivered. This was where the Vampires slept.

Several coffins were obviously new, others ancient. Some were well-kept while many appeared neglected. I began to notice a pattern as I walked through the honeycomb of burial chambers.

Many of the coffins had an odd symbol on them. I couldn't read the symbol, but these were the coffins that for the most part looked dusty, old, and untouched, although some were more recent. The coffins probably housed their "dead."

The other coffins in the catacombs were generally in better shape and likely for their "undead."

I wondered which coffin might be Volod's. Now that would be some very useful information.

At the end of the network of burial chambers, I saw a set of stairs leading upward. I frowned. Shouldn't the prisoners be down here somewhere? A lower level maybe? Prisoners were always kept in dungeons. I should know. I'm from Otherworld which remains in medieval times, disdaining the modern.

I'd searched with my earth magic as well as by foot, and there was nothing below the catacombs. So I went for the stairs.

I headed up.

And up.

And up.

Eventually I realized I had to be aboveground in the pyramid. The walls slanted and the stairs were leading to the center of the structure.

Based on what the outside looked like, I'd expected to be able to see out. But the pyramid was made of granite so thick my elemental magic couldn't penetrate it. The mirrored surface must be a way to escape detection.

The fact that the walls were made of granite that I couldn't get through with my magic set my nerves on edge. I'd been locked in a granite room before, with all of my elements taken away from me, and it was one of the worst experiences of my life. I didn't care to repeat it. No thank you.

As I climbed higher, I heard noises. Faint at first,

then louder. I came to a door. The stairs continued up to more floors above me, but the noises were loudest here.

I listened and reached out with my air magic. No one stood on the other side of the door, close to it, but there were beings in that room. Not paranorms but norms.

Slowly I pushed open the door, holding my breath as I hoped that the hinges wouldn't squeak or someone would notice a door being opened by, well, by nothing.

I let out my breath as I slipped inside the dimly lit room.

Cages.

Empty cages along with a cage filled with three bound and helpless norms. One was crying, another whimpering, the third silent.

My heart hurt. I held my hands to my chest as I looked at the norms who would be killed if we didn't save them. Again I wanted to set everyone free, but again I had to remind myself that I couldn't.

I hated this impotent feeling. I was so used to being a paranorm version of a superhero, able to leap buildings in a single bound—sort of. It was my job to protect those who needed it. A job I took on because I wanted to help make things right in the world.

And this was wrong. So very wrong.

I set my jaw. I'd make it right again. I just hoped it wouldn't be too late for these norms.

Forcing myself to turn away from the norms, I slipped back out the door and headed up another level. It was silent all around me, but the closer I got to the next floor, the better I was able to sense that beings were there. Magical beings. Paranorms.

When I reached the door I placed my palm against it and closed my eyes. Yes. Three paranorms. I sensed a Sprite, a Witch, and a Doppler. Maybe Vampires didn't know Witches aren't true paranorms because they're part human, or maybe the Vampires just wanted to experiment. Whatever the case, it was sick.

I swallowed and stared at the door. I couldn't go in there because paranorms—with the exception of the Witch—would possibly be able to see me. I didn't want anyone to notice me, call to me, or in any way bring attention to me.

No, I needed to get back to Manhattan. I needed to run as fast as I could to the closest town, the closest telephone, so that I could call Rodán.

It wouldn't be long before the sun came up and I was human again and wouldn't have the speed of the Elves. I'd have to hitch a ride back to the city if I didn't get hold of Rodán.

Once I was back, once we laid our plans, we'd take care of these Vampires.

We'd take care of Volod.

We'd get the serum and antiserum back and destroy them for good.

Right now though, I had no idea how.

EIGHTEEN

I brushed my hand over my belly and looked at my hand. No jagged claw marks remained from the now headless Vampire's fingernails. No slashes on my hand from her fangs.

The gray dawn had just peeked through the trees and I'd changed from Drow to human behind a small all-night diner. The marks that did remain were the ones in my thoughts, the ones that made my head and heart hurt. The ones that made my stomach ache.

When my skin had lost its amethyst hue and my hair had returned to black from cobalt, I left the cover of the trees for the front of the diner, a shack of a place just off an isolated part of the freeway. It wasn't going to be easy being inconspicuous since I was still in my two-piece leather fighting outfit.

The steps leading to the diner's front doors were old and weathered and the diner itself looked like it belonged in the nineteen sixties.

Bells jangled and the warm smells of bacon and eggs made me queasy after last night. Only three patrons and a waitress were in the diner but it might as well have been a roomful the way they stared at me. I hoped I hadn't gotten leaves in my hair after I said the Elvin cleansing spell that had also mended the few tears in my leathers.

But likely it was because I was wearing a leather half top, tight leather pants, and leather boots. I probably looked like a biker babe and they were checking the parking lot for a Harley with a dude driving it.

I did my best to put my emotions about last night aside and approached the cute little ponytailed blond behind the counter. She wore a pale blue T-shirt with *Pa's Diner* on it and faded Levi's. I thought about the Vampires and how close the diner was to their lair and prayed that she wasn't going to be one of their next meals.

Not if I could help it.

"I need to borrow a phone to make a call." I gave a pretend smile when I reached her. The diner was completely silent as she stared at me. I added, "My ride died about a quarter mile back. I need to call my guy."

The blond blinked then shrugged before she dug into her front jeans pocket. "You can use my cell phone."

She handed me the phone and I started to dial. "Thanks a bunch. It's a long walk back."

"Back to where?" she asked but I already had the phone to my ear and was turning away to talk with Rodán.

"Nyx," he said when he answered and I heard more concern in his voice than I'd expected. I was calling from a number he wasn't familiar with yet he knew it was me. "Where are you?"

The blond gave me the address and I relayed it to Rodán who said he'd send someone to get me. Then I told him quickly and quietly as much as I could.

It had been a long night, but I knew I couldn't relax during the time it took to get from where I was in New

Jersey back to Manhattan. Maybe I could unwind a little as I processed what I just experienced.

After what I'd done and seen last night, there was no true relaxation in the near future for me. Not until we stopped Volod and the rest of the Vampires.

Nothing could take away the chill I felt as I sat on the worn steps of the diner to wait for whoever was going to pick me up. As Drow I don't really feel temperature changes, but when I'm human sometimes they affect me a little more. I think I shivered, though, more from what had happened just a couple of hours ago, than from any chill.

Images of what I'd seen at the Vampire lair kept pounding at my head and I wanted to get them out. The backs of my eyes ached as I remembered the norms being offered up as sacrifices to the Vampires.

Cars and trucks whooshed back and forth on the freeway. A couple of vehicles came and went out of the diner's parking lot and then a very familiar SUV pulled up near the steps where I was sitting.

I smiled when Adam climbed out of the SUV. Warmth replaced the cold I'd been feeling inside.

"Adam." I ran up to him and wrapped my arms around his neck and let him hold me for a few moments.

He drew back, then gave me a light kiss before he said, "Are you okay? We've been worried about you. Olivia's been threatening to hunt down Vampires and stake them in their sleep."

"I know exactly where she can start staking, too." I reached up and kissed Adam before he could say anything else. "There is so much . . . so much."

He hugged me tight for a long moment. Then we got into his black SUV and I collapsed against the seat. Adam started the engine and warm air poured in through the air vents.

Adam touched my chin with his fingers, bringing me around so that I was facing him and looking into his eyes. "Nyx, your tone right now . . . Are you okay?"

"I'm not okay. Not really." I shook my head and drew away from him. "This threat is unbelievably worse than what we've seen before. We've faced a lot of evil in the past, but these Vampires are beyond evil."

Adam frowned as I continued. "The monster in the Vampires has awakened and it's out for destruction." I clenched and unclenched my fists as I spoke. "The world as we know it could change. The world for paranorms could actually end. And norms—if the Vampires aren't stopped, their world could be a terrifying one."

"It sounds worse than any of us thought," he said, his jaw tight, his gaze intense.

"An evil has been released," I said, and I heard fear in my own voice. "Right now, I'm afraid. I'm afraid for everyone."

Adam looked at me with deep concern. "I've never heard you sound like this before. I've never heard or seen the slightest bit of doubt in you."

"They have the means of destroying every para-norm." I gripped one of his arms and forced myself to relax my grip. "They not only know the destructive power of what they now possess," I said, "but I have no doubt they'll use it if they have to in order to control any and all paranorms to get what they want."

"Damn, Nyx." Adam took my face in his hands. "Don't give up hope. No matter what it takes, we'll get the bastards."

I closed my eyes, but when I saw the images replay in

my mind I opened my eyes again. "I don't even want to think about or tell you what I watched."

Why couldn't Dark Elves cry? Why couldn't I have inherited the human ability from my mother?

"I couldn't do a thing." My voice came out in a choked whisper. "Not a thing."

He stroked my hair. "I've never seen you like this," he repeated. "It's not like the Nyx I know."

"They're unleashing their thirst for human blood." I pulled away from Adam again. For some reason I felt an irrational anger against him, but only for a moment. "I saw three humans taken. There was a frenzy unlike anything I've ever seen. Humans will be attacked and either slaughtered or turned into Vampires and added to their ranks."

I couldn't stop myself as I went on. "They fear no repercussions at all. And they do have the control. We have to do everything we can to get it all back and destroy it. Everything they've taken needs to be destroyed."

I looked at him and sighed. "I could sleep a whole twenty-four hours."

Adam brushed my hair again with his fingers. "We'd better get back." He put the vehicle into reverse and gravel crunched under the SUV's tires as he started to back out of the parking lot. The weight of it all settled on my shoulders and I wanted to slide down the seat into a puddle.

"What exactly happened?" he said.

"It was a very long night." I propped my elbow on the passenger door window and rested my head in my palm as I looked out at the passing trees and growing hints of civilization. "So much happened that it's really hard to know where to start."

"From the time we left the Sprites' meeting place is a good place." Adam reached over and squeezed my free hand, then held it as he brought both of our hands onto the center console. "All the way until this moment."

His hand was so warm and just having him there holding it settled me a little inside. Grounded me.

I told him all that had happened, beginning at the point where I started chasing the motorcycle after we fought more Vamps outside of the manhole.

"You chased a motorcycle on foot?" He cut me a sharp glance before he focused on guiding the SUV onto the freeway. "You're kidding me."

"I'm pretty quick as Drow and I have my air element to push me along even faster," I said.

"Quick would be an understatement." Adam kept glancing from the road to me. "I have a feeling this is a long story."

"You could say that."

I told him everything. I have a photographic memory, as norms would call it, and I didn't leave out anything.

As a cop he'd seen it all when it came to violence, so I didn't feel like I needed to spare any details. Of course he hadn't seen humans used as hors d'oeuvres before, but by the time this Vampire nightmare was all over, I wouldn't be surprised if he witnessed norms being attacked firsthand.

"Man, Nyx." His features looked hard, tough, like a cop about to make a bust. But when his eyes met mine his concern and caring for me was so obvious. "You shouldn't have taken off by yourself the way you did. You were lucky, real lucky that those Vamps didn't discover you."

Automatically I wanted to argue. To show how tough

I was as a Tracker. Those feelings fizzled as I looked at him.

"You're right." I linked my fingers through his on the console. "Like I told you, I had the cell phone and had planned on calling for backup."

"This is the Wonder Woman act. It belongs only on TV." Adam shook his head. "You found the place and you should have come back and let us all go tonight."

I opened my mouth, then shut it. My Drow warrior instinct was so strong that it was hard to back down from being told I should have asked for help.

"You're right," I said.

Adam raised an eyebrow. "You're agreeing that maybe you're not invincible?"

"Yeah, believe it or not, I am." I turned my head away from him to look at the dead trees and bushes flying by as he drove. "It's hard for me to admit it, but I already told you that much."

"How are you feeling about it all?" That concerned look was in his warm brown eyes when I glanced back at him.

"Sick inside." I straightened in my seat and put my hand on my belly, like that might still the queasiness. "I've busted Vamps sucking on norms before, but I've never witnessed anything like this."

His expression was hard to read now. He'd gone from concerned to cop tough to unreadable.

"They were crazed, Adam." I swallowed back the harsh feeling at the back of my throat. "I'm afraid of what might have happened to norms last night."

Adam gave a nod to the police radio which I hadn't even noticed was off. "Too many reports of people being attacked savagely and murdered. Still others missing."

I held my hand over my mouth before I said, "How many?"

"Reports were still coming in when I pulled up to the diner," he said. "I turned it off for now so you and I could have a chance to talk."

"I was so afraid of this." My words were hardly a whisper. "I knew it was going to happen, but I'd hoped that they wouldn't kill their victims. I'd hoped that maybe they'd just drink some of their blood." I rubbed my temples with my thumb and forefinger. "A naïve hope."

"Not naïve, Nyx." Adam released my hand and brushed his knuckles over my cheek. "We always have to have hope no longer how bad it looks like it may be."

"If only this whole thing was just a bunch of Sprites creating chaos." I reached up and clasped his hand. "I'd take a pink Statue of Liberty over humans being Vampire meals."

"You and me both." Adam moved his hand from mine and brushed my hair with his fingers. "What you saw tonight would have been hard for anyone to go through."

"I've always heard Belize is a nice place to go to escape." I gave him a half-hearted smile. "I've never been farther from Manhattan than the Catskills or New Jersey."

"When this case is over, how about we visit Belize?" Adam said. "I have plenty of vacation coming."

For just a moment I felt a little lighthearted. Like my mind had taken a brief escape. "I've never worn a bathing suit."

"You sure look great swimming without one, though." Adam said with a look in his eyes that told me he was thinking about our time together in the Catskills. "Although you would look terrific in a little leopard-skin bikini."

I lightly punched his arm. "This isn't the time for thinking about me in a bikini."

"No. It's not." His smile faded. "Nyx . . . I'm starting to care for you too much. I don't know—I just don't know what I'd do if something happened to you."

I froze in my seat. Adam had showed me affection but he'd never said anything like this before. I wasn't sure how to process it.

He put both hands on the wheel and focused on driving. "I've never cared for anyone this way." His gaze remained on the road ahead, then he shoved his fingers through his hair. "And I don't know what to do about it."

I reached for his hand and clasped it in mine again. He looked at me and I pressed my lips against the back of his hand. "We'll just have to work on this together because I feel the same way."

We drove in silence for a while. A comfortable easy silence where we clasped hands and I felt the comfort of his presence. I felt wanted, protected, needed. All of the things I'd pushed aside for so long.

Long before we arrived in Manhattan, I fell asleep with Adam's hand holding mine to keep me from traveling to dark places my mind didn't want to go.

Sunshine did a really poor job of trying to reach me through my bedroom window. The sky was gray but in one spot it looked like the sun was trying to tunnel its way through and it just wasn't working.

I rolled over onto my stomach and looked at the clock. I had a pretty good internal clock, so I couldn't believe it when I saw that it was noon. I'd slept four hours and I didn't feel like I had the luxury of time.

Kali was sitting at the end of the bed, looking regal as ever, and just staring at me.

Purposely I did not think about last night or the wee hours of the morning. I wanted a shred of normalcy, if only for a few moments of make-believe. That everything was going to work out and that no one else was going to be hurt or killed.

"What?" I said to Kali as I scooted up in bed. "I fed you last night before I left."

She looked down her cat nose at me before lightly bounding off the bed and striding out of my room. I blinked as I saw the shredded panties all over my floor. I groaned and flopped back down on my pillow. Not the panties again.

Urgh.

I climbed out of bed and took a hot shower just because it felt good. Elvin cleansing spells were nice, but sometimes the real thing was better.

Especially after last night. I felt like I had so much slimy gunk on my skin from being around the Vampires and seeing what I had seen.

After Adam took me to the Pit, I had debriefed with Rodán. Adam had wanted to take me straight home, but I'd wanted to get that part over with. He'd headed off to the NYPD and I'd gone into the Pit.

When I'd finished telling Rodán everything that had happened, he ordered me to go home and get some sleep because I'd need it. We had a long day and night ahead of us. He would be calling a meeting this evening and then he and I had to appear before the Paranorm Council.

Once I'd dressed and tossed the scraps of panties into the garbage, I grabbed a cereal bar out of my pantry and a bottle of green tea from my fridge. I chased the cereal bar with the tea, then headed downstairs to the office.

The moment I walked into the office, Olivia said, "Turn your purple ass around and head back out."

"Excuse me?" I said as I looked at the dead-serious Olivia. "I know I didn't call, but—"

Olivia turned her large-screen computer monitor toward me. My lips parted and I wanted to take a step back in horror as I read *The New York Times*' online headline:

TWENTY-SEVEN MURDERED CITYWIDE KILLLING SPREE

"That doesn't count all of the missing people." Olivia grabbed her sweat jacket. "Twenty-seven is just the number of bodies found around the city."

I held my hand over my mouth as if that might repress the memories of mere hours ago while trying to pretend I hadn't read a headline and heard the words that came straight out of nightmares.

"Boyd called." Olivia took me by my elbow and turned me back around so that I was headed out the front door instead of in. "He wants us at one of the murder scenes at Amsterdam and 114th Street."

"Columbia University?" I managed to get the words out through my horror as Olivia led me back out into the cold, windy afternoon.

"Five college kids."

I pressed my hand against my belly. If I had taken out those Vampires somehow. If I had used fire to roast them and force them to have to regenerate, maybe the college students and the others wouldn't have had to die.

"You couldn't save them." Olivia's voice was stern as I walked with her toward the garage where I kept my black Corvette. "Boyd filled me in on your adventures last night. I'll kill you later. But for now we need to get to the scene."

I wrapped my arms around myself, drawing my coat

tighter around me. It did nothing for the cold seeping into my bones.

My friend James, a Gorilla Doppler, was a professor in the School of Engineering and Applied Science at Columbia University. I made a mental note to call him to see how things were being handled at the university level. James kept tabs on everything.

I was really missing my XPhone when Olivia drew a new one out of the pocket of her sweat jacket and handed it to me. "Boyd told me what happened to yours," she said as I took it. "You're still going to get your ass kicked, but you might need this at the scene. I set it up and charged it for you while you were resting."

"Thank you." I took the phone and slipped it into my handbag. I would have said how grateful I was, but she might have started kicking my butt right then.

"I even set your ringtone," she said as she gestured to the phone.

I raised my eyebrows as I looked at her.

"George Thorogood's *Bad to the Bone*."

A song played in one of my favorite movies from the eighties, *The Terminator*.

"I sort of feel like a Terminator right now." I clenched my teeth. "And I'm not stopping until I terminate every one of those damned Vampires."

"I'll be right beside you blowing out Vampire hearts," she said.

It took only a few minutes to make it from the office to the university. The scene itself wasn't hard to find. Considering the twenty or so emergency vehicles crowded around.

We had to park so far away we might as well have jogged from our office. All of the flashing emergency lights were enough to cause someone to go into a seizure if they stared at the scene too long.

"This is way too much for one of the Soothsayers to handle." Olivia's breath fogged in the air as she spoke.

"A dozen Soothsayers even," I said

We looked around us at all of the cops and crime scene investigators, news reporters, bystanders, and people who were being interviewed.

I would take Sprite chaos over this horror any day of the week.

"Only because so many people were murdered last night." I gripped my new phone in my pocket and rubbed my thumb over its smooth surface. "Twenty-seven." I kept saying the number over and over in my mind because it was so hard to imagine. Even when we fought the Demons we hadn't lost that many paranorms in one night.

We had to show our PI credentials and shove our way through the crowd and get past the barricade. Olivia called Adam to let him know we'd arrived, and he told us where to meet him.

On the way, we passed a young guy, probably a student, who looked like he'd been up all night drinking. He was sitting on a gurney while paramedics attended to something on his neck and a police officer took notes as he asked the young man questions.

A girl, more than likely a student as well, was on a gurney next to an ambulance, and she was fighting off police officers and ambulance attendants. She was pale, wild-eyed, her whole body shaking. She started screaming for them to let go of her and I turned away as they strapped her to the gurney.

Adam was always all business when we met up on a

case. He cocked his head toward a woman who I recognized as police captain Alex Wysocki. I'd met her once and had liked her genuine, forthright personality. Olivia had an altogether different perspective on the captain, but Olivia had a different perspective on lots of things.

"I think you might want to help me try to explain this to Captain Wysocki," Adam said as he guided us to where the captain stood. "The city is nearly paralyzed," he said as we walked.

"Twenty-seven," I repeated, still unable to comprehend the number.

"Yes, and others missing." Adam's strides were long and Olivia and I had to jog to keep up with him. He was so focused he likely didn't realize it. "We've got a citywide panic with national attention. This morning we thought it was only a few, but bodies keep turning up. Mostly in groups," he added as he gestured toward two body bags being loaded into ambulances.

My stomach ached and my heart hurt as I saw bags disappear into the interiors. "Did those two see it happen? Were they hurt?" I asked as I gestured to the young man and then the young woman. The woman's gurney was being lifted into the ambulance while she screamed.

Adam lowered his voice. "The girl has been hysterical from the moment help arrived and almost incoherent. Every now and then she stops screaming long enough to say a woman with fangs bit her, but there are no marks on her neck."

He gave a short nod to the guy. "That student has two puncture wounds, the wounds still bleeding when we got here."

"The Vampires could have started the process to turn those two." I looked from one student to the other. "I think it only takes two bites. They may plan to find these students again. From what I've learned in the past, once Vampires bite a human, there's some kind of connection that lets them find the human again."

"Shit." Adam scrubbed his hand over his face. "On top of that, five students, dead. Three appear to have been drained completely of blood, another victim's throat was gouged out, and one"—he looked at me like he didn't want to say the rest—"one torn apart."

I swallowed back the desire to throw up. If only I could have destroyed them last night, this would never have happened. None of this.

"What's up, Boyd?" Wysocki said to Adam after acknowledging Olivia and me with a nod.

The police captain was tall and slender, her blond hair short and smooth. She was feminine in appearance but her voice was hard, a seasoned officer who didn't put up with anyone's bullshit, as Olivia would say.

"Got any damned thing for me? You said on the phone you knew something about this," Wysocki added.

"You're not going to find this easy to get down." Adam looked at Olivia and me as we stood close to her. He looked back to the chief, his features hard, tense.

"Vampires, Captain Wysocki," he said. "We're dealing with honest-to-God Vampires."

NINETEEN

Captain Wysocki stared at Adam, an even harder look on her features than before. "I don't have time for this, Boyd. I've got thirty-one confirmed dead now. Sixteen missing."

Thirty-one dead? My whole body wanted to convulse. Sixteen missing?

"He's telling the truth." I stepped forward trying to control my shaking. "I've dealt with them before."

"Before? Bullshit." The way the captain looked at me I could tell that my words meant nothing to her. After all, I was a PI, not a police officer.

The captain's attention snapped to Olivia when my partner raised her voice and said, "Boyd and Nyx aren't imagining things and they're not making shit up."

Wysocki took her gaze from Olivia to Adam and back, not even looking at me. I didn't care, I just wanted her to believe us.

"DeSantos, I've never known you or Boyd to be delusional." Wysocki gave a sharp nod to one of the officers who called to her before she returned her attention to us. "But right now I want to know what you've been smoking."

"You may not believe us now," I said, "but when you see more bodies turn up like this, you're going to wonder if we're right about what we're telling you.

"That girl." I pointed to where the student's ambulance was just starting to leave. "There are no marks, but she probably *was* bitten. Vampires have healing power in their saliva. All they have to do is lick a wound and it heals."

The captain looked ready to draw the Glock beneath her jacket and shoot us. "I'm going to have all of your asses—"

"The others," Olivia interrupted, "bite marks, mutilation, things no human being should be able to do. Vampires are powerful and vicious."

"I think the Vampires let those two live as a message," I said. "They want people to know it was them, that they're back and they think they can do whatever they want to."

I continued, "You might not want to hear it but if those students get bitten a second time and become fully infected, it would be better for both of them, and for all of us, if they were dead."

"What the hell?" Wysocki looked at Adam. "Get these two out of here, Boyd, before I put you on involuntary leave."

"We need you need to listen." Adam held his ground without giving an inch. "Give us five minutes."

The captain narrowed her eyes. "I'll give you three minutes to convince me why I should believe you."

Adam dragged his hand down his face in a frustrated movement.

Olivia returned Wysocki's hard look. "That's not enough time but we'll give you the best summary we can."

"There's a whole paranormal world that hardly anyone

is aware of," Adam said. "Those of us who do—we're sworn to secrecy. It's the only way the paranorms will let us help protect norms—I mean our citizens."

"Paranorms. Norms. Right." I heard the sarcasm in her voice when she stared at me. "Okay, so you say we have Vampires to blame. How about giving every officer a few cloves of garlic, some holy water, and a cross?"

"The Vampires will just feel a little sick," I said. "Those things don't actually stop them. Don't come close to stopping them."

"We're serious, Captain," Adam said.

"What Boyd's trying to say is that there's shit out there you can't begin to imagine," Olivia cut in. "We don't have enough time to explain, and honestly, you don't have time to listen to it all. We're telling you because you need to know what in the hell is happening."

The hardass captain looked conflicted. It was in her eyes, something I'd never have believed before.

"Vampires were defeated in a paranorm rebellion in the eighteen-hundreds," I said, hoping that I was helping, not making things worse. "We thought we had them under control until now."

I think the only reason why the captain looked like she was even considering what I had to say was because Adam and Olivia had started speaking first.

"Long story," Adam said. "But the Vampires have possession of something that makes it damn near impossible for paranorms to control them anymore."

"No," I said. "It makes it *completely* impossible for us to control them."

"Us?" Wysocki frowned at me. " 'Us' as in 'us paranorms'?" She didn't miss anything, did she.

I didn't answer and Adam said, "The paranorms are

working on a way to stop the Vampires. Because they're supernatural beings, it's not going to be easy."

"Supernatural beings." The captain shook her head. "If I did believe you, what could the NYPD do?"

"Figure out a way to keep people off the streets at night," Adam said.

"By telling the people of Manhattan that Vampires are responsible for all of the attacks and missing persons?" Wysocki looked even more grim. "That's not going to fly."

"I know that, Captain," Adam said. "Some other way, but any way possible to keep more people from being slaughtered."

Captain Wysocki put her hands on her hips, pushing aside her jacket. "I'm going to do what I can," she said. "Not necessarily because I might believe you. Because there's something out there and we need to keep the people safe. I've never known you to be crazy, Boyd. It sounds outrageous, but possibly wannabe vampires out there at least think they really are Vampires. After looking at the results of these attacks, I will at least give you that."

"They'll kill cops, too," Adam said. "Hollowpoints to the heart are the only thing that will stop Vampires, but won't necessarily kill them."

"Cutting off their heads will do it, though," I said. "Or a stake to the heart."

Wysocki gave me a strange look, then glanced from Adam to Olivia. "I'll do what I can and you do whatever you need to and keep me updated," she said to them. "But you say one word to any other law enforcement officer or public figure and your asses are mine."

"You bet, Captain." Olivia's sarcasm matched Wysocki's earlier comments. "And while you're at it—"

I caught Olivia by the upper arm and jerked her away from Wysocki before she could put us under the police captain's gauntlet with her big mouth—it was likely a good thing for Olivia that she was no longer a NYPD officer.

"Thanks," Adam said to Wysocki. "We've got one hell of a lot of work to do. I'll let you know when we have something."

Wysocki gave a brief nod and turned away. She'd given us more than three minutes of her time, but I didn't think it had been enough to truly convince the captain that Vampires were responsible for all of the murders and the missing.

Rodán and I approached the Alice in Wonderland unbirthday party sculpture but he stopped, bringing us both up short.

"Nyx." He took my hands in his as we stood on grass. "Be careful on this case."

"I'm always careful." I kissed his cheek. "Thank you."

"Are you all right?" Rodán said as he studied me.

I shook my head. "New York City is paralyzed." I swallowed, anger and fear like a vise clamped around my throat. "Everyone in the city is talking, wondering what's going on."

"We will prevail." Rodán squeezed my fingers. "Do not lose hope now."

"I've never felt this way." I took my hands from his. "It feels wrong. So horribly, horribly wrong. And humans—"

I rubbed my forehead with my fingertips. "It's crazy. Newscasters are even reporting wild rumors that what the norms call 'cult groups' of wannabe Vampires are responsible. If they only knew, New Yorkers would be more terrified than they already are."

"We will get the serum and the antiserum," Rodán said. "You must have confidence in that."

"I have never seen the city like this." Something in me kept rejecting what Rodán was saying. It was the first time in my life that I had felt any sense of hopelessness or helplessness. Somehow this seemed more powerful of a threat than anything I had ever seen, including Demons.

A prickling sensation crawled up my back. I put my hand on my dagger at the same time I whirled around to face the empty park. Rodán turned at the same time I did.

"Pardon," came a voice before Negel appeared in front of me.

I wanted to put my hand to my pounding heart, but I gripped the hilt of my dagger instead. "Have you ever heard of strike first, ask questions later?" I said. "You might think about letting a Tracker know you're there with a little more advance warning."

"My apologies." The Sprite did look sorry as he gazed at me with his big bulbous eyes. "I guess I was so excited to see you I didn't think. I have been waiting here to talk with council members as they enter." His ears drooped. "I could not even get one to accept my offer to help or to acknowledge my sincerest apologies for the despicable acts of some of my people."

"Why didn't you contact me?" I asked. "I could have talked with them for you."

He held up a cell phone. "I tried to call."

"Oh." I put my hand on my new replacement XPhone. "I have a new number."

His cell phone disappeared into his rags. "I wanted to attend the council meeting myself."

"It's a secret, urgent, last-minute, emergency meeting." I stared at the Sprite. "How did you find out about it to begin with?"

"We are often overlooked," Negel said. "But we are also often at the right place at the right time."

"Uh-huh." I put my hands on my hips. "I don't think the council will allow you to attend. Sprites aren't exactly welcome and these council members aren't the friendliest or most inviting types."

Which was understandable—considering—and obvious from the council members' response, or lack of.

Negel straightened and raised his chin. "It was my people's fault. We are not evil and we must make amends."

I relaxed. The Sprite had just caught me off guard. "It was brave of you to show up here considering all that Sprites had been up to lately."

"You don't understand," Negel said. "I would give my life for this cause and to, in some way, right the wrongs that a few of my people have caused. The ones who are not truly representative of us."

"It takes time to overcome many years of prejudice," Rodán said. "We will do what we can to right that wrong that has been done to your people. But that may take time."

"We are mischievous, that is true," Negel said. "Strange to many. But we are not evil."

Negel shook his head, his eyes looking big in the night. "We are not evil as a whole. Tobath became intoxicated with the power he thought he had. But he was not us. I want to help and I will do whatever it takes." The Sprite took a deep, audible breath. "Including giving my life to right this horrible wrong. Please . . . let me help."

The intensity of the Sprite's declaration and his plea tugged at my heart. "Thank you, Negel."

"I admire and trust you," he said, looking at me.

"It means a lot to me that you would say that." I smiled. "You have no idea."

"You deserve it," he said. "That is how I feel."

Funny how a Sprite was giving me the warm fuzzies when just days ago I was ready to staple them all to every billboard in Times Square.

"I would like to help you tonight," Negel said. "I know you will go after the Vampires."

I narrowed my eyes. Warm fuzzies versus undisclosed information . . .

"Thanks, Negel, but not tonight," I said. "You're not a Tracker and I can't be worrying about your safety and still do my job."

"I do not need watching after." Negel straightened and raised his chin. Maybe he was regretting being so nice.

"I know and I apologize." I rubbed my temples with my thumb and forefinger. "Just not tonight, okay?"

He gave a brief nod before he turned his attention to Rodán. "I will get back to you," Negel added before he vanished.

My stomach hadn't settled since last night, and I didn't think it was going to any time soon as I stood before the Paranorm Council and waited for my turn to speak.

I felt nervous, off-kilter, anxious to meet with the other Night Trackers and make plans. This meeting would be a waste of time because Trackers would do what we had to do regardless of what the council had to say.

Rodán stood next to me, the only Peacekeeper other than myself at the secretive council meeting. His long blond hair was a sleek, shining stream down his back and his features regal. As usual his expression revealed nothing of what he was thinking. His flesh was golden next to my pale amethyst skin and his robes were almost the same cobalt blue as my hair.

Smells of smoke and crushed rose petals hung heavy in the air, the light trails of smoke coming from torches burning in brackets along the medieval-looking walls. Shadows cast by the torchlight gave the warm chamber an eerie feel that added to the crawling sensation along my skin.

Council Chief Leticia, a Doppler, perched on a throne at the center of the crescent-shaped table. Leticia was not only the chief, but she represented all Dopplers. Generally a peaceful race of beings, Dopplers were usually the easiest group of paranorms to get along with.

Like I'd explained to Joshua, out of all fifteen-plus races of Fae, a Siren had been voted in as their representative. How I don't know, but that's how it was. Bethany was gorgeous—as a Siren that really went without saying—but I'd never liked the haughtiness in her sea-blue eyes.

Even though there are a number of different kinds of Weres, they didn't seem to mind that Eric, a Werewolf, was the envoy for all Weres.

The elderly Shifter, Reginald, who represented all Shifters, including Shadow Shifters, was tight-faced. As in his whole face seemed drawn forward, lines and wrinkles coming to a point at his nose and lips.

Dark Elves didn't generally get into Otherworld politics, but my father had expressed his displeasure that one of the Light Elves, Caolan, was the delegate for all Elves, Dark and Light.

My father had ranted about that for a good two weeks before he pretty much disavowed anything to do with a council that would allow Light Elves to represent Dark Elves, too.

My skin felt hot and it itched more as I thought about how soon the Vampires might be out to feed on norms. It was just after sundown—I'd barely had time to shift—and time for Vampires to wake from their sleep in the catacombs.

Trackers had seen Vampires attack norms from about ten at night to three in the morning. Before and after those times, things were usually quiet on the Vampire front.

But who knew what they'd do now?

I glanced at Rodán to see him studying the five council members, as if to gauge their abilities to understand what we had to tell them.

It wasn't that long ago that I'd helped save all of their lives, but you wouldn't know it to see the way they were looking down their noses at me now. Arrogant, egotistical—

Council Chief Leticia settled her gaze on me and I could see *her* appreciation. Out of all of the council members, Leticia was the only one who truly knew what the Trackers had done that night, because she'd actually been there.

The rest of the council members seemed clueless to the fact that if the Trackers hadn't saved their lives, then they'd all be mere memories right now and paranorms would have been governed by a bunch of Metamorphs.

"Nyx of the Night Trackers," Leticia began. "Thank you for your prompt appearance at this emergency council meeting."

The Siren, Bethany, who represented all Fae spoke up. "Tell us what you know about the Vampire situation."

Situation? Vampire *situation*? Bethany lost major points with that description of the devastation and the threat to paranormkind that was happening right now.

Without the usual formalities of addressing each council member, I began speaking. "We are facing a threat more devastating to all paranorms than anything we have faced before." I managed to keep my voice steady as I spoke.

Bethany frowned but we didn't have time for formalities and tradition and I wasn't going to give in to it.

"The decision to keep the paranorm virus to create an antiserum was a huge mistake," I said and then realized my own mistake when I saw the council members bristle like a bunch of male peacocks.

In his calm yet powerful way, Rodán took over. He spoke formally as he usually did when in front of a bunch of paranorm bureaucrats. "You have already been informed that the Vampires now have both the serum and the antiserum. Nyx and I are here to provide you with any information you believe you need and to answer any questions you might have."

"We will be working on a plan to stop the Vampires." I wanted to get past the explaining part. We didn't have time for that. "The Night Trackers are meeting after Rodán and I return from this session."

The Shifter council member looked like he was starting to speak, so I hurried to talk. "What the Vampires are doing is beyond atrocious."

Can't show weakness. They would trample me with their bureaucratic boots if I did.

The doors of the chamber opened and the council members frowned when a young Shifter messenger girl jogged to the front of the room, carrying a piece of paper.

"This had better be extremely important." The elderly Shifter council member, Reginald, looked down his long pointed nose at the messenger. "You are disturbing a most important meeting."

The girl bit her lower lip but went to the back of the crescent-shaped table and handed Council Chief Leticia the piece of paper. The messenger waited beside Leticia's chair as the council chief read the note.

Leticia's expression shifted to a mixture of concern and alarm before settling into a businesslike demeanor again. She passed the piece of paper to the council members on her left and then the paper was sent to the right side of the table so that all council members were able to read it.

Varying shades of concern, anxiety, and anger radiated from the members. They conferred in low voices but I caught the words "Volod," "demands," "now," and "must."

Leticia took the piece of paper and the quill in front of her and dipped it in the inkwell. She wrote something on the bottom of the paper before folding it in half and handing it back to the girl with a brief nod.

The Shifter girl jogged back through the open doors of the chamber before they were closed behind her.

I barely kept from pressing my palm to my belly that was queasy from nerves—and something else. The sensations now in my mind and body reminded me of how I'd felt just before one of my closest friends, Caprice, was murdered by Demons.

At that time it had felt like a premonition, like something extremely bad was about to happen. And something beyond horrible did happen and Caprice lost her life because of it. In the end I hadn't been able to save her.

This time I was sure the feeling was because I knew

devastation for all paranorms was going to come to pass if we didn't stop the Vampires.

"It appears we will now have a meeting with the Master Vampire and we will bring in our bargaining chip, so to speak," said the council chief. I'd heard Leticia was a gambler, so I wasn't surprised by her analogy. She made a gesture to the guards behind me and I looked over my shoulder.

Shocked couldn't begin to describe how I felt when the chamber doors were opened and Danut was led through by two Doppler guards.

They had put Danut into a compression suit.

Not just any compression suit, but one made especially for Vampires. It was like a norm straightjacket, but with very important enhancements. A cross was fastened to the front of the suit, the cross burning the Vampire if he made any quick movements.

Garlic cloves and holy water filled the lining, the mixture making the Vampire in the suit perpetually ill and weakened. Danut looked like a human who'd been drinking too much alcohol then slept in the gutter, a side effect of the holy water/garlic mix.

Two more enhancements were even more vital. So that the Vampire in the suit couldn't be helped out of it, there was a Dryad-wood piece infused with Dryad magic and fastened over the Vampire's heart. The moment a being other than a Doppler PTF agent tried to take the suit off of the Vampire, the wood disc expanded into an eight-inch stake that immediately pierced the Vamp's heart.

If for some reason *that* failed, what was around the Vampires neck likely wouldn't fail. It was a thin metal wire made from an alloy mined by the Dark Elves. If triggered by an escape attempt, the band contracted and the Vampire's head was cut off.

I wished Volod and every one of his followers were in those suits—just before both the stakes and the collars were triggered. But right now, this was insane.

"Bargaining chip . . ." I stared at Danut who appeared too ill to recognize me. "No." I turned to face the council. "Holding Volod's brother hostage is going to make things a lot worse."

The council members looked taken aback.

"The Drow female is correct."

At the sound of the Master Vampire's voice I whirled to face him, one hand going to my buckler, the other to one of my dragon-clawed daggers. What was Volod doing here?

Volod appeared calm but fury radiated from him, a heavy layer beneath that calm veneer. The air was so tense around him I felt like something was going to explode.

Two Vampires were with him, one standing to either side of him. Elizabeth and Drago.

Elizabeth wore a sparkling sequined gown of bronze that would have looked stunning with her red hair and fair complexion—if she wasn't an evil being.

Her brother, Drago, emanated power that was only superseded by Volod's.

My heart pounded and I gathered my elements around me, drawing them to me and strengthening me.

Next to me, I felt Rodán's magic grow along with my own. His magic was a tangible, powerful thing. But would his kind of magic work now? As much as I wanted to believe it could, I didn't truly think so.

Volod strode forward, with sweeping looks at everyone in the room.

The Master Vampire gave an arrogant sneer. "Looks like a little party. Another party we Vampires were not invited to. All you paranorms should just post a sign above your doors, 'Vampires Not Invited'. Doesn't really matter anymore, however, as you will soon find out. We are here to stay whether invited or not."

The Master Vampire reached into his pant pocket. My body went cold as he brought out a small syringe filled with an all-too-familiar green fluid.

Volod tapped the safety cap at the end of the needle. "I am not here to bargain."

TWENTY

"Thank you for honoring my request for an audience with the council." Volod tossed the folded note on the floor in front of him. The note slid across the stone, coming to stop before the council table. The note. How could the council have allowed him in here?

Elizabeth looked at me with hate in her green eyes and I remembered her determination to bleed me dry to avenge her cousin's death. Drago's green eyes were narrowed at me, too.

Considering Volod had it in for me they might as well get in line.

Then the Master Vampire's eyes met mine. The intensity of his gaze nearly made me look away, but I held my own.

As he stared at me, blood rushed in my ears and I began to feel lightheaded. Dizzy.

Volod. He was doing something to me with his mental powers. I could feel him trying to get inside my head. I could see his black eyes. Feel the darkness inside of him trying to get into me.

I had to get my concentration back and control my emotions. But still fear clawed at me. I threw up my air shield with as much power as I could channel.

Volod looked as if he'd been slapped.

Relief flooded my body to have his horrible blackness out of me. It had felt . . . dead to have him inside my mind. It was a feeling I never wanted to experience again.

His recovery from his surprise was almost instant. So fast that I didn't think anyone else but me—and possibly Rodán—could have seen it.

The Master Vampire turned to look at the council in a deceptively casual manner, as if dismissing me. "You will release my brother, or"—he looked at the syringe and then back to the council—"I will inject a paranorm and release him into paranorm society. If you try and do anything to me here, my brothers have been instructed to do the injection for me."

I could almost hear the collective intake of breath by the council.

"We do not negotiate with terrorists." The Shifter council member's pinched face looked pale but stolid.

"A terrorist? Call me what you will, it does not matter." Volod gave the Shifter a look that was so dark I wondered if he was doing the same thing to the Shifter as he had to me. "But as I said, I am not here to negotiate."

Volod then met each council member's eyes. "You should be well aware of what could happen to all paranorms who carry the mutated gene if this virus is released."

"Set the Vampire free." Rodán spoke with his usual calm exterior. He could not possibly have been so calm inside. Or was he? "The Vampire called Danut has no value to us in the given situation."

The council members looked at each other. One at a time, the members gave Leticia a nod before she made a gesture to the Doppler guards who held Danut.

"Release the prisoner." It was obvious the words were sour on Leticia's tongue as she said what she did not want to.

The guards turned and faced Danut, then each put a hand on the cross at the front of the compression suit. Danut took a sharp intake of breath as they removed the cross from the suit and one of the Doppler guards pocketed it.

Danut's eyes remained crazed and he still appeared sick.

The guards each put a hand on Danut's shoulders. Simultaneously they spoke a chant in an ancient language that I didn't know but had heard somewhere in Otherworld. The Dopplers' voices were low and I could barely hear them, even with my enhanced hearing.

Volod never took his gaze from his brother who seemed to be in a complete stupor.

When the guards finished the chant, the thin band around the neckline split in half and retreated into the suit. The compression suit itself went slack and the guards began to take it off Danut, sliding it off his shoulders and then pulling his arms out of it.

The moment the suit was off Danut, the guards let him go, not bothering to help him stand. Danut stumbled forward and he dropped to his knees. His eyes began to look less crazed, less glassy.

Drago left Volod's side, went to Danut, and picked the Vampire up under his arms. Using his Vampire strength, Drago made it look as if Danut weighed nothing. Drago put Danut's arm over his shoulders and half-carried the Vampire who stumbled as they rejoined Volod, then stood behind him.

As Volod watched Drago and his brother, fury clearly rose in him, and I could tell the anger was close to making him snap. "I should punish one of your own right now for what you did to my brother."

No one said a word. The chamber was silent except for the pop and hiss of the torches in their brackets. That sound seemed suddenly too loud to bear.

"Injecting a paranorm is an extreme measure, of course." Volod's jaw tightened as he seemed to rein in his anger. "But it is one we are prepared to take."

He held up his hand as if to stop anyone from speaking. "We also know every paranorm's weakness thanks to information also provided to us from the Sprites, which they gained from your very archives."

Volod didn't have to tell anyone not to speak because it was as if something held us all in silence. "We will use those weaknesses against any individual being who goes against us."

"What is it you have to present before the council?" Leticia finally said.

"You will listen to our demands." Volod's fangs gleamed in the torchlight and he looked like he was ready to start ripping out throats.

"What are those demands?" Leticia said with a calm that I had to give her credit for.

"You will no longer hunt my kind." He looked directly at me. "Trackers will never harm another Vampire."

Angry words stuck in my throat as I did my best not to show any kind of emotion that would betray what my thoughts were at that moment.

Volod rolled the syringe in his palm and I caught my breath. What if he dropped it, broke it open somehow, released a drop?

He returned his gaze to the council. "Vampires are to be left alone to be as we were meant to be."

"May I ask what that is?" Leticia said.

"We will feed on humans at will," he said, and a word Olivia frequently used went through my mind but I didn't say it out loud. No way was that going to happen—I wasn't about to let it. "We will also choose qualified humans and turn them into Vampires to improve our ranks."

Reginald thumped his fist on the crescent table. "We cannot allow you to slaughter or infect humans to turn them."

"Allow?" Volod cocked an eyebrow. "The question is, will you be the first paranorm we inject if anyone tries to stop us?"

The elderly council member's lips tightened into a thin line and he didn't say anything else.

Council Chief Leticia folded her hands on the table. Her knuckles were white. "If humans are hunted, not only is it a horror I would not wish on any being, but it may expose the paranorm world to norm scrutiny. It could harm our way of life."

"A horror?" Volod's lips curled back, exposing all of his teeth as well as his fangs. "They are a food source. There are so many humans that it makes no difference when we take the lives of a relative few."

"All lives are important," I said even though I should probably have kept my mouth shut. "Don't you have the tiniest bit of humanity left in you? After all you were once human."

"Watch yourself." Volod hissed the "S" as he bared his fangs at me. "You have been in my way far too often, purple one."

Rodán applied light pressure to my wrist, telling me without words not to say anything else.

Volod turned his gaze back to the council members.

"Vampires will also have a seat on the Paranorm Council, meaning that I will represent my kind.

"You will be permitted your votes on any issues which will not impact the Vampires, and I will abstain from voting. I could care less about any of you paranorms or your issues unless they affect my kind and you can be of service to me. Therefore my vote on anything I chose to vote on shall be considered the majority."

I thought Reginald was going to self-combust as Volod spoke. The Shifter's mouth tightened until I couldn't see his lips anymore.

"As a matter of fact," Volod continued. "I will serve as council chief, replacing Leticia."

I found myself admiring Leticia more and more for her calm, strength, and aplomb as she said, "We will take your requests under consideration."

"My dear Leticia." Volod laughed in a way that sounded almost friendly. "Your humor does my undead heart good. You know of course these are not requests. This is how it will be from this point on. We do not fear you or any paranorm."

He gestured with the syringe as he talked. "As a matter of fact, I have more to explain to you." Still gripping the syringe of green death, Volod started to pace before the council. "Paranorms will live their lives. We will live ours. However," he said, "we may need or want things from the paranorms. We will make that clear at the time."

Volod continued his slow pacing. "We have a list we will produce. But for now that can wait. Our major demand and law now, is that no Vamp will be investigated, detained, arrested, prosecuted, or persecuted," he said.

"We will control our own." Volod seemed positively

happy at the moment, obviously feeling that he had the entire upper hand. "We have our own rule of law as well. We shall pursue and punish anyone who comes against us." He looked at me. "The Trackers will assist in those situations and report to me."

"Trackers report to you? No way." I was incredulous, but I shut up when Rodán squeezed my wrist again.

"Especially you." Volod smiled. "And I shall take great pleasure in punishing you. I know your weaknesses, Drow Tracker."

My face went hot. The thought of my weaknesses being used against me made me want to throw up. To be completely helpless, useless . . . I couldn't let that happen again.

"Actually"—he tilted his head and looked as if he was considering something—"for your transgressions against us, purple one, I should take you now for persecution. However, I sense we will meet again and we will be at odds."

My skin went from hot to cold with every word he spoke. "I took care of you once," he said. "The next time you cross me you will be committing suicide . . . and it will not be a pleasant end for you. You cannot win."

Volod took a step forward. With the nightmare look of death—death for me—on his pale features, I barely kept myself from backing up.

"Do you understand, Tracker?" He said "Tracker" in a growl.

Rage poured through me. The desire to destroy him, destroy all Vampires was so strong I wanted to do it now. But I was powerless at this point and time.

"Do you hear me? Do you understand?" Volod raised

the syringe, a look of fury on his features. "I want an answer from you, purple bitch."

I forced myself to nod.

"I want to hear your answer." Volod's voice sounded like thunder, reverberating through the room.

"Yes." I spit out the word. "I understand."

Satisfaction relaxed his features and my fingers itched to go to my daggers.

I had never felt so helpless while still having all of my powers available to me. I could do nothing. Nothing.

"My brethren have much to accomplish tonight." Danut gave a slight bow to the council. "I will be calling a council meeting soon at which you will swear me in as Leticia's replacement."

Volod started to turn away, then paused. "If anyone follows us or tries to locate the whereabouts of the serum or antiserum—it will mean their death."

Silence as Volod passed through the doors. Then Elizabeth, Drago and Danut left, Drago supporting Danut, helping him leave the chamber. No one said a word until the council doors slammed shut behind the Vampires.

Rodán leaned close and pressed his lips to my ear. "Your team awaits you at the bank on the northern end of Conservatory Water. They are in their natural forms so the Vampires should pass them without sensing them."

I nodded and kept my voice as low as his. "Olivia and Adam?"

"I felt this too dangerous for humans." He drew away. "Your friends will not be pleased, but it is for the best."

"I agree." I turned and gave a slight bow to the council. "Thank you for the audience," I said before I hurried toward the huge chamber doors. The guards opened them, letting me out even as I heard protests from the council members that they still needed to discuss the situation with me.

Rodán would handle them and relay anything that needed to be discussed.

My heart seemed to permanently be flying as fast as my feet flew as I rushed up the stairs. I wrapped myself in a glamour before I exited the door at the back of Alice's unbirthday party.

When I reached the bank of the northern end of Conservatory Water, Mandisa approached me from out of the darkness, her bow and quiver full of arrows slung across her back.

A bunny hopped forward and grew, slowly transforming into Kelly. Joshua rose from the shadows and Ice landed in a run as he shifted from a falcon to his human form.

Nadia walked from my left, her slim serpent swords glittering in the park's low lighting. A Siamese cat gave a meow before Lawan took the place of the cat. A wolf seemed to appear from nowhere, then the Werewolf, Ondrej, was where the wolf had been standing.

"We don't have a lot of time," I said as my team gathered around me. "As long as the serum and antiserum are in the Vampires' hands we're powerless to stop them from slaughtering humans."

"Where do we start?" Kelly said with an intense expression.

It shouldn't have amazed me how professional Kelly became once she was tracking. Kelly was all business, her attitude completely at odds with her behavior when not tracking.

Of course Rodán would pick no one who wasn't a team player when out on the field. I'd learned that with Ice during the Werewolf op. He might be a real jerk, but he was one kickass team player on a mission. I would choose to have him at my back any day.

I addressed the seven team members who were present, looking at them one at a time as I spoke. "I have a lot of information to share but not the luxury of time to give more than a brief rundown."

They remained silent as I updated them, obviously recognizing the fact that interruptions would hinder our mission.

Being as brief as possible, I told them about my chase after Drago to Volod's pyramid compound in New Jersey. I explained what I had seen there and what I had learned. I ended my briefing with what had happened in the council meeting. By the time I had finished, each member of my team looked grimmer than ever.

"We need to get to the pyramid as soon as possible and find that serum and antiserum," I said. "Using the transference, I will reach the compound first, Ice likely second traveling by air. The rest of you will need to find some pretty fast transportation."

"You shouldn't go ahead of us, Nyx." Nadia didn't look pleased with me at all. "We can go together. We're safer as a team, not any one of us on our own."

"I'm going in for reconnaissance," I said. "I'll wait for backup before I enter the pyramid."

"You should not even be inside the compound," Lawan said. "Wait for us."

"I am your team leader." My tone was firm, emphasizing the fact that I wasn't about to change my mind. "No arguments. Get there as fast as you can."

I told them where to ditch and hide their rides, and how to enter the compound where they wouldn't be seen.

"We may be rushing things, but the sooner we recover the serum before they move it the better. I'll try and rely on glamour and speed. Therefore, for this part of the op," I said, "I would prefer going it alone and doing the recon myself. However, Rodán insists I go with my team."

"Damned right he should," Joshua said.

I chose to ignore him. "You'll be there if I need you. We can't afford more than just one paranorm inside the pyramid tonight," I said. "It's too dangerous. These Vampires have a power sense I never knew existed. After I'm through inside, I'll meet you in the area of dense trees just northwest of the main garage entrance."

Nadia looked both concerned and upset with me as I backed away. Maybe it was anger toward Volod, maybe it was the sense of urgency in saving lives. Maybe it was the fear in losing the opportunity of knowing that the serums were in that pyramid. Whatever it was, all I could think of was that I needed to do something now.

"If I don't come out within an hour after you arrive, send a two-man team in to look." I pointed to Joshua and Ice. "You two—you'll be that team. As shadow and as a mouse, they shouldn't be able to detect you."

I explained how to get in and showed them a basic layout of the pyramid which I'd sketched and saved in my phone. Then I sent the drawing to their own XPhones to have with them.

"Volod should get back to his compound in forty-five minutes at best," I said as I started to mentally prepare myself for the transference. "That means I'll have that long to do some recon before I meet all of you."

The whole team looked unhappy with the plan to let me go ahead. Mandisa had her eyes narrowed as she studied me and I could see even she was displeased with my decision.

I could feel my fear of Volod diminish somehow as I thought of the unspeakable evil he represented. I had to have more information and I had to have it now, so that a plan to defeat that evil could be outlined and pursued. I felt the world as we knew it depended upon it.

Only yesterday I'd been in the pyramid, so I didn't feel like I was taking a big risk.

It was time to do the transference. By focus, thought, and magic, I would move myself from Central Park to Volod's lair.

I closed my eyes and concentrated on my memory of the catacombs. With all of its nooks and hidden corners, I would easily hide be able to in there.

The sense of my team members still around me gradually grew dim. My awareness of them completely faded as the intensity of my focus grew.

The image of the catacombs grew stronger in my mind. Stronger and stronger yet.

Then I was flying through darkness, spinning. Air compressed around me, squeezing the breath from me. My elements were not my friends during the transference, that much I had realized the first time I spun through the black void.

My hands and knees hit hard-packed earth as I came out of the transference. The impact jarred my head and dizziness made my mind spin. Vomit rose up in my throat in a rush. Pressure kept my eyelids shut as I lost what I'd eaten for dinner.

I was vaguely aware of my surroundings. Without opening my eyes, I knew I'd made it into the catacombs and that nothing living was near me.

But then I tried to get up too fast, before I'd caught

my breath and before my limbs had recovered enough to support my body.

This time my face hit the dirt along with the rest of me. Even as I struggled to regain consciousness my mind was slipping closer and closer to darkness.

TWENTY-ONE

I hate the transference, was my first thought as I opened my eyes and spit the acidic taste out of my mouth. I wiped the back of my hand across my lips before I raised my head and realized I had passed out. *I really need to work on that*, I thought.

My internal clock told me I'd been out for a good half hour.

Not good. Really not good. That meant I only had fifteen minutes at most before Volod arrived. So much for using the transference to get here faster.

I clenched my teeth together. How could I have let myself pass out? I'm a Drow warrior. Drow warriors don't pass out.

Apparently this one did.

I pushed myself up to my hands and knees and glanced around the part of the catacombs I was in. I frowned. My photographic memory didn't recognize whatever part of the catacombs I was in. I knew I hadn't seen the coffin standing against the wall nearby, that was for sure. It was funny to think of a Vampire sleeping standing up. Wasn't that just for Mummies?

At least I made it into the general vicinity of where I'd wanted to—I hoped. By the strong smells of graveyard dirt, must, and age, I knew that yes, I was in the right place. Not to mention all of the nooks and crannies and the coffins around me.

A rat was the only creature I sensed near me, nothing else. I was safe for now. no other living beings were around.

My eyes widened as a coffin in front of me started to open.

It was then that I remembered Vampires didn't qualify as the living.

I had been about to get to my feet but I froze, still on my hands and knees next to the remnants of my supper.

Cold realization washed through me. I could have been in a roomful of Vampires and I wouldn't have sensed anything living because I'd been paying attention to the wrong senses. Something about the transference had knocked a wire loose in my brain, apparently.

Every coffin around me could contain a Vampire. I could be in a nest of them for all I knew.

I froze as I heard a sound to my left. As a Vampire climbed out of the coffin, I wrapped myself in a glamour, but I was sure the Vampire would be able to smell the vomit.

If I hurried at least he wouldn't see it. I whispered, "*Avanna*," and the Elvin cleansing spell erased all traces from the dirt and from me.

The Vampire was a male, a tall one, dressed in a tux. Some of these Vamps appeared to be so pretentious it was almost funny. But there was not a single thing to laugh about in this whole ordeal.

When he was on his feet, the Vampire straightened the jacket of his tux, including the sleeves and then the wrists. His hair was parted slightly to the side and had a slight wave to it. He had the appearance of someone in his mid-thirties from the roaring twenties. I almost expected a female Vampire "flapper" to climb out of the coffin next to him.

When he was finished primping himself, the male paused. Sniffed the air. He frowned and wrinkled his nose like he smelled something really bad. He looked in my direction and scowled before he walked my way.

I rolled to the side away from him, then scrambled to my feet. The Vampire looked at the earth in the spot where I'd just cleaned up the mess. He paused a moment, then seemed to give a mental shrug and strode on through the catacombs.

Before I followed him, I dusted dirt from my leather pants, more from an absentminded action than from the need to get dust off me. I jogged after the Vampire who had disappeared around one of the corners.

The coffins in this part of the catacombs were old, covered in cobwebs and a thick layer of dust. Elaborate coffins were obviously for wealthier Vampires, where the plain wood ones likely housed those who'd had little money. Vampires apparently had a social structure even when it came to coffins.

There were more different types of coffins than I'd ever imagined, reflecting styles of the times throughout the ages. I thought of what I'd told Nadia about how Vampires came to sleep in coffins. Taking it to their graves had a whole new meaning when it came to humans being turned to Vampires.

I kept a good distance behind Mr. Roaring Twenties while taking inventory of where I was and what was around me. The earth sloped upward and I realized we were farther under the building than I had gone before.

The Vampire rounded a corner but I came to a stop. I sensed something strong, something powerful.

Now that I was focused on the undead, I sensed Volod. Not the Vampire himself, but his essence, his scent. I closed my eyes and reached out with my senses and my elements and found what I was looking for. A private chamber was behind a series of cubbyholes and twists and turns.

This chamber was larger than any of the other places in the catacombs. I peeked around the arch leading into the chamber and saw a polished black coffin in the center. It was simple yet elegant, and still masculine.

Volod's coffin.

It was open, obviously because Volod wasn't there. I walked over to it and almost touched the gleaming surface but drew my hand back before my fingers brushed it. The inside of the coffin was lined in white pillowed satin with red accents. Dark Elves mine not only metals but jewels, and the red accents were blood-red rubies.

How difficult would it be to come back after Volod had taken to his coffin, open it, and stake him?

No time for fantasies. I needed to do my recon, then get out to my team.

Mr. Roaring Twenties was gone, of course, but I followed his scent until I was in an area I recognized and was able to find my own way out.

After I exited the catacombs, I went to the set of locked double doors that I had been sure was a scientific research center when I'd been here before.

It was logical that the serum could be in the research center. In the meeting of Vampires that I'd witnessed, Volod had said about the contents of the box, *"We will use them in whatever ways we deem necessary, from experimentation to threats."* Volod probably had Vampire scientists working on experiments already.

Again I peered through the clouded glass set into the

doors, sent my air elemental magic through every nook and cranny, and closed my eyes. Using my air magic, I both sensed and saw with my mind the enormous room filled with scientific equipment. Fortunately I didn't sense anything alive or undead.

I used my air magic to unlock the door and eased my way inside.

The research chamber was enough like the ones in the abandoned NORAD facility that it made my stomach churn. Something I never expected in a Vampire lair. Everything smelled like a hospital and looked sterile, normal, not like some medieval torture chamber that I'd expected Vampires to have. Actually, I'd never thought of Vampires having a research center to begin with. It made me wonder what they had used it for before now.

I kept my glamour tight around me, trusting in the fact that I couldn't be seen.

In my mind I saw flashes of the Vampires last night. Their frenzy, their fervor. And then I remembered the two college students who'd been bitten, and their friends who had been brutalized or ripped apart.

Earlier, according to Captain Wysocki, the count was up to thirty-nine dead, fifteen injured, and five missing.

The thought of the Vampires and all of those deaths made me ill. I had to get the serum back along with the antiserum. Had to.

I looked in cabinets, drawers, anything that could be opened and closed. I didn't think I'd find anything, but I had to make sure it wasn't here. This was the place they'd be using or had been using, to experiment on both norms and paranorms.

The chamber was divided into two rooms. I went

from one part of the research center into another when I turned the corner. At the back of that room was a door.

The door drew me. There was something about it that made my heart pump faster, made me feel like I had found something. Something *important*.

It was just a door. Blond wood. Brushed silver hardware. Window with frosted glass. Nothing special.

But I knew something was there. What I was looking for was in *there*. I had never sensed the serum before, but I knew Volod had been in that room. There had to be a reason.

My senses focused totally on that door. Something important, yes. I paused at the door and listened. Silence. Everything was absolutely quiet.

I grasped the door handle, opened the door, and went inside.

The door slammed shut.

An alarm sounded.

My heart started pounding like mad.

Red fog rolled out from the doorway and around me.

The putrid rotten egg-smelling fog burned my lungs, burned my skin.

I started coughing so hard that my chest hurt.

Gas. I was being gassed. I'd walked into a trap.

Something about the gas stole everything from me. What kind of gas could do this to me?

My glamour faded away. I couldn't hold onto my elements.

I tried to turn and run, but my legs wouldn't work.

Every part of my body went limp. I collapsed onto the chamber's sterile white floor.

Waves of panic made me feel like my heart would give out.

I struggled to remain conscious. I couldn't pass out and let Volod find me. Had to get out of here. Had to.

My limbs gave out every time I tried to push myself to my feet.

Finally I lay on the floor, choking and gasping. Unable to use my limbs, move my body. I couldn't use my elements.

It was as if everything had been taken from me and I'd been left an empty shell of a being.

My sense of hearing and my sight were dulled. I could smell nothing but the gas and taste it on my tongue. My fingertips were numb. And my sixth sense was muted. Almost gone.

Real fear, terror, vibrated throughout me before my body started to relax.

The alarm stopped and I heard the door open. And then I heard muffled sounds above my own coughing. I tried to look up to see what it was but the red fog made my impaired vision worse.

Shapes stood over me. Humanoid shapes. Then one crouched next to me and its face moved closer to mine, like in slow motion.

Volod.

The Master Vampire wasn't wearing a gas mask, it was like the gas didn't affect him at all.

His expression was amused and I didn't have the strength to even wish I could punch him.

I just wanted to rest.

Sleep.

I needed sleep.

Volod said something that sounded like orders about a tank, but the words were wavy, bending in and out of shape.

Two other humanoid figures came from behind Volod.

One grabbed me under the arms and the other stuck some kind of mask on my face. Then they put a small tank on my back that was connected to the mask.

I felt like I was suffocating. Like I couldn't draw a full breath.

"A rebreather," a muffled voice said close to my ear. "We had expected you sooner or later and prepared a little gift for you. We know that air which is not fresh will block that power source," the voice said. "Any new air that comes in is filtered to have a minimal amount of oxygen in it—just enough to keep you here with us, but not enough to restore your power. No, there is no fresh air for you.

"By the way," the voice added, "we have included a small amount of the gas in the rebreather which will continue to incapacitate you. The gas will ensure that you are kept in a conscious but weakened state and unable to use any of your powers."

I felt so lightheaded, so limp, that I didn't want to fight it anymore. Whoever was talking to me was telling the truth. The lack of fresh air and the small amount of gas I was breathing had stripped me of my control over the elements. My magic.

They carried me. I couldn't see where, couldn't tell what they were doing. But it did feel like we were going up and up and up. Maybe it was the gas, or maybe they were moving up into the pyramid.

Eventually we reached a door that they opened. I saw Volod following behind me and the two Vampires carrying me by my arms and legs. Through the glass of the rebreather mask, Volod looked like a norm's version of the Devil or even the one-eyed Demon, Balor, from Underworld.

We entered a room and I heard sobs and groans. The

Vampires held me upright even as my limbs wouldn't hold my weight. I was forced up against something hard, like a wall. The rebreather tank dug into my back.

I was aware of something being put onto my head, above my gas mask. It appeared to be some kind of head cage. I screamed behind the gas mask. The head cage, which was hinged in the center, closed around my head. I heard what sounded like bolts being screwed until I felt a pointed end pressing against my temples and the base of my skull.

Something was latched onto the top of the head cage. I realized it was a chain as metal scratched against metal. I was lifted by the head, only slightly supported by a Vampire, and I was suspended over the floor. I could feel the pressure on my neck as it felt like it was being stretched to the breaking point. Was he going to just let me go and hang there?

No, please no, I begged in my mind. Then a Vampire put something under my feet. A small block of wood or stool, but it was barely enough to rest my feet on.

They cuffed my wrists and cuffed my elbows behind me, and shackled my ankles with heavy iron bands. They shackled my elbows to the ceiling as well.

I knew if I lost my balance, my shoulders would be pulled out of their sockets. Or if my head was tethered any tighter than my elbows or wrists, I would be done. My neck would break, being supported by nothing but the head cage.

My muscles didn't want to hold me up then any more than they had before. But something told me I couldn't relax, couldn't let my muscles give way. I couldn't lose that little bit of control I had. I was barely able to keep myself from swinging by the head cage.

One of the Vampires bent so that I couldn't see him.

He touched my waist with his cold hands and I wanted to shrink from him. Then my weapons belt wasn't on my hips anymore. The familiar weight of it was gone.

Volod came close enough that I could see his smile that looked so, so evil through the glass in my face mask.

"Aren't we lucky?" he said. "Out of all of the paranorm Trackers, we have you. You have just become a very favorite captive, though you will not be with us long." Volod laughed and my stomach churned at the sound of it.

Lucky, I thought. *So freaking lucky.*

"Well, purple one. I'm sure you didn't forget the fact that I said I would take care of anyone who followed me." Volod patted me on the shoulder and I flinched. I hadn't realized my entire body hurt so much or how sensitive my skin was, side effects of the gas. "Just two hours ago, I warned you. Yet here you are," he said. "You can't imagine the pleasure I will get from your coming fate."

Lucky me.

It was like an endless half-conscious loop going through my head. *Lucky me, lucky me, lucky me.*

Volod took strands of my long hair and stroked them. "It would be interesting to turn you into a Vampire," he said. "Such pretty blue hair and unusual skin. But alas, you made your choice. And you will have to live with it." He released my hair. "Or rather, die with it."

The cold chill that flowed through me only made the burning in my lungs and in my body worse.

"Remember that compression suit you put my brother in?" Even if he could hear me I didn't have the strength to argue that I hadn't been the one to do it. That as a matter of fact, I had been against it because Volod had the upper hand with the serum and the list of paranorm weaknesses. I knew we would only make him angrier by taking his brother captive, which was exactly what happened.

"The head cage," he continued, "is like one of those suits, in that it's important that you don't move. Otherwise there are very dire consequences."

I choked on the gas-tainted rebreathed air and tried to keep from moving. I wasn't sure why, but I was certain he was about to tell me.

Volod tapped me on the temple. "If you try to escape," he said, "these spikes around the head cage have been cocked and will be triggered. The spikes will enter your skull. If anyone tries to help you escape, same problem for you. Without the cage spring mechanism being disengaged with a key, you are a dead Drow female."

Horror seeped into my pores as he spoke and I started trembling hard enough that I was afraid I'd fall off my support. It took so much effort to keep myself still that my body ached from it.

Through the glass of the face mask I saw the evil of his smile. "That will be the end of this poor little Night Tracker. But please keep your balance. I'm truly hoping you don't die this way. I have better plans. This is simply to keep you waiting until I am ready for you."

I wanted to cry from the helpless, hopeless, desperate feelings he was instilling in me. Feelings I wasn't used to, feelings I didn't like. But this was beyond not liking something. This was heading toward terror. I'd never experienced true terror in my life.

The terror was not only for myself but for everyone whose lives were in danger who I couldn't help now that I'd gotten myself caught.

Volod leaned close to me, so close I could feel his

breath on my ear. "Looks like we've found another weakness for Nyx of the Dark Elves and Night Tracker."

I wanted to struggle against my bonds and fight the Vampire scum, but he had stripped me of any ability I had to defend myself or others.

"Oh," Volod said. "I am certain there are other Trackers somewhere around my compound. We will deal with them in an appropriate manner, just as we are going to deal with you."

No. I closed my eyes. My team members could walk right into a trap if they weren't warned. And how would I manage that?

"I will see you. Soon." Volod patted my shoulder and I opened my eyes to see him smile broad enough to bare his fangs.

Volod moved and then he and the other two Vampires were gone from my line of sight.

"Clean up that Doppler mess," I thought I heard Volod say as he walked away from me.

I had to force myself to calm down to keep from hyperventilating.

The pressure of the head cage was more than enough to remind me that I shouldn't lose consciousness. If there was a way to make it out this situation alive, I had to stay alert—as alert as possible in my circumstances—and I had to keep calm. Very calm.

I didn't move my head but I looked around me with my gaze, the best I could. For the first time I saw that there were other prisoners. Other paranorms.

They weren't wearing rebreathers, but they all had head cages. Their wrists, elbows, and ankles were shackled and attached to rings suspended from the ceiling and pulled taut. A solid bar was attached to their ankles, separating them. They were going nowhere.

A horrible sick feeling churned in my belly when I saw a Doppler female hanging from a head cage, her neck broken from probably passing out, hanging herself before the chains of the shackles could support her.

Is this my fate?

"Don't look," a Shifter female said from across the room from me. The Shifter didn't move her head as she spoke. "She wasn't the first to succumb, but I'm hoping she's the last."

Being a Night Tracker, being who I am, I wanted to reassure her that everything was going to be okay. At that moment I wondered if that would be a lie.

TWENTY-TWO

Breathing the same oxygen over and over through the rebreather made me lightheaded.

"Nyx," came an urgent whisper close to my ear.

My whispered name startled me enough that I almost lost my footing on my block.

"Do not move," the familiar voice said. "It is me, Negel."

Negel couldn't be here. Was the lightheadedness causing me to start hearing voices?

I couldn't turn my head, but even from the corner of my eye I saw nothing.

"I'm in glamour," he said. "No one can see me."

"Then I'll just sound like I'm talking to myself." I sounded slightly drunk, my muffled words slurring through the face mask.

"I heard Volod tell you what this head cage will do to you, so I fear I cannot help you." If I could see him I was sure he'd be wringing his hands. "Not yet. Somehow I will though. I will save you."

What could a Sprite do to save me? "How did you get here?"

"I hid inside Volod's limousine when he drove from the city to this place." Negel said. "He was alone in his car so I sat across from him. Sprite glamours are too strong for even Vampires to sense us."

"You rode in the limo with Volod?" I half laughed, half choked. I was afraid I was getting delirious.

"Yes." Negel's voice was serious while I had the insane urge to giggle. "When we arrived I slipped out and followed him to this room."

"My team." I had a hard time swallowing with as little oxygen as I had. "I need you to take a message to them. I'll tell you where they should be waiting for me."

All of my words were hard to get out and probably would have been hard to hear if he wasn't a Sprite. Those huge ears apparently came in handy.

"Tell them what you have seen and that I said to go to Rodán now." My tongue felt thick and heavy. "They have to come up with another plan because Volod believes they are outside. They must leave now."

"I will do this," Negel said. "And then I will come back and help you, Nyx of the Night Trackers."

"Don't." I wanted to shake my head. "I don't want anything to happen to you. Go back with them to the city."

"I will go find them now," Negel said. "But what I do after that is my choice."

It was too hard for me to argue. I felt tired, lethargic. "Be careful," I said.

"Don't lose hope, my friend," Negel said and then he was gone.

I don't think I'd ever felt so completely alone before as I stood there with the head cage and rebreather on. Bound, shackled, helpless.

My internal clock didn't seem to be working because I had no idea how much time had passed as I stood, staring straight ahead, not moving. It felt like a few hours had gone by, but I just wasn't sure. It was as if the gas had screwed with my mind.

Had it been an hour? Two? More?

Whatever amount of time, it had to be before dawn because I hadn't shifted. I couldn't even sense what time of day it was—if sunrise was coming soon. I wondered if I could survive shifting into my human form, if that would trigger the spikes in the head cage. I change not only in appearance, but my body shifts into a slightly different form.

The click of the door being opened was muffled. I couldn't turn my head to see who had just come in.

Volod walked in front of me with Vampires to either side of him, four total.

"Take her down." Volod gestured to me. "But do be careful. I would hate to lose my prize."

I swallowed, finding the action even harder with the rebreather.

Two of the Vampires took me by my upper arms and raised me while another unfastened the head cage and the fourth kicked the box out from under me.

Breathing became more difficult with every moment. When the Vampires set me on my feet, my knees gave out. But they had a hold on me and didn't let me fall.

They fastened a chain between the cuffs on my legs so that I had just enough space to shuffle, like a prisoner on a chain gang. It never occurred to me how humiliating it would feel to be forced to walk this way.

The gas mask itched, and the rebreather tank felt cumbersome and heavy on my back. The head cage had given me an intense headache and I had a never-ending dizzy feeling.

While I shuffled past, the other paranorms who were

in the room watched me. Their eyes looked sad, as if they already knew my fate.

My body ached with tension that grew and grew as we went through a doorway that led to a stairwell with concrete steps. It reminded me of just days ago when Joshua, Olivia, Angel, and I had gone to Volod's penthouse. The Vampires were careful to make sure that I didn't fall down the steps and had to support me half the time because my legs really didn't want to.

With all my being, what I was really wishing I had were my abilities and one of my daggers. I could take Volod and all four of his Vampire thugs out at one time.

Especially Volod. When it came down to it, I was going to take immense pleasure in dealing with him.

And I would. If I died, I would take Volod with me. Regardless of whether I lived or died, Volod was going to be history.

My stomach clenched and unclenched as we went down the stairwell from the upper part of the pyramid. We were in the same part of the pyramid where I'd seen norm and paranorm prisoners the first time I'd come here.

After several flights of stairs down, the Vampires stopped with me on a landing in front of a door. One of the Vamps opened the door and the others half pushed, half dragged me over the threshold into a long dark hall.

The longer it took, the more my heart raced and felt like it pounded inside my throat. Through the gas mask and my foggy vision, I realized that I'd been here before. This was the same hallway with the room where I had overheard Volod speaking with Drago. That had been only yesterday but it felt so long ago.

We passed that room coming from the opposite way I had the other night so that we were headed out toward that huge ballroom where the Vamps had held their frenetic rally.

As they pushed me onward, the muffled sounds of laughter and beings talking came to me through the mask.

No.

No. They were taking me to a roomful of Vampires. A place where a hundred Vampires could tear me to pieces.

Cheers, heckles, and laughter came at me in a rush as I was shoved and pulled into the ballroom. Through the glass of the mask, I could see too many Vampires. It looked like another cocktail party, only this time I imagined there was a different reason to celebrate. Probably my capture. Maybe my death.

The louder the Vampires became, the sicker I felt.

I was taken to the front of the ballroom, before the fireplace. The same spot where Volod had showed the red box to the crowd that had gone into a frenzy with every word Volod had said . . . just last night.

Danut stood to one side, fury on his features. Drago was beside him with his sister and Volod's lover, Elizabeth.

Volod stood in front of me as I stared out at the rows of Vampires. Fangs looked long and white, prepared to sink into their evening meal. Would I be one of their appetizers?

The Master Vampire raised his hands and the room quieted.

"First, before we proceed, I believe we must show this creature the Vampire way of justice."

"Justice, justice, justice," the crowd chanted.

Volod stepped toward me. An eerie sensation crawled up my spine before acute fear as the Master Vampire bared his fangs and grabbed me by my shoulders.

I wanted to scream. Wanted to jerk away. Wanted to hurt him. But I was powerless.

Volod was a blur as he dove for me.

I did scream then as he buried his fangs deep into my neck.

The pain was intense at first, a burning wildfire sensation. Gradually it dimmed and I could feel Volod drawing blood from me and taking it for himself.

I hoped the Drow half of my blood killed him.

The lightheaded, dizzy feeling grew stronger and I started to slump. But Volod had hold of me in his vise grip and didn't let me fall.

Blood was on his fangs as he raised his head. I wanted to kill him so badly I could taste it, as much as he had just tasted my blood. He went for my neck again and I stiffened, but this time I felt his tongue as he licked the wounds and the blood around them.

"So that is what Dark Elves taste like." Volod licked the rest of the blood from his lips. "Tastes like chicken."

I was in such a fog that I barely heard the Vampire laughter as I stared at Volod with hate suffusing my entire being.

Not only was he doing his best to humiliate me in front of these Vampires, but he had violated me by taking my blood. That violation was a sick, sick feeling in the pit of my stomach.

The Vampires who had brought me here half lifted, half forced me to step up and onto a stool. Two of the Vampires kept me steady while the other two rigged something to the ceiling, then attached it to my head cage.

"Today we show the paranorm world that we are serious about our threats to their way of life," Volod said.

Vampires cheered and called out and jeered at me.

"Paranorms have been a threat to our very existence for over a century," Volod continued. "But no more. Never again will they get in our way. Tonight will be all the proof they need that our rule will be absolute."

Screams of laughter mixed with shouts of anger.

"Death to all paranorms!"

"Feed on them, bleed their powers."

"No more synthetic crap. Nothing but the real thing."

"Let *us* rip into the lavender monster."

There were more important things at risk than even caring about being called a lavender monster. Not only my life, but lives of countless paranorms.

Volod raised his hands again and finally the Vampires settled down. "We have another special guest."

The room went totally silent.

Hair prickled at my nape and goose bumps spread across my skin. The Vampire bite on my neck tingled. I had a strong feeling, a strange feeling, that this guest would not be who I expected, but some being who held my life in the palm of his hand.

Why I felt that way, I didn't know. But I waited with everyone else.

Rodán strode into the ballroom surrounded by four large Vampires.

Frenzied hisses, screams, and howls met Rodán.

The shock of seeing Rodán was enough to make me wobble on my perch. Volod reached for me and clamped one hand on my calf. "Don't die on me just yet," he said as he steadied me.

"Nyx." Rodán's calm veneer looked like it had cracked a little as his eyes met mine. "I have come to negotiate your release."

Vampires burst into laughter.

"We don't negotiate with terrorists." The shock I felt edged my voice even if I was hard to hear through the gas mask. "You shouldn't be here."

"As I said at the council meeting, I don't care what you call me, but I am not a terrorist." Volod's features were tight. "I am the leader of my brethren and we have no need to negotiate."

Was that fear in Rodán's eyes? Fear for me? I'd never seen Rodán scared of anything.

"I warned all in the Paranorm Council meeting what the new order is." Volod drew a syringe full of green fluid from out of his jacket pocket. "I detailed what will happen to those who don't follow my command."

More voices cried out for the horde of Vampires.

Two Vampires took hold of my upper arms on either side of me and kicked the support from beneath my feet. My heart pounded. My body trembled. I was going to hyperventilate. If the Vampires let go of me, I was as good as dead.

I looked at the needle. I might be as good as dead, anyway.

"Despite my warning, in less than two hours' time," Volod continued, "your Tracker invaded my compound, and I know you have others outside. Apparently you, Rodán, the council, and even your Trackers did not take me seriously. You defied my law, a law which came with consequences for ignoring it."

The crowd became frenzied, their madness a tangible thing.

My stomach churned as Volod raised the syringe he had taken from his pocket. "In less than two hours you show defiance." Volod's expression grew dark. "You will now experience what happens when my law is ignored.

This will be the sign for all paranorms that not living the new law, my law, will result in dire consequences."

"Kill the purple one," someone shouted and others took up the call until it became a chant. "Kill the purple one."

"Set her free." Rodán spoke coolly, evenly, as if Volod didn't have a syringe filled with the virus in his hand.

"Oh, I intend to release her." Volod neared me. "But she will now become a symbol for all paranormkind to see the power I possess and to see that I have no fear in using it."

I'd never seen helplessness or fear in Rodán's eyes until that moment. If he tried to stop them, the Vampires would let me go, the spikes would enter my brain, and I would die. If Rodán didn't stop them, Volod was going to inject me.

There was no way out.

"Leave her be." Dark storm clouds churned in Rodán's eyes and the look on his face was pure fury. "If you harm Nyx, there is no place you can hide where I will not find you."

The crazed audience laughed.

"Threats, Rodán?" Volod grasped my arm. "Out of all of the paranorms who could walk into my lair, this is the one I will enjoy annihilating most."

I gritted my teeth. I couldn't see but I felt Volod's hands on me as he stretched out my arm.

Sweat broke out on my skin. My heart raced so fast my chest hurt.

My gaze met Rodán's as my whole body trembled. I couldn't read his expression, but his eyes told me how much he cared for me, feared for me.

"Kill her, kill her," came the chant from the crowd.

Volod positioned the tip of the needle by one of my veins. "I want you to watch."

"No," I said. "Please don't."

"Too late for begging." Volod jabbed the needle into my arm and injected the virus into my veins.

TWENTY-THREE

The fluid felt warm as it entered my veins, and the heat of it spread throughout my entire being. The Vampire bite burned as if I'd been branded.

Yet I was numb. Completely numb.

The Vampires had increased their frenzy. I was vaguely aware of their crazed shouts and expressions.

"According to the scientist's records," Volod said, "you have forty-eight hours before you become contagious and then ill shortly after. However, for all we know it could take less time." He smiled as he added, "Our records indicate that your human half will not compensate for your paranorm half. You carry the mutated gene."

Volod looked from me to Rodán. "You might want to quarantine her from the world as she dies a slow and very painful death."

Rodán said a word in the language of the Dark Elves that was so dark, so foul, that I expected the room to go black and everything begin to shake with Rodán's wrath. Light Elves do not say curses, but Rodán was not like other Light Elves.

Even though he couldn't possibly have understood the word Rodán had spoken, Volod looked amused. "The next time you cross me, more paranorms will be injected. You will not be told which ones. They will infect every paranorm they come close to. There will be no time to quarantine."

Volod continued, "You will not find out until sickness and death begins, and by the time you discover those who are sick they will have infected numerous others."

The Master Vampire's expression changed and he no longer looked amused. "You see, I don't care about your little paranorm world."

"Return the serum and antiserum," Rodán said. "To use it would be genocide."

Volod shrugged. "I am rather indifferent as to whether your paranorm world continues to exist, unless it can improve the Vampire way of life. If it harms my world, the paranorms can be vanquished." His voice and his words were cold as ice. A being with no regard for the lives he could easily take.

"The choice of whether your world goes on or is ended is the choice of your leaders." His gaze settled on me and he had a hard, cruel smile. "So the purple one becomes my message to the paranorm world." He turned and focused on Rodán. "You, Rodán, are but the mailman. Yes, she is the toxic package."

The Vampires in the room started clapping and laughing. The sick feeling in my belly magnified.

Rodán's fingers twitched as if he might cast some kind of spell, but he didn't move, didn't change his expression. "Tell me what you want in exchange for her life. Give her the antiserum. Inject me. I will be your message, not her."

Volod glared directly into my eyes. "She got what she deserves. She and you had fair warning and there will be no deals for her life. None."

Rodán maintained his fixed expression.

"I am willing to tolerate paranorms, but if your kind cannot live in a Vampire-dominated world, they will not live at all. Do you understand, Rodán?"

Rodán's jaw tightened almost imperceptibly.

"Do you?" Volod's voice boomed. "I want to hear it."

Rodán sounded like the calm at the center of a storm before the storm unleashes all its power. "I understand."

"Take her and begone." Volod dropped the syringe into a nearby wastebasket. "The head cage and rebreather will remain on your Tracker until you have been escorted out of the compound."

"Give the Elves to us," a Vampire shouted.

"Let us bleed them dry," another Vamp said.

Volod motioned to the Vampires to calm down. "You will have plenty to feed on this night. Every night."

The rebreather was tightened on my face. Everything had a surreal feel to it. Like this was happening to someone else.

I couldn't truly comprehend the fact that Volod had injected me. That the virus was now in my body and within forty-eight hours, I would become contagious, and I would start to die soon after. If I did become contagious and if I wasn't quarantined, thousands of paranorms would become infected. A slow, painful death . . .

My entire body continued to be numb from shock. I met Rodán's gaze again and this time I wondered if that was a tear in the corner of his eye.

"Now go," Volod said to the crowd of Vampires as he waved his hand toward the entrance to the ballroom. "Feed at will and with the freedom we deserve."

The Vampires cheered, then heckled me some more as they left.

As the Vampires were leaving, I felt a strange sensation, as if I was attached to something moving away from me. I turned my head in just enough time to see Volod walk down the same hallway we had come in.

Was the feeling because he had taken my blood and he had a part of me with him? The thought was so horrible I shoved it away.

Then he was gone. The Vampire who had administered to me one of the most painful ways to die. Slowly, and with the knowledge that there was a cure, but I couldn't have it.

Even in the haze in my mind I knew I'd get that antiserum to not only save myself, but to save every paranorm from this terrorist of a Vampire.

I thought about the Vampires who had just left to go feed on norms and anger rose up in me. The flux of my emotions combined with everything else was making me more ill.

The Vampires who had taken me from the room where I'd been held prisoner, then strung me up in the ballroom, were the same Vampires who now unfastened the head cage from where I was suspended. The Vampires held me steady as they lowered me to my feet.

Still wearing the head cage and rebreather, I was pushed from the ballroom and back down the hallway, past Volod's chamber, and to the stairwell. I was still shackled at my elbows, wrists, and ankles.

My mind spun as I shuffled out like a prisoner on death row. I was on death row. In forty-eight hours I would become infectious. Within a short time after that came illness, then ultimately death.

Getting the antiserum in time felt suddenly hopeless. I could barely grasp onto the thought as Rodán followed the four Vampires and me down through the pyramid and outside.

The moment we walked into the night, a blast of cold air hit me full on. I was freezing. It was as if I weren't Drow and I was fully human. But from what my returning sense of time was telling me, the sun was a few hours yet from rising. Enough time for Vampires to tear apart more innocents in Manhattan.

The Vampires escorted me and Rodán to the huge iron gates of the compound. I watched as the Vamps tossed something near me. My weapons belt. Apparently Volod felt no threat at all from me.

For that one moment I wondered if I would have the opportunity to be a threat to him.

Yes, I will be a threat to the vile creature.

If I die, he's coming with me.

That was all there was to it. I had the fervent hope that Vampires went to Underworld or the norm version of Hell.

And I had an even greater hope that I would go on to Summerland, should I pass from this Otherworld. I wasn't sure Dark Elves went to Summerland, and I wasn't sure if everything I'd ever done would be counted against me even though I'd been protecting paranorms and norms by doing it.

At the gate the Vampires took the rebreather mask and tanks off me. They unshackled my limbs, then unlocked and unbolted the head cage from my temples and the base of my skull.

Life flowed back into my body and soul. Even through the numbness I felt my magic stir within me. I hadn't lost it to the virus. Yet.

The moment the Vampires finished releasing me,

they backed away. If I didn't think it might make things worse with Volod, I would have taken them out in an instant. We needed to bide our time and that might make things more trying with the Master Vampire.

I was still a little dizzy and not totally with it as Rodán half carried me through the gate to his waiting red Lamborghini. Rodán practically shoved me in before he climbed into the car and gunned the engine. He spun the sports car away from the compound and onto the dirt road leading away.

My lungs burned and I didn't think I could catch my breath any time soon. I leaned against the sports car's seat and tried to grasp hold of reality.

An evil Vampire had just injected me with a virus that could wipe out countless paranorms.

For one moment I would have burst into tears if I could have.

"Nyx." Rodán looked at me as the Lamborghini tore through the woods as if the car was cushioned all the way around by air. "You will live. We *will* get the antiserum."

No words came to me. Nothing. I just watched the road as Rodán drove.

"Do not lose hope. We will come up with a plan that will get us in." The intensity of his words carried through to my still numb mind. "If there was no antiserum, there would be no hope. But you are alive and the antiserum exists, so there is still hope."

My throat hurt as I spoke. "I know," I said in a tired, quiet voice. My voice went from quiet to angry. "*I* will get it. It may be a suicide mission, but I have nothing to lose. I've already been handed a death sentence."

"The Trackers will get the antiserum and the serum,"

Rodán said. "We will meet and determine the best timing and develop a strategy." He looked at me. "Nothing can stop the Night Trackers when we work together as a team."

He was right. We couldn't risk me screwing up on my own and Volod deciding to take the serum and antiserum away from the compound. We needed a team to take him down.

"There are a few things I need to tell you." I closed my eyes and rubbed my aching temples. The bolts from the head cage had left temporary indents in my head.

When I opened my eyes, I told Rodán everything from my transference into the catacombs to being gassed, and Negel coming to me in glamour.

"The draftsman no doubt finished the layout from my memory when you debriefed me after my first visit to the compound," I said. "We can add to it from what I saw tonight . . . before I was captured, and use that for our mission plan."

An ache in my throat made me wince when I swallowed. "More importantly," I said, "I believe there is more information we can add to it from what Negel may have learned. Who knows what else Negel saw when he was in the pyramid."

Rodán nodded. "We will interview Negel before the planning session."

I thought about what to do with the Sprite. "We should also include him in on the planning session— he'll be an invaluable resource."

"Agreed," Rodán said.

I gave Rodán Negel's phone number, then frowned. "That's assuming he got out of the compound."

"Negel did get out and he gave the other Trackers

your warning and your orders to return to base." Rodán guided the Lamborghini onto a highway. "That's how I learned about what happened to you." He glanced at me. "And how I came to contact Volod for your release."

"Thank you." I studied Rodán who had the regal bearing of a prince. "I can't believe you came for me . . . I can't believe you offered your life for mine."

Rodán's expression was serious when his gaze met mine again. "You are special to me, Nyx. I could never leave you with the Vampires." His normally calm expression darkened. "But I never expected them to inject you."

I rubbed the sore spot on my neck where Volod had bitten me. Such an incredible violation.

All Volod had to do was bite me one more time *with intent* and I could be "made" into a Vampire. A fact that sent chills through me. I wondered if my Drow half would fight off the infection that allowed Vampires to turn humans.

Then I realized it didn't matter, and obviously Volod hadn't intended to turn me because he had just handed me my death sentence. No, he had done it to humiliate me.

I thought again about how I had felt a strange connection to him when he left the room after injecting me and wondered if it had anything to do with the bite. Just thinking about the Master Vampire made my neck tingle.

"Where do you want me to take you?" Rodán's voice was soothing as he met my gaze with his leaf-green eyes. "You should not be alone tonight."

I pushed my hair off my cheek and behind my ear. Only one place on this earth Otherworld or any Otherworld was where I wanted to be right now. No matter how much I loved my friends and my parents, right now there was only one person I wanted to be with.

"Take me to Adam's house."

"Nyx?" Adam's eyes were blurred from sleep as he looked from me to Rodán when we stood on the doorstep of his small house in Brooklyn. "Is everything okay?"

I was still weak from the gas and Rodán was helping to support me with his arm around my shoulders. "No, it's not okay." I wasn't going to lie, but I would say what I truly believed. "But it will be. I intend to make sure of that."

"I will leave Nyx in your hands," Rodán said before he turned me so that his gaze met mine. He took my face in his palms, then kissed the top of my head. When he drew away he said, "After you rest, come to the conference room at the Pit. I'll contact Negel as we discussed as well as notify your team and the other Trackers. I also intend to be in touch with leaders from all of the paranorm races," he added.

"Thank you, Rodán," I said quietly. "Thank you for everything."

Rodán's expression grew dark. "I didn't do enough."

"You were there for me," I said. "You tried. You offered your life. That means everything."

Rodán was quiet for a moment. "I'll let you tell Olivia." He paused before he said, "Bring Adam with you to the planning meeting."

I blinked in surprise and Adam looked like cold water had been thrown over him. Rodán had never allowed Adam to join a Tracker meeting.

That Rodán had even let Olivia come to the meetings had been unbelievable. Making her a Tracker had been even more stunning and shocking to all Trackers, including myself. Maybe I shouldn't have been so shocked because she was more than equipped to be a Night Tracker, even if she was human.

"What's going on?" Adam's demeanor changed almost instantly from someone who had just been dragged out of bed to a tough cop interviewing a witness. "What happened? What do you mean offered his life?"

"I'll explain." I laced my fingers through Adam's, needing to feel him. With my free hand I gave a slight wave to Rodán after he retreated. He eased into his Lamborghini and I watched him drive down the narrow street until the car vanished around a corner.

Adam tugged at my hand and drew me into his house, then closed the door behind us. He took me by my shoulders and he pushed my blue hair away from my cheek as he cupped my face in his palms. "Tell me, Nyx. You've got me worried."

I closed my eyes and rested my cheek in his palm. If somehow we didn't get the antiserum, these could be my last moments with Adam. I hated to ruin this precious time with him by facing reality, but I didn't have a choice.

"Nyx?" His tone was growing more and more concerned. He moved his hands and grasped me by my upper arms. "Tell me."

I opened my eyes and swallowed. I managed to keep my voice steady as I finally got the words out. "Volod injected me. He injected me with the virus."

The shock in Adam's brown eyes made my heart hurt. For a moment he just stared at me. Then he released my shoulders, wrapped his arms around me, and he nearly crushed me as he squeezed me to his chest.

I gasped for air, but right then I didn't care if I

couldn't breathe easily. I could feel Adam's fear for me as much as I could feel my own fear.

"No." He started rocking me back and forth. "You're not going to die from the virus. Not going to happen."

"I have forty-eight hours." I said against his T-shirt. "Forty-eight hours before I become contagious and before I start to die if we don't have the antiserum."

He drew back and grabbed my face in his hands again, holding me in a firm grip. "I don't care what it takes. We're going to get that antiserum."

I nodded, my cheeks brushing his palms, but I could say nothing.

Adam scooped me up in his arms and my head spun a little with the movement. He carried me to his bedroom where he laid me at the center of the bed.

He settled himself beside me and kissed me so gently, so lovingly, that every kiss was etched into my heart and soul.

"I love you, Nyx." Adam's voice was hoarse as he met my gaze. My body felt warm and my skin tingled from head to foot at the surprise of what he'd just told me. "I'm not going to lose you."

"I love you, too," I said before I kissed him. "I've loved you for a long time, and I don't plan on leaving you anytime soon."

Adam kept kissing my lips, my cheeks, my forehead, my hair, until he brought my body against him. His heart was a hard thump beneath my ear as he pressed me close to his chest and held me the few hours until after dawn.

Sleep never came. All I could do was revisit everything that happened last night and what the future held.

In some part, I began to think, what happened to me didn't matter. What mattered was getting the antiserum and the serum to save countless paranorm lives.

What also mattered was saving innocent humans from being slaughtered, bled to death, or infected and turned into Vampires.

The only way I could help though was to remain alive.

My mind kept racing. I knew my life or death did matter. Not just to me, but to my family, to my friends, and to people who counted on me to protect them. My life mattered.

As Adam held me I nestled in his embrace and allowed myself to feel the comfort of his presence, of his love.

And I stared up at the ceiling and planned.

TWENTY-FOUR

Olivia punched me in my arm the moment she walked up to me and Adam at the back entrance of the Pit.

"Ow." I rubbed my upper arm. "What was that for?"

"For not including me and Adam last night in your little Vampire compound raid." Her features grew tight and she was definitely pissed. "And for getting yourself injected with that damned virus."

Her eyes looked a bit red, but Olivia never cried, so that couldn't have been it.

I had told her everything over the phone from Adam's house. I wasn't sure what her reaction had been because all she said was, "I'll see you at the Pit."

When I saw her black shirt I blinked. "There's nothing on it." I looked up at her. "You're wearing a blank T-shirt."

"Wasn't feeling particularly funny today." She leaned toward me. "Although I did almost wear the shirt, 'Stupid Kills. Unfortunately Not Near Enough.'"

I gave a little smile. "That's better. I needed that."

For a moment I thought Olivia might hug me, but she kept to her sarcastic self. That was better than a hug coming from Olivia. It was familiar and made me feel a little more like everything was going to be all right.

It was afternoon, extraordinarily early for Trackers to meet, but this was an emergency situation.

Adam maintained his arm around my shoulders. He'd kept me close ever since I'd gone to his home, like he was afraid I might get away from him.

We slipped in a back entrance of the Pit and went to the conference room from that direction. It was a Friday night and in case the forty-eight hours estimate was wrong, I didn't want to infect countless paranorms.

I hadn't even wanted to meet with all of the other Trackers just in case, but Rodán had insisted it would be fine and as a precaution everyone on the team would be given a small dose of the antiserum once we got it.

We would get the serum and antiserum. I refused to doubt otherwise.

My father always told me that doubt leads to uncertainty, uncertainty leads to fear, fear leads to mistakes, mistakes lead to failure.

Drow warriors never entertained doubt.

I am a Drow warrior.

Those feelings I'd have after being injected I tossed aside in favor of what I'd been taught all of my life by my warrior king father.

All of the Trackers were in the room when Adam, Olivia, and I arrived. My cheeks grew hot because of the way each Tracker was looking at me. I couldn't tell if the anger I saw in some faces was for me or against me, and I didn't want to acknowledge the concern for me in the eyes of my friends or the look of pity in others' gazes.

What I did acknowledge was the determination that each Tracker also showed, a determination to accomplish the mission, something every Tracker was trained for extensively.

"The Trackers have been given a choice," Rodán said

before I entered the room and was standing in the doorway. "They have unanimously chosen to be on the team that goes to the Vampire compound to recover the serum and antiserum."

I took a deep breath just before he added, "They have also chosen you to lead the team."

A well of emotion rose up in me with a knot in my throat and it pressed behind my eyes. I straightened and walked into the conference room.

When Adam came in just behind me, his hand resting on my shoulder, expressions changed again, this time to surprise. I expected Ice to be openly hostile but amazingly he wasn't. Maybe it had to do with Adam showing up on the Werewolf op and working with my team, which had included Ice.

On the other hand Kelly was scathing. "What's the norm doing in here? Bad enough we have one," she said referring to Olivia.

I had to grab Olivia's arm to keep her from walking past me, straight for Kelly. She'd probably do more than just punch Kelly's arm.

When I wouldn't let her by, Olivia made little kissing sounds. "Here, bunny bunny. I've got a carrot for you."

Kelly scowled and Joshua interrupted with, "I'll see your carrot and raise you one."

Rodán ignored the exchange in favor of moving on to what was important. As Olivia, Adam, and I took our seats he was saying, "There is much to accomplish. Others will be joining us in just moments, as they are already here."

Ondrej, the Werewolf from Beketov's pack, came through the nightclub door just as Rodán finished speaking. He stood near the back since there was standing room only.

The same door opened again followed by low murmurs from the Trackers as at intervals several different
beings filed through, representatives of almost every race
of paranorms. A Doppler, Shifter, Shadow Shifter, Witch,
and Tuatha Fae warrior each made their way into the conference room. The last was a Sprite—Negel.

"We are adding to our forces." Rodán gave a nod to
those who now gathered around the conference table,
"One representative of every race has been invited to
this meeting. Each will then select their best paranorms
to participate, as we need as many fighters as possible to
join our mission."

Rodán allowed no time for questions or comments.
He gestured to a wall beside the conference table. The
layout the draftsman had prepared was fastened to the
wall. The draftsman was Fae and his drawings were
three-dimensional and interactive.

Negel's additions were added in glowing red as opposed to my contributions in neon blue. According to the
layout, it looked like Negel's knowledge of the pyramid
and compound was far beyond mine. I quickly studied
the enhanced layout and memorized it.

Rodán and I had gone over everything on the phone,
but this was the first time I'd seen the composite.

We'd discussed all that Negel had learned when debriefing him as well as sharing with Rodán plans I had
come up with the night before. From those details we
developed a general compound invasion and serum/an-
tiserum rescue plan.

"Nyx." Rodán jarred me from my thoughts as he
called my name. "As you will be leading this mission,
you may take over now."

My belly flip-flopped a little as I pushed back my
chair and walked around the conference table to the

wall. Some Trackers were looking at me with a different kind of interest, and I realized this was the first time some of them had seen me in my human form.

Fair skin instead of amethyst and black hair instead of blue, not to mention no pointed ears and no little fangs, as well as less defined musculature, made for a very different-looking Nyx Ciar. The fact that I was in Dior slacks and a cashmere sweater instead of a two-piece black leather fighting suit might have made them look at me differently, too.

For some strange reason I felt a little nervous being in charge of the entire team of Night Trackers and representatives of various races of beings. Despite the fact that I was compromised as a carrier of the virus, they were willing to follow my lead.

"Negel, please." I indicated with a slight movement of my hand for him to join me at the front of the room.

Tension filled the air as the Sprite walked toward me. He looked nervous and his form wavered a bit, like he was seriously tempted to disappear behind a glamour. Sprites hadn't exactly been welcomed before and this was a stretch to have him in the meeting.

"This is Negel of the Sprites." I looked slowly around the room, meeting the gazes of each Tracker, including Kelly. "Thanks to Negel," I said as he stood beside me, "we have detailed information about the Vampire compound."

I cleared my throat. "Negel was extremely brave and resourceful in coming to the compound, finding me, and giving my Tracker team my warning. Not only that, but he has given us detailed information that I will show you on the layout."

With the interactive layout, Negel and I proceeded to show the newly expanded team all of the entrances and exits we had discovered first. We also went into descriptions of the various rooms, chambers, and other locations in the pyramid, including the catacombs with the Vampire coffins.

Negel provided invaluable information about where guards were stationed as well as where weapons were stashed.

"Volod told his brother and the other Master Vampire that he wanted the number of guards increased as a precaution," Negel said. "Now that the paranorms know the Vampires do have the serum and antiserum and we now know the location of the pyramid, they could face some opposition. They are arrogant enough to think they are safe in the pyramid, though, with their doubled guards and the treatment of the serum."

"Doubled up on their guards . . ." Ondrej shook his head. "That means nothing. We will take them out."

"The best time to attack is during the day while the Vampires are still in their coffins, when they are completely helpless." Joshua leaned back in his chair. "We should get there before night falls. That does not give us much time."

"We considered a daylight attack," I said. "However, we would give away our element of surprise because their human guards would alert them. Not only that, but all of the Vampires would be in the pyramid and would wake and be ready for us."

"As opposed to waiting until most of the Vampires have left for the night to hunt," Negel said.

I explained how the pyramid was designed so that no light could get through, meaning the Vampires had no chance of daylight entering their sanctuary. Even their entrances were deep belowground, including their parking garage. The Vampires had their full abilities during the day, so long as they remained in the pyramid.

"We should infiltrate the pyramid when most of the Vampires are out hunting," I said.

"That would be close to midnight," Nadia said.

I nodded. "It's definitely the best time to get into the compound and the pyramid."

"What then?" Ice gave me a hard look. "You go in alone again and this time get yourself killed?"

My face burned hot. As Drow my cheeks don't show red if I'm embarrassed or angry. It's another story when I'm human.

"A select team," I said, "will go into the pyramid first and prepare for the next team to aid in securing the area. If we are successful in securing the serum and antiserum, we will make our way out. If we have problems and you are called, or once we have the serums, the rest of the team will storm the pyramid."

"You mentioned getting the serum and antiserum when the first team goes in," Angel said. "Do you know where it's being kept?"

I gave Negel a nod indicating it was his show now.

"I know the exact location of the serum and I believe the antiserum as well." The Sprite's ears wiggled. "It is in a safe beneath the carpet, under a bookcase, in Volod's office."

"How do you know that it's in that safe?" Ondrej asked from the back of the room.

"I followed Volod who returned the large bottle of serum to the safe after injecting Nyx," Negel said and I flinched at the sound of Volod's name. The Vampire bite on my neck burned.

Negel looked at me with fear for me in his big eyes.

"His brother Danut was there and Volod told him if only the purple Tracker knew the antiserum was so close in that safe."

The room went quiet as everyone looked at me.

"Amethyst," I said to lighten the mood since almost everyone knew I hated to be called purple. "Not purple, amethyst."

"Excellent work," Nadia said to Negel and there were other murmurs of approval.

Lawan shifted in her chair. "What about getting into the safe? Is there a lock or combination?"

"I watched Volod open it himself, saw the combination number he used, and memorized it," Negel said. "I was looking right over his shoulder as he stooped over."

Tracey leaned forward, her forearms braced on the table. "Great job, Negel."

This time the Sprite looked like he was blushing.

"Thank you, Negel," I said, and his mottled cheeks turned even redder.

"There is something that makes this more urgent than you realize." The room quieted as I spoke.

"According to what Negel overheard," I said, "Volod is planning on dividing up the serum into three parts. I tried not to flinch from saying the name which was followed by a burning sensation where the bite mark was. "He is keeping each part at separate locations. A scientist is coming tomorrow."

Negel's ears flopped as he nodded. "During the day. The scientist is human."

I clenched my hands into fists. "In addition, the scientist is supposed to develop a misting method of distributing the serum throughout the city if the Vampires believe our threat to them is too great."

"It could be spread on the wind," Negel said, "and kill us all within days."

"There is no telling how potent the serum is." I rubbed my temples, almost feeling the imprints of the head cage bolts still there.

Deep concern was in Negel's voice. "Volod is also considering having the scientist destroy the antiserum."

My stomach pitched even though this wasn't the first time I'd heard that fact. Rodán had told me all of it earlier over the phone when we discussed Negel's debriefing.

Murmurs of concern over all of the news sped through the room.

"Can I ask an obvious question?" Joshua leaned back in his chair. "Why don't we simply develop more antiserum right away?"

"We had recovered only a small amount of antiserum." Rodán stepped forward. "We never recovered the formula from the antiserum . . . that recipe died with the scientist."

Rodán met the gazes of paranorms around the room. "That was why the serum was at the Paranorm center. The council planned to have the serum and antiserum studied in order to develop more antiserum in case other quantities of the virus serum turned up. The only antiserum that we know of is in the Vampire's safe."

"This makes everything more urgent." I touched my collar by habit, then drew my hand away. "We have to take control of the compound tonight. We have no choice."

All of the Trackers and others in attendance nodded in agreement.

"We have plans for this mission," I said. "However, all Trackers are resourceful and we are open to brainstorming."

Everyone at the meeting was all business as we got down to our plans. I assigned leaders for each team after we estimated the totals of paranorms which included each race represented.

At least twenty compression suits were available in the detention center. In storage from the Paranorm Rebellion were the countless small crossbows used to shoot stakes at a Vampire's heart. The crossbows and stakes had been fashioned from Dryad wood, making them even more accurate because they were infused with a little Dryad magic.

In large supply were plenty of garlic tablets and holy water, along with a few other items that would help in a battle against Vampires.

"We know what's at risk, we have a plan, we know our enemy." I put my hands on my hips as my gaze traveled the room and I saw the seriousness in every paranorm's eyes. "Now let's go destroy that enemy."

TWENTY-FIVE

My heart pounded as Team One and I eased through the dark forest and approached the Vampire compound. Through a break in the clouds, moonlight cast a silver glow on everything except the pyramid which absorbed the light.

The smell of rain edged the air. When I looked up, dark clouds closed the gap and hid the moon. A raindrop hit my nose.

When we were at the edge of the tree line and were a hundred yards from the front gate, Mandisa came up on my right, Ice on my left. Behind us were Lawan and Joshua. Taking up the rear were three big Doppler males.

Three Vampire guards stood at the huge black iron gate that was between the high stone walls. One of the Vampires paced back and forth from one end of the gate to the other. The razor wire on the stone walls glittered in another patch of moonlight that peeked through the dark clouds.

I gripped the hilts of the two extra daggers I'd brought with me. My weapons belt was heavy with my dragon-clawed daggers, my buckler, my new phone, one of the small stake crossbows along with a few wooden stakes, and some other items that might come in handy.

Adam had procured twenty radios with earpieces and we were using them to relay instructions and responses from both teams that were going in covert, as well as communicating with the leaders of the force surrounding the perimeter of the compound.

The fact that I'd been injected with a deadly virus was always at the back of my mind. I tried not to think about the virus being in my blood, but the thought was still there.

I couldn't allow myself to dwell on it at all. What was important was getting my people in and out without injury and procuring the serum and antiserum.

My muscles tensed as I got ready to roll with our plans.

Heat burned in my belly when I thought about the reports already pouring in to the NYPD and to the news stations tonight.

Captain Wysocki had told Adam earlier that there had been even more attacks over the last few nights—people murdered, injured, or missing—than the NYPD had released to the news stations. Tonight had started earlier than the other nights and reports were coming in fast.

The city was in an all-out panic. Adam said Captain Wysocki was starting to believe that they were dealing with Vampires. Real Vampires. Not wannabe norms, but truly real Vamps. Nothing human could be doing what was happening to countless innocent people.

I narrowed my eyes at the gate. We would stop the Vampires from attacking humans ever again.

Team Two consisted of the rest of the Trackers. That team was being led by Angel and would come in on my signal.

The balance of our forces had gathered in an enormous circle around the compound, far enough out of range that they wouldn't be spotted. Despite the size of the force, it would be difficult for the Vampires to know that we were stationed as close as we were. There were benefits to having the variety of races of beings on the force.

Shifters could shift into any type of warm-blooded creature that lived in the forest.

Dopplers often had forms of forest animals, like Angel who was a squirrel. She and the Doppler leader had selected only those Dopplers who could fit in undetected.

Of course since wolves lived in this area of western New Jersey long before man drove them out, Werewolves were essentially indigenous.

Elves and all races of Fae belong in nature and are just as difficult to identify by scent or sight.

I had the gift of a keen sense of smell, but even I was having a hard time distinguishing one race of paranorm beings from another by scent in the forest tonight.

The middle Vampire guard continued his pacing while the other two stood sentry to either side of the gate.

I looked over my shoulder and nodded to the three Doppler males who each gave a nod in return before they separated. They would come at the gate from three different directions. One Doppler shifted into a great horned owl, another into a skunk. The third morphed into a large black bear.

The owl hooted and flapped its great wings as it took to the sky and flew silhouetted against the filtered moonlight over the guards.

"Look at the size of that thing," one Vampire guard said.

"Never seen one so big before," added one of the other guards.

The skunk strolled out of the forest, its tail high, as it approached the guards. They were preoccupied by looking at the owl that had landed on one of the stone walls.

A guard glanced down in time to see the skunk raise its tail. "Shit!" he cried out and started to run from the gate. "A skunk! Kill that thing!"

The other two guards scattered but none of them made it far enough to avoid getting sprayed by the Doppler skunk. Then the skunk shot after one of the guards who kept running.

A second guard was trying to beat off the owl that had taken flight, then swooped down to claw at the Vampire's head.

The third guard ran straight into the black bear. It tore the guard into pieces before ripping out his heart.

Once they were away from the gate, the owl and skunk shifted back into their human forms and slammed the Vampires to the ground.

I took the two extra daggers I'd been holding and flipped them end over end toward the former skunk and owl Dopplers. They each caught a hilt in their hands, then used the large daggers to carve out the Vampires' hearts.

Within moments the Dopplers had tossed the Vampire bodies into the forest. The males took their places at the gate, replacing the Vampire guards.

I wiped away a raindrop that hit my forehead, then pressed the tiny button on my earpiece. "Team One. Break," I whispered into the mic. "Team Two, hold until I give the word."

In case the gate opening and closing triggered some

kind of notification in the pyramid, we would find alternate ways of getting into the compound.

Joshua slipped into his shadow form and skimmed a moonlit patch of grass before he disappeared into the dark forest. His objective was to find a crack, any opening to the garage, and slip through it. He would enter the pyramid from that angle.

Lawan morphed into a Siamese cat. She stepped with a cat's delicacy and grace through the shadows and to the front gate. She easily slinked between the bars of the gate and headed for the north entrance of the pyramid.

Ice smirked. "Lawan can play cat and mouse with me anytime." And then he was gone. I looked down and saw a white mouse who skittered under leaves and low-hanging branches on his way to the pyramid. Ice would make it in through the south entrance.

"Your turn." I glanced at Mandisa, who gave me one of her hard, unreadable looks before she moved.

I expected her to approach the gate and scale it. Instead, one second she was there, the next second she was gone. I took a step back in surprise. Abatwa Fae could use glamours? Nice.

As a paranorm I could still see her milky white outline, but humans or Vampires wouldn't be able to. I watched as she went up to the Doppler guards standing at the gate.

Mandisa walked through the bars.

Not in between the bars. Through the bars. Like a Specter or Shadow Shifter.

Mandisa looked over her shoulder at me before facing forward and walking toward the west entrance.

The beating of my heart increased as I wrapped myself in an air glamour.

To gain momentum I went at a hard run from the forest to the east wall. Several feet from the wall I jumped up and forward-flipped over the wall and razor wire. I landed in a crouch on the ground on the other side of the stone fence.

I looked around me, taking in the compound with a sweep of my gaze. Everything looked normal on the outside. I saw no signs of my team. I hadn't expected to since the pyramid was too big for me to see around from the middle point.

But I did see the guard who stood at the entrance where I would be going in.

A few more raindrops hit my face as I ran in glamour toward the east entrance that led down below the pyramid. The smell of rain grew stronger as I ran for the guard.

The skies opened up and began to pour. By the time I reached the Vampire guard, I was soaked. I stood a few feet away from the Vamp who looked irritated at being out in the rain. It was one of those who had shackled me and bolted the head cage onto me.

I drew one dragon-clawed dagger, held the hilt in a two-fisted grip, and walked up to the Vampire. Just to let him know it was me about to take his life, I released my glamour at the same time I swung my blade at his neck.

The look of shock was still on the Vampire's face as his head dropped to the wet ground and his body collapsed.

I kicked the Vampire's feet off the square of stone that covered the east entrance. I used my earth magic to make a quick search to make sure no Vampires were in the passageway that led into the depths below the pyramid.

After I moved the heavy slab covering the entrance, I

climbed down, leaving the entrance open for Team Two. I tapped my earpiece as I jogged down the steps. "Team Two, come on in."

"On our way," Angel said. "We'll be right on your tails."

I hurried into the black darkness when I reached the bottom of the steps and along the earthen passageway. A strong sense of déjà vu overcame me. I'd been at this very place only two days ago? So much had happened since the time that I'd first walked down this passageway that it seemed longer.

My skin felt cool and wet from the rain as I dodged the roots dangling from the earthen ceiling. After running down the slanting passage, I saw the strip of light beneath the black door. I paused to search what was on the other side of the door with my elemental magic.

Another guard, just like Negel had said.

From my belt I withdrew a small periscope and slid it beneath the door to get an idea of exactly where the guard was standing. He was almost dead center from the doorway, maybe a foot away at most.

I replaced the periscope on my belt and in a pocket on my weapons belt I reached for a disc that was about the size of a quarter that humans used for currency. I knelt, pressed down on the center of the disc, then slid it beneath the doorway.

The strong smell of garlic was followed by a grunt, like someone was in pain. Then a loud thud against the door. The intense mixture of holy water and garlic would throw the Vampire off balance and I could picture him slumped against the door.

It was too bad large quantities of the stuff couldn't be used on more than a Vampire or two at a time. The power of the combination was diminished when not used in a form this concentrated. It was also hard to trigger and get to the Vampire before he or she moved.

I wrapped myself tight in an air glamour again.

Holding one dagger, I jerked the door open with my free hand. The Vampire guard stumbled backward, followed by the pungent odor of garlic. Before he had a chance to right himself, I brought my dagger down on his neck. His head dropped on the passageway floor and his body fell beside it.

I picked up the expired disc and tossed it into the passageway before closing the door and leaving the headless Vampire in the darkness.

Once again I was standing on the black marble of the foyer, the crystal chandelier hanging overhead. I looked at the sweeping staircase and listened. Coming from behind it, in the direction of the ballroom were voices.

My throat tightened as I walked toward the ballroom at a brisk pace, still in glamour. I reached the entrance and looked in to see more Vampires than we had expected.

I started to back out so that I could tell Angel that we had a bigger problem than we'd thought. But two Vampires came up behind me and I had to step away inside the ballroom.

To my right was the office where Negel was positive Volod now had the serum and antiserum hidden. I had to get into that office, but so many Vamps were crowded near the hallway that I didn't know how I was going to get past.

Volod walked into the ballroom from the hallway.

The bite mark on my neck burned like white-hot fire and I slapped my hand over the bite. The heat of it traveled through my fingers and I felt it throb.

At the same time, Volod raised his head, but he didn't look at me. I bit my bottom lip as the burn continued. Volod reached inside a suit jacket he was wearing tonight.

Faster than I could see or react, Volod whipped out a small knife and flung it at me.

I cried out and my glamour dropped as the knife buried itself to the hilt in my thigh.

TWENTY-SIX

My leg gave out from under me and I dropped to one knee. The knife had penetrated the muscle of my thigh.

"Ballroom!" I shouted into the mic. "Storm the compound now!"

Vamps who had been standing near Volod started toward me. I jerked the knife out of my thigh at the same time I gathered a powerful shield around myself.

Blood poured down my thigh and pain burned in it enough to make me grind my teeth as I got to both feet again.

How appropriate to have this battle in the same room where I'd watched Vampires go crazy not only once, but twice. The second time with me as the exhibit and victim.

Resting my weight on my left leg, I drew my dagger along with my buckler.

A Vampire came at me from my left.

I was too close to go for his neck so I ran him through with my dagger.

It was only enough to make him pause before he began to heal.

He went for me with fangs and claws even as I jerked the dagger out.

I dropped to the floor and rolled between his legs and came up behind him.

As he whirled I had my dagger ready for him. I sliced into his neck.

My momentum wasn't enough. The blade only made it three quarters of the way through.

He backhanded me with a Vampire's amazing strength and slammed me across the room against a wall.

I fell, landing on my knees. More pain burst through me from my thigh. The Vamp's neck was already starting to heal as he charged me.

There was barely enough time to jerk the small crossbow from my belt, load it with a stake, and fire.

The stake buried itself deep inside his heart.

With a pained cry the Vampire tumbled forward, landing on the hilt of the stake and driving it even further.

He lay still.

I looked around me.

A madhouse.

The entire pack of Vampires from across the room raced toward me. Where was my team?

Then it looked like almost every Tracker from both Team One and Team Two had descended on the room from all four entrances.

My teams rushed the Vampires and began battling them.

More Vampires flowed in from the main entry which was closest to the stairs from the catacombs. Must have woken a few late sleepers. There were even more Vampires in the pyramid than we had suspected.

Candle flames flickered in the wall sconces and I considered frying Vampires with my fire elemental magic. But there were too many Trackers around and I didn't want to take the chance of roasting anyone who wasn't a Vampire.

When I saw Adam and Olivia, my heart started pounding so hard in my chest that it hurt. They were human and didn't belong here no matter what they thought. Vampires were too powerful.

But they tag-teamed again. Olivia shot a Vampire in the head with garlic and holy water bullets which caused the Vampire to come up short. That gave Adam a clear shot to stake the Vamp with a loaded crossbow.

My neck still burned where the bite marks had been, but the burning lessened. Volod was walking farther from me. I swung around and saw him heading toward the hallway leading to his den.

I started after Volod, who shouted orders which I didn't understand in the chaos. He had stopped behind three vampires engaged in a fight with Angel and Mandisa. I had to reach that room behind him and he knew it.

I rushed forward but two Vampires got in my way.

One of the Vampires flung himself at me with fangs bared and claws extended.

The other Vamp circled me to come up from behind.

Blood rushed in my head and pain pounded in my thigh.

Before either Vampire could touch me, I dove to the side, dropped, and rolled a few feet away.

The Vampires smacked into each other as I scrambled to my feet.

Almost without pause they came after me again.

The burn of the bite mark on my neck was fading more. Volod was getting away.

Had to get to him!

I called to my fire element and sent huge flames rushing at the two Vampires.

They screamed as they were engulfed in fire.

I took both of my daggers and with a full swipe of each, beheaded both Vampires at the same time.

To my left two Vampires came up behind Olivia. She didn't see them. I called my fire element and torched them, exploding them in flames.

Olivia nodded before pulling the trigger on her small crossbow with the stake. The Vampire she nailed didn't see it coming. He was dead before he hit the floor.

I looked and saw two Dopplers engaged with four Vampires.

Three Trackers were to my right fighting off seven Vampires.

I sensed an attack from behind. I whirled with my dagger sweeping neck high. I grazed one Vampire but crumpled under the weight of another as he flew into me. Pain screamed through my leg as his weight landed on my thigh. He raised his hand and a wicked-looking knife was clutched in his fist.

He slumped forward, his dead weight on me. Ice stood behind the Vampire with his emptied crossbow. A stake was buried into the Vampire's back, straight through to his heart.

Love that weapon.

I limped to my feet and looked for Volod. The Trackers had all but crushed the Vampires. Six Vampires stood with their hands up, surrendering to the garlic, holy water, and stake weapons.

Two Vampires bolted through the doors leading out of the ballroom.

There was no escape for them. Our forces had the exits blocked and we would find any surviving Vampires.

What mattered now were the serums. I had to get them.

Volod had disappeared, but I would find him.

I ran to the hallway where the office was.

Four Vampires emerged from the office and rushed us.

Where had they come from? What were they doing in that room?

Just in time to avoid one of the Vamps' fangs and claws, I dodged to the side.

I ground my teeth against the pain in my thigh. "Team leaders," I said as I ignored the pain to keep from limping and hurried past the four Vampires. "Assign squads to search every room for remaining Vampires."

Before anyone had a chance to respond, I was already going after Volod.

My earpiece crackled.

"Nyx!" It was Negel's voice and he sounded panicked. I didn't know how he'd gotten hold of an earpiece but it didn't matter. Static made it hard to hear him clearly.

"Volod . . . get . . . away . . . dark . . . running . . . text . . ." Then again I heard "text."

"What?" I said as I ran down the hallway, leaving the melee behind. But all I heard was a crackle and then silence.

I reached Volod's office. The door was wide open.

My skin prickled as I peered around the doorframe.

A bookcase had been moved aside and there was an opening in the floor.

My stomach pitched. No one was in the room and what I was seeing couldn't be good.

I limped toward the opening. It was a safe and it was empty.

The earpiece crackled as I whirled around. I felt suddenly helpless and off kilter. My neck no longer burned, not at all.

Where was he? Volod might release the serum now with all of the paranorms around.

A few garbled words were all I could hear Negel say over the mic.

"What?" I shouted again as I ran back to the door and looked up and down the hallway. Where could Volod have gone? "I can't understand you, Negel."

"Stand-up coffin . . . catacombs . . . tunnel," I heard him say through the static. ". . . text. . . . phone."

I bolted out into the ballroom. Three more Vampires ran from the entry to the ballroom. They were immediately met with a barrage of wooden stakes launched from crossbows that Trackers had aimed at them. At least two of the shots were bull's-eyes as the Vampires collapsed.

"Secure the perimeter. Volod is gone and so are the serums," I said into the earpieces. "No one, I mean *no one* gets beyond our perimeter but Trackers only. I want additional paranorms at each exit now. Volod cannot be allowed to escape."

Volod is here somewhere and he will not escape, I thought. *He cannot escape. We have him.*

I reached for my transmit button. "Negel, where are you?"

Nothing.

What was going on? Could Volod have actually escaped?

"Negel, tell me something."

The room was all but secured. As the torched Vampires began to reform, they were put into compression suits before they got their strength back.

The radio crackled. A few garbled words, then the word, "text" again.

What did that mean? "Text."

My phone vibrated. Oh. That was what Negel had been trying to tell me. He'd sent a text message and in the fight I hadn't felt the vibration.

When I looked at the screen I clicked on a message from him. *Can't talk. Following Volod and two vamps. Long tunnel. Entry in stand-up coffin. Volod has the box. Help!*

I replied into the transmitter. "I got it, Negel, I'm coming. Don't lose sight of them, but don't try and take the box yourself." I was so glad Olivia replaced my phone.

Stand-up coffin . . . Stand-up coffin . . .

I frowned. Where—

Then I remembered the stand-up coffin in the catacombs at the place where I'd done the transference. Pain made me grind my teeth even harder as I raced there.

Over my earpiece I told Olivia, Ice, and Adam where to find the tunnel entrance and to follow it. I also ordered the team leaders to have the perimeter moved out, that Volod may have exited through a tunnel beyond our net.

As I bolted for the catacombs, thoughts raced through my mind. How could there be an exit we didn't know about? Why didn't I sense it with my earth element? Maybe it was the lack of fresh air in the dank catacombs. At this point it didn't matter. I couldn't let Volod get away.

Shouts and cries from paranorms battling in other parts of the pyramid continued.

I rushed out of the ballroom and headed downstairs toward the kitchen, past the infirmary, and beyond the research center until I came to the stairs going down into the catacombs.

Wary that some Vampires might still be in their

coffins, I dodged through the dark, dark place carefully. Fortunately I didn't run across any and I made it to where the stand-up coffin was.

The lid of the coffin had been moved aside and instead of a bottom to the coffin there was an entrance into a dark tunnel.

I looked at my phone again. Another text message from Negel.

Volod running from exit. Still with two other Vampires. Beyond the perimeter.

I ran into the tunnel. Earth and air elements told me how long the tunnel was. A little over a quarter of a mile, farther out than our five-hundred-foot perimeter like Negel had said.

My heart pounded, blood racing. I used my air element to propel me to the tunnel exit. A quarter of a mile was normally hardly anything when I ran, but the wound in my thigh slowed me down some.

Finally I reached and stopped at the mouth of the tunnel. I listened. I saw moonlight break through the clouds. The rain had stopped.

In the distance were sounds of running—shoes snapping small branches and wet leaves slapping against bodies. The rain had not drenched the forest enough to quiet it.

The sounds were still loud to my ears as I stopped and whispered into my earpiece. I told the Trackers how to reach my position from the pyramid exits, including the one in the catacombs.

Water trickled from branches like tears as I started running through the forest, following the sounds again.

I came to an abrupt stop.

Listened.

Now everything was quiet.

No more sounds of running.

Where was Volod?

My neck started to burn. White-hot fire seared it and the wound in my thigh.

I sensed Volod and I spun around.

Volod was barely five feet away. Behind him was Danut.

"Purple bitch," Volod shouted as he raised his hand and shot power at me.

I flung up my air shield and backed it up with magic I took from the earth and water from the trees and puddles.

My shield was so strong that Volod's power bounced off of it, shot past him, and slammed into Danut.

The Vampire was flung against a huge tree, which cracked like the sound of thunder.

Volod's face was twisted into a furious expression. He raised his hand again, sending his incredible power at me.

My shield held, but barely. The strength of his blast knocked me on my backside. Pain burst through me as I scrambled to my feet while at the same time trying to enhance my elemental magic.

I didn't have time to go on the offense as another ball of power slammed into my shield.

This time I felt my whole body burn as some of it invaded my protection.

Before I could recover, I felt Volod in my head again. Just like he had at the council meeting, only this time stronger.

The pain in my bite mark intensified as I fought against Volod's mental assault. He was trying to get inside my head. His darkness was working to seep into my mind.

My shield completely buckled and I dropped to my knees.

Volod walked toward me with an evil, hateful expression on his face.

I dropped my daggers and clapped my hands to the sides of my head.

Had to get him out. Had to get him out.

The slimy feel of his presence inside made me want to vomit.

Had to get him out.

I summoned everything I had.

And attacked him.

Earth buckled at his feet. Air blasted into him at the same time. Rainwater gathered and shot toward his face, temporarily blinding him.

The combination of three of my elements slammed him up against a tree.

I sent the same elements at Danut, who'd gotten to his feet.

Volod's hideous darkness, the deadness I'd felt inside, left me in a rush.

It was too late when I sensed Drago behind me. I had put all of my magic into the shield between me and Volod.

I glanced over my shoulder in time to see Adam bullrush Drago, knocking the Vampire on his side.

Before Drago realized what had happened, Adam had his crossbow pressed to the Vampire's heart and he fired.

The stake drove into Drago's chest, piercing his heart.

My neck burned and I gathered my elements for a strong shield. Volod was coming back after me.

Volod hit my shield with another blast of power.

I could feel myself weaken again. Both Danut and

Volod raised their hands at the same time. I wouldn't be able to keep my protection up if it was hit with blasts from both of them.

Adrenaline pumped through me as I back-flipped, then dove behind a tree. The tree caught on fire as if lightning had struck it. A crack loud enough to hurt my ears and then the top half of the tree started to fall on me.

I scrambled away from the tree and came face-to-face with Danut. I didn't have time to draw a dagger so I grabbed his head and head-butted him. He shouted out. Immediately I jerked his head down and slammed my knee into his face.

Danut screamed but then his fangs flashed in the moonlight and he came at me.

I almost faltered in my mad scramble to get away when I saw a sword flash through the air—and nothing holding the sword.

The steel blade came down on the back of Danut's neck. Danut's body dropped. His head rolled away from his body.

Negel appeared beside me, holding the sword, a pleased look on his face.

The bite marks on my neck burned. I twisted. Volod was coming at me, all fangs and claws and fury.

I grabbed the sword from Negel.

Swung at Volod.

The blade connected with his head.

The metal sliced his skull straight across the top, above his ears.

From the powerful momentum of my swing I fell back hard onto the ground.

Volod wouldn't survive even part of his head being sliced off.

But the next thing I knew he was running.

Volod was running.

With his hand holding onto his head, he tore through the forest, away from me.

What?

It couldn't be.

I must not have sliced all the way through.

Right before I started to run after Volod, I heard a cry.

I turned to see Chuck run a sword through Negel's belly.

"No!" I shouted.

Chuck raised his sword as he ran toward me.

I took fire from the burning tree and ordered my element to fry him.

He went up in flames, his screams echoing through the dark forest. I finished him with my buckler, severing his head from his shoulders.

"Negel." I dropped to my knees beside the Sprite.

The burning in my bite mark was gone. My thigh was numb. But my skin felt like it was going to freeze off from my fear for Negel's life.

"You're going to be okay," I said. "We just need to get you to a Healer."

Negel shook his head. "I am done." He gave a weak smile. "But it was a great fight, wasn't it?"

The backs of my eyes burned as I nodded. "You saved my life."

"Here it is." He pointed to a box on the ground at my side. "Volod set it down before he attacked you." The Sprite smiled. "Now you shall live."

If I could have cried, tears would have been rolling down my cheeks. Instead the rain-wet trees sprinkled tears for me onto Negel's face.

He was starting to fade. I saw it on his face, in his eyes.

"Tell my brother, Penrod, to watch over my wife and sons." Negel's words caused me to gasp as pain wrenched my insides. "Tell him . . . that I love them all."

"I will." My voice choked as I said the words. "Thank you for saving my life. You are one of the bravest beings I know."

"Bye, Nyx." A peaceful expression was on his face. "Good-bye."

And then he was gone.

TWENTY-SEVEN

Even though it was night, my skin was still warm from a day on the beach in Belize. This trip was the first time I had ever been out of New York State, other than New Jersey, and I loved it.

Adam and I had moved onto a more private area when the sun went down. Now we sat next to one another, holding hands with me resting my head on his shoulder.

Silver moonlight bathed us both and a breeze teased my hair and ruffled his.

"The last time we saw moonlight was the night we took down Volod's operation," Adam said, sounding like he was deep in thought.

"No you don't." I raised my head from his shoulder. "I so do not want to talk about business." I shook my head. "We recovered the serum and antiserum, everyone involved in the battle was given a tiny dose of the antiserum and an epidemic was avoided. End of story."

"We never had a chance to talk," Adam said. "You've been in quarantine with the other paranorms who came in contact with you." He tugged on my hair. "Then you and I were on an airplane to Belize and you slept the whole way."

"Okay. Details." I sighed. "But only a little."

"Fair enough," he said. "How does the council know they got all of the serum?"

"It was measured before Volod got hold of it," I said. "They were able to determine how much was injected into me and believe every drop is accounted for."

"Captain Wysocki is breathing a few sighs of relief," Adam said, "now that the attacks have stopped. I told her how we put a stop to them. I'm not sure she can quite get herself to fully believe that real Vampires were behind it all."

"I can understand that," I said with a nod. "After all, she's just a norm."

Adam tickled me and I giggled. "You're a special norm, Adam." It was hard to speak as I giggled. "You're not just any norm."

He kissed the top of my head. "Any leads on Volod?"

I shuddered at the name. "None. It's like he evaporated."

"Or e-vamp-orated," Adam said with a laugh.

"Not even funny." I lightly punched his shoulder. "At least all of his forces were wiped out and many of those captured have already been tried and executed. The others will never see the light of day—or moonlight—again. They'll rot in jail."

"Paranorm justice is sure faster than the human system of justice," he said.

"When you're working with magical beings," I said, "things are easier to investigate with more accuracy, too."

"Volod may not have been captured, but he has nothing left." I shuddered at the mention of his name. "He will be tracked down. Rodán said he will not quit the pursuit until the monster is captured or destroyed."

I swallowed. "Volod may have something left." I cringed at the thought. "We never recovered the list of paranorm weaknesses from the pyramid. It's possible Volod somehow had it on him that night and got away with it. It's a thought that frightens me."

"It is a scary thought, but that's in Rodán's court now," Adam replied.

I nodded, but still felt a shiver.

He smiled. "Okay, we can stop talking about business. Back to vacation now . . . where were we, Nyx?" Adam said as he started tickling me again.

"Yes, I know you needed all the facts, Detective Boyd." I said through my giggles.

Then he took my face in his palms and kissed me so fast and sudden that he stole my breath. His kisses were soft and wonderful, then hard and more urgent, and just as wonderful.

He ran his hands over my body, skimming my breasts in my little black string bikini.

"We can't do this here," he murmured in my ear. "Let's go back to the beach house."

"Yes." My voice was a hoarse whisper before we kissed again.

Adam helped me to my feet and we started walking down the beach toward the beach house. "Dang, I forgot the backpack." He brought me to a stop. "Wait here."

While I waited, my gaze traveled the dark waters with moonlight sparkling on its gentle surface. Then I looked at something that sent chills through my body.

A male standing just beyond the edge of the beach, near a group of palm trees, was looking at me. He was so far away I couldn't make out who he was through the moonlight.

The bite mark on my neck burned. Feeling almost

dazed, I brought my hand to it and felt heat when I touched it.

"Volod," I said, my voice a hoarse whisper.

"What?" Adam came up from behind me.

"Look," I said as I glanced at Adam over my shoulder. I turned back and blinked. The male was gone. "Volod was there." I pointed. "Volod is *here*."

"You just need to relax." Adam massaged my shoulders with his strong hands. "Take some time away."

Maybe he was right.

Maybe it had been my imagination.

"You do need a vacation, Nyx." Adam grasped my hand. "I shouldn't have brought the subject up."

Instead of worrying about what I might have seen, I squeezed Adam's fingers and we turned and walked back to the beach house.

FOR CHEYENNE'S READERS

Be sure to go to CheyenneMcCray.com to sign up for her PRIVATE book announcement list and get FREE EXCLUSIVE Cheyenne McCray goodies. Please feel free to e-mail her at chey@cheyennemccray.com. She would love to hear from you.

Read on for an excerpt from

ZOMBIES SOLD SEPARATELY

the next Night Tracker novel from Cheyenne McCray
and St. Martin's Paperbacks!

Icy wind and water whirled around me as my hair whipped across my cheeks. Wind spun so fast, fierce, and cold that a growing storm roared with power.

Hail stung my face and arms. Rain splattered my face and rolled down my cheeks and skin. Water blurred my eyesight.

Thumps on hard surfaces. Loud crashes. The sound of smashing.

An object glanced off my forehead as it spun in the storm.

Hurricane. I was trapped in a hurricane.

So hard to breathe. Water in my nose. In my mouth.

No sound came out as I tried to scream.

The storm wasn't natural.

Not natural at all.

It wasn't supposed to be happening.

The storm wasn't natural . . .

Because it was caused by . . . me.

My elemental magic. Air and water.

"Nyx!" I shouted over the shrieking storm. I clenched my fists and dug my nails into my palms. Fought to gain control over my magic. *"Stop!"*

My control over the elements had never been so fragile.

Again I screamed into the wind. Tightened my muscles.

With all I had I grasped the reins of my magic.

The storm ended like a car slamming into a concrete barrier.

Things that had been spinning in the storm crashed to a hard surface.

Shock immobilized me.

I blinked water out of my eyes.

My surroundings came into focus.

I was in my bedroom in my apartment in Manhattan.

For several moments I sat on my sodden mattress and stared at the devastation around me.

How had I lost control in my sleep? I wasn't a child. Only younglings would do something like this without near the destruction I had just caused.

Without realizing I was doing it, I reached up and touched the collar around my neck that signified my Drow station in life. No, I was nowhere near being a youngling. I was of age by Drow standards. By Earth Otherworld standards I was fully an adult.

I looked around me. Almost everything in my room was smashed and broken. Trinkets I had purchased since I had moved from the Drow realm to New York City were cracked, broken, torn, shredded.

As a well-paid Tracker and PI, and thanks to my wealthy Drow heritage, I could replace everything that had been ruined. But I couldn't replace the memories that accompanied a good many of the objects.

I let my hand fall away from my collar and it splashed in the water pooled around me on my mattress. I inhaled and exhaled with long, slow, deliberate breaths.

Even though Dark Elves don't get cold easily, the storm

had chilled me enough that goose bumps broke out along my skin. I shivered.

A nightmare.

The same one I'd had countless times since I was a youngling. The worst part of the nightmare was seeing an elder, a man with long, graying red hair in a world with lavender-streaked skies. The vision of the man made me sick.

Unlike every other time I'd had this nightmare, this time my entire being had reacted to the nightmare. It had never happened before. I'd never woken in the middle of a storm I had caused to happen.

My heartbeat slowed while my mind started to clear.

A sick sensation, like thick, black sludge weighted my insides. It reminded me of just weeks ago when I'd been sentenced to death by a Vampire. The thought had bile rising in my throat. I didn't want to think about that. Not at all.

I moved my palms to my belly, over my soaked lingerie. I lowered my head and closed my eyes.

It had been a long time since I'd had such intense nightmares—nightmares that I never remembered when I woke.

During most of my adolescence I'd woken up screaming, wind whipping around my room from my elemental magic. Sometimes the room would be filled with mist. Sometimes a slow, drizzling rain.

Never a storm.

Mother would come in, rock me until I stopped crying and the rain ceased or mist cleared or wind subsided.

When I got older the nightmares came less frequently. I gained control over my elements and woke with nothing more than a sore throat from screaming.

Even though I never remembered the dreams, somehow I knew they had all been the same.

Once I came of age at twenty-five, they stopped.

I frowned and opened my eyes, blinked more wetness away as I raised my head. The nightmares started again two weeks ago. Over two years since they had stopped.

"Why now?" I said, the sound of my voice loud in my bedroom that was still, save for the sound of water dripping from the doorframes.

The sludge in my insides only worsened.

Winter sunlight slashed through the French doors and into my bedroom. I stared at the fractured pattern reflected in the sheen of water on my hardwood floor.

Light.

Light here, in the Earth Otherworld, often means renewal, rebirth.

In the lives of the Dark Elves, light means death. Death to any Drow who dared to go aboveground during the day.

To all Drow but me.

The mattress made squishing sounds as I shoved the comforter off my legs. I found a place on the floor where nothing was splintered or broken, slid out of bed, and got to my feet. Water ran down my body in rivulets, joining the puddles on my floor.

Had Kali gotten caught in the storm? I hoped not. My blue Persian would never forgive me.

I stepped through the water and felt melting bits of hail beneath my feet. My floor would be ruined if I didn't take care of it. Other than my elemental magic, I knew little Elvin magic, but I did know the word for "clean."

"*Avanna,*" I said and the room dried, including my hair, skin and the lingerie I wore. My things still lay broken on the floor and I wished I knew an Elvin word for "repair."

I stepped over a broken crystal clock, grabbed a shortie robe, and slipped it on.

A frame with a photograph caught my attention and I stooped to pick it up. The glass shattered but it didn't look like the picture of Adam and me in Belize was ruined.

I smiled and traced my human lover's image with my fingertip as my heart skipped. Love for him flowed through my veins, warm and sweet, as I took in his boyish grin and that dimple I loved. In the sunshine of Belize he looked sexy, adorable, and intensely masculine, all at the same time.

I set the picture with its broken frame on my nightstand where my lamp should have been. It too was on the floor in shambles.

I avoided everything sharp and pointy and walked toward the window next to the French doors leading to the balcony from my bedroom.

Ice-laced sunlight touched my face and body as I peered out the window and the cold made me shiver again.

By day I look a lot like my human mother with my fair skin and sapphire blue eyes. The exception is that my hair is black with blue highlights and hers a pale shade of blond.

When the sun sets, my skin turns a pale, pale shade of amethyst and my hair a deep cobalt blue. When it's dark I look more like my father with my pointed ears, small fangs, and Drow-pigmented skin and hair.

I am not human then, and have no choice but to avoid humans who know nothing about the paranormal world. Which is just about everyone.

My mind filled with the fragmented emotions both the nightmare and the storm had left me with. A storm in my house. How had I lost control like that?

I pushed aside the sheer curtain and the glass felt cool against my nose as I stared out at the street from my apartment.

It had snowed last night. From the corner of my apartment at 104th and Central Park West, I had clear views from the terrace of Central Park. No one from Otherworld is used to snow because there is no change of seasons there.

I love Manhattan. I love all the seasons. Each season is beautiful and unique in its own way.

The Earth Otherworld holiday season had been pleasant so far and Christmas was just days away. The city was locked in winter's grasp and everything was white and beautiful.

Sometimes I tugged on a jacket and boots, and waded through the new powder while throwing snowballs at statues, taunting the Gargoyles hidden inside them.

Today the weight in my belly grew heavier as imprints of the nightmare pressed against my soul. Dread, terror, anger, pain . . . the kind of pain that makes a person's heart hurt as if someone close to them has died.

I tried to swallow but my throat was too dry.

For the first time the image of a face with blurred features shimmered at the edge of my consciousness. Somehow I knew it was the face of someone I cared for.

I brought my hands to my chest. The contours of the image seemed so familiar.

And then the ghostly face was gone, like it hadn't been there at all. . . .